Karen Clarke

Summer at the Little French Café

Bookouture

Published by Bookouture in 2019

An imprint of StoryFire Ltd.

Carmelite House
50 Victoria Embankment
London EC4Y 0DZ

www.bookouture.com

ISBN: 978-1-78681-800-3
eBook ISBN: 978-1-78681-799-0

This one's for Mandy,
my partner in romance and crime (not literally!)

Chapter One

Here, at last.

After propping my suitcase against the harbour railings, I pulled the postcard out of my bag and held it up, comparing the image on the front to the tall, whitewashed café across the cobbled street. It looked so much more vibrant in real life, but the picture must have been taken in the eighties, so it was hardly surprising the colours looked rather vintage.

Chamillon – Île de Ré was printed at the bottom of the postcard; a fishing village on an island on the west coast of France that I'd discovered via the internet, weeks before booking my flight.

The café, which overlooked a boat-filled harbour, hadn't changed much in the intervening decades. The red-and-white striped awning was the same, as were the tables set out at the front, draped with gingham cloths. Only the old-fashioned sign above the door had been changed, replaced by gold lettering on the window, spelling out Café Belle Vie.

Mouthing the name, my heart did a kangaroo leap. It had been behaving oddly since finding the postcard among my father's things, to the point where I'd started to worry I was developing a condition.

Slipping the card back into my bag, I tipped my face to the sun and drew in a calming breath. The first thing I'd noticed, climbing out of the taxi that had brought me from the airport at La Rochelle, was how good the air smelled in Chamillon. Back home, a scorching summer's day tended to concentrate the odours of the busy Camden Road, where my photography studio was based. A mix of petrol, tarmac and fried doughnuts that I'd never learned to appreciate, but represented 'life' to my friend Toni. She couldn't understand why I preferred commuting back to my childhood home in Hertfordshire. It backed onto sheep-filled hills, and the nearest shop was a good three miles away.

By contrast, the air here was rich with the vibrant scents of sea and sunshine, and the piney shrubs separating the villages that made up the island. I'd seen a surprising number of cyclists as I arrived. Cars were discouraged due to a lack of road space, adding to the picture-perfect prettiness cultivated by the local council. Apparently, no overhead cables or new constructions were allowed, and window shutters had to be painted one of sixteen shades – eight of which were blue, and eight green. The island's unspoilt beauty attracted celebrities, and it wasn't unusual to spot film stars hanging out. Just a few months ago, the actor Jay Merino had filmed his final film in the capital, Saint-Martin, before retiring. Not that I cared about celebrities, but I hadn't been prepared to fall in love with Chamillon at first sight. I was tempted to forget my mission and go exploring – though that might be difficult with a suitcase in tow. I should have gone straight to the guest house I'd booked online, but I was early, as well as hot and thirsty, and once I spotted the café, had asked the taxi driver to drop me off.

I adjusted the thick strap of my camera bag, resettled my cross-body bag (I possibly had too many bags) and grabbed my suitcase handle. Wheeling it across the cobbled quayside was a noisy and tricky process, the wheels bouncing and twisting as I tried to avoid bashing the ankles of passers-by. It was lunchtime, and although Chamillon (according to TripAdvisor) was less touristy than some of the adjoining villages, the area was still busy with visitors, and day trippers from the mainland, dipping in and out of shops, or taking in the view.

As I approached the café, feeling too hot in the long-sleeved T-shirt and 'comfy for travelling' jogging pants that had seemed like a good idea in the damp, London morning I'd left behind, I imagined explaining to the café owner why I was there.

Hi! I wonder if you can help? Thirty years ago, my father had a liaison with a young Frenchwoman while visiting London and nine months later, I was born! It turns out she didn't want to be a parent so gave me to my father to raise and he never saw her again! I know! They didn't even exchange names! Anyway, he died a while ago, and I found this postcard when I was sorting through his things, and a message suggesting my birth mother was born in Chamillon! So, I thought I'd come and find her! Only thing is, I know nothing except that her name begins with M and she has terrible handwriting! Anyway, do you think you might know what happened to her?

I would say it in exclamation marks, to show I was in on the joke – that I knew it sounded like the far-fetched plot of a tragic movie – but also to prove that it wasn't tragic, because after Dad had married, I'd had a wonderful, nurturing Mum after all. Until she died when I was eighteen. Which was actually pretty tragic, by anyone's standards.

No wonder Toni was worried. I hadn't really thought this through properly.

'Are you *sure* you want to go on your own?' she'd asked me yesterday, her face flexing in agony as Freddie grabbed her swinging ponytail. 'You know I'll drop everything, Elle. You only have to ask.'

'I'm positive,' I reassured her, plopping a kiss on my godson's russet curls. 'You can't drop a baby, a job, a husband *and* a business.'

'I'm tempted to drop this one right now,' she'd muttered, attempting to unfurl Freddie's chubby fingers as he giggled, and kicked his dimpled legs. 'And Mark would survive without me for a week.'

'The business won't.' We'd been through it several times already. 'Petra can easily do what I do, but you *have* to be around if I'm not.' As well as being my oldest friend, Toni managed my photography studio, Perfect Moments – 'Specialties: Family Portraits and Weddings' (though I did an awful lot of corporate-style headshots for websites too).

'Petra's your assistant.'

'You can't deny she's a brilliant photographer in her own right, and I'll be back before you know it.'

Toni had tutted, knowing she was beaten. 'I just don't like the thought of you over there on your own, dealing with… *this*.' Finally freed from her son's clasp, she'd indicated the crumpled bag I'd found tucked in a rucksack in my father's wardrobe while sorting out his clothes a couple of months ago. A move intended to kickstart me towards the next phase of my life – which had worked, but not in the way I'd anticipated.

'It's France, not North Korea,' I'd said, my heart kicking up a gear. 'And you keep telling me to take a break and do something different.'

'I meant a holiday, not go off on a quest to find your birth mother.' She'd plopped Freddie down on his playmat in her cluttered but cosy living room and retrieved the postcard, turning it over to read the scrawl on the back.

'*Donnez à la fille les bonnes chaussures et elle peut conquérir le monde,*' she read out, exaggerating the French vowels.

'It means—'

'"Give the girl the right shoes and she can conquer the world." I know, it's a quote by Marilyn Monroe, which is kind of spooky when you look a bit like her.' I'd been told before that I bore a similarity to the actress, but couldn't see it myself. I had too many freckles for a start, and no one would notice if I wasn't wearing a bra.

'I thought I was the spitting image of Dad.'

'Just as well, considering he didn't demand a DNA test when she dumped you with him.'

'I wasn't *dumped*, and he never had a moment's doubt that I was his daughter.'

'Only because you didn't have dark hair and eyes, like her.'

'I did have eyes. Two, in fact.'

Toni had laughed, but begrudgingly. Like a dog, she'd been reluctant to let go of this particular bone. '*Dark* eyes,' she clarified. 'Do you think he carried a torch for her, if he kept that postcard tucked away?'

'Toni, you know Dad wasn't like that.' The good thing about us having been friends since primary school was sometimes the not-so-good thing – Toni knew way too much about me and my life. 'By the time he found out about me, he was madly in love with Mum, and I'm sure they'd have loved me whatever I looked like.'

'Of course they would, I'm sorry.' Toni had returned her cat-green eyes to the postcard, reading out, '"I only ask that you call her Eloise and give her the life she deserves, which I am unable to do. Maybe, one day, she will come to see the village where I was born. M." Not even a kiss,' she'd huffed. 'Or a name.'

'Their night together was meant to be a one-off,' I reminded her. 'They were both a bit drunk, and Dad didn't expect to ever see her again.' It had been so hard to imagine my serious father, who curated exhibitions for a museum, being singled out in a bar in Covent Garden by a stranger. He'd confessed to 'getting tipsy' that night, after visiting the British Museum with a couple of friends, and 'acting recklessly' – though he'd been single at the time and entitled to act how he wanted.

'And I'm very glad I did,' he'd said, holding one hand while Mum gripped the other as he told me the full story, which I'd demanded in more detail when I was twelve, after watching a documentary about women exchanging babies for cash, and worrying I was one of them. As it turned out, the facts were more mundane. My birth mother had remembered Dad mentioning the museum where he worked and tracked him down there nine months after their close encounter, waiting in the car park until he left work, alone.

'She said she had something that belonged to me, thrust you into my arms, said you were exactly one week old, and vanished. It was a bit of a shock,' he'd said, with classic understatement. Everything about Dad had been understated, apart from the lavish moustache he'd sported in the eighties, which was perhaps what had drawn her attention in the bar. 'But I loved you from that very moment.'

'And the second I held you, so did I.' Mum's blue eyes had been brilliant with tears. 'I was so grateful she gave you to your father, so I could love you too,' she said, and I'd thanked my lucky stars that she'd applied for a job at the museum, and Dad had fallen for someone with such an enormous heart. A lesser woman might have been jealous, or ended their relationship rather than take on another woman's child, but not Mum, who'd always believed that people were intrinsically good, and rarely spoken ill of anyone.

Once they'd registered my birth – 4 June, according to my birth mother – and introduced their startled parents to their brand-new grandchild, Mum had suggested bringing the wedding forward 'so we could start our life together as a family'. They'd married when I was eight weeks old and my sister Jess was born a year later. No one outside the family had ever suspected that I wasn't Mum's natural daughter.

'Good for him for stepping up, and I'm not saying he wasn't a good father, but he knew all along where your birth mother was born and should have given you this stuff,' Toni had said, looking as shocked as the first time I'd shown her the postcard, which had been wrapped in a gossamer-fine shawl and accompanied by a gold bracelet loaded with charms.

'What good would it have done?' I'd argued, in his defence. 'It's not like there was an address, and an invitation to visit whenever I liked.' Even so, I'd imagined my parents discussing what to do, but guessed it was a topic they'd decided to leave for another day. A day that had never arrived, and now I could never ask them and know the truth.

'I suppose it's obvious she didn't want to be found,' Toni had reluctantly acknowledged. 'And it could have done more harm than good for you to know back then, but I can't believe they went ahead and called you Eloise, just because she wanted…' Toni's words had petered into a wince. 'Sorry, Elle. I'm just worried, that's all.'

'I know, but don't you think it's fate?' I'd persisted. 'I was only meant to find the postcard once Mum and Dad were gone, and now I have to find *her*.'

'My suggestion of hiring a private detective stands.'

'Not enough information.' I'd already been on a genealogy website and accessed birth records for everyone born in Chamillon whose name began with M, but there were over 14,000 entries dating back to 1602 and I'd soon given up – plus, I'd realised, after reading the postcard for about the fiftieth time, I'd felt a strong pull to go to Chamillon myself. 'I want to try and find her, even if I don't have much to go on.'

Toni's face had softened. 'But what if you don't?'

'Well, at least I'll have tried,' I said, with a pragmatism I hadn't really felt. 'I'll be able to move forward, one way or the other.'

Now, I dithered, staring unseeingly at the café window, wondering whether I could find a free table inside, when a man bowled through the door and careered into me.

'Whoa!' His hand shot out as I was thrown off-balance, but my heel caught the edge of my suitcase and I tumbled to the ground, my camera bag bashing the cobbles.

'Oh no!' Scrabbling to a sitting position, I unzipped the bag and looked inside, but there was so much padding my camera hadn't budged.

'Is anything broken?'

'I don't think so.' I gingerly twirled my wrists, but the man had dropped to his haunches and was peering in the bag. 'That looks expensive.'

'It is, but no harm done.' I whizzed the zip back round, my heart thumping in my chest. 'It was the last thing my father bought me before he died, so it has sentimental value.' *Way too much information.* The fall must have wobbled my brain. 'It's a Nikon 7200 digital SLR. I'd wanted one for a while. The sensor on my old one wasn't working properly, which isn't good when you're photographing a wedding. It was a birthday present…' My voice quavered and I bit my lip. 'Sorry,' I said, fixing my eyes on the bag, which was rather tatty on the outside, giving no clue to its valuable cargo. 'He died eighteen months ago,' I blathered on. 'It was an aneurysm. Sudden, so not painful, but a shock, him being there at the start of the day and gone by the end, but at least he didn't suffer.'

I shut my eyes against a prickle of tears, recalling the phone call to the studio from his research assistant Carly, who'd found him in his office. *He looked really peaceful, Elle, as if he was having a nice dream.*

'He died at the museum where he worked and was at his happiest, so that was good, and we'd said I love you before I left the house that morning as usual, so nothing was left unsaid, but I suppose I thought I'd have him for a lot longer.' Oh God, I was sitting on a cobbled street in France, babbling to a stranger, like someone who didn't have boundaries. Praying he'd do the decent thing and move away, I jumped when he spoke again.

'I'm really sorry, that must have been awful for you.' I nodded, not daring to speak, or open my eyes until I was sure they weren't going to leak. I'd cried so many tears in the weeks after his death, I wasn't sure I had any left. 'And now, I've sent you flying,' the man continued, and I registered that he was British, his accent similar to mine, and wished for a moment he'd been French. At least then, he wouldn't have understood my outburst and I might have exited our encounter with some dignity intact. 'Let me help you up,' he said.

Sensing movement, I flipped my eyes open and saw two outstretched hands, strong and capable-looking. Aware I was blocking the doorway, I placed my palms in his and let him pull me up. Slamming against his chest, I gaped up into a pair of chestnut eyes that flickered over my face as though absorbing every feature and took a self-conscious step back. The rest of him came into focus: dark blond wavy hair, a tanned and friendly face, and soft stubble that wasn't quite a beard, but suited him. He looked like someone people would turn to in a crisis, with an easy-going aura that made me think he might be a surfer. Weren't surfers supposed to be chilled? Something to do with being at one with nature, though he probably wouldn't be wearing dark trousers and a white, short-sleeved shirt if he was going surfing. He was nice-looking—

No. I wasn't looking for a man, despite Toni urging me to 'at least have a shag' as she charmingly put it, while I was here. I wasn't on holiday, despite being in what looked like the perfect spot to have a relaxing break.

'I'm Charlie Croft.' The man seemed to break free of whatever he'd been contemplating. 'Are you sure you're OK?'

'I'm fine, thank you, Charlie.' Actually, my wrist was throbbing a bit, but I could see he felt bad. 'I'm Eloise Matheson, but everyone calls me Elle.'

'Which begs the question, why introduce yourself as Eloise?'

Stumped, I gawped at him. 'I… suppose, because I like it,' I said, even though no one had ever used my birth name.

'So, why not just say your name is Eloise?'

'Because I'm used to being called Elle.' Irritation rose. He'd knocked me over, and now he was questioning my name?

'Sorry, I'm being an idiot.' His grin was so engaging my annoyance melted away. 'It's good to meet you, Elle, and I really am sorry for not looking where I was going.' He moved aside to let an elderly man with a little black dog tucked under his arm enter the café. 'Listen, I'd buy you a drink, but—'

'No, really, there's no need.' I reached once more for my suitcase, dusting a hand on my jogging pants, wishing I was wearing something that didn't scream *watching television on the sofa while recovering from a bout of flu*. 'Thanks, anyway.'

'I suppose you're here about the job?' He angled his gaze behind me, and I turned to see a sheet of paper taped to the glass, the words STAFF VACANCY in big letters at the top. I caught the words 'part-time' and some words in French that I didn't understand. 'Just go through and ask for Dolly,' he said, eyes crinkling into a smile. 'Maybe I'll see you later.' He backed away with a wave while I tried to form a coherent reply, and was quickly swallowed by a crowd of tourists taking photos of the harbour.

'So, you're here about the job?'

I swivelled to see a full-fringed woman in an apron, carrying a tray of empty glasses, wearing an expectant smile. Her eyes swept over my luggage and back to my fiery cheeks. 'Looks like you've come a long way,' she said. 'You'd better follow me.'

And, without knowing exactly why, I did.

Chapter Two

It was pleasantly cool in the café, despite bright sunshine streaming through the windows, bouncing off an array of gleaming crockery behind the counter, where a youngish man was pouring foaming milk into a metal jug, while an older woman chatted to a customer at the front of a snaking queue.

'As you can see, we're extremely busy,' the woman – Dolly, I guessed – called over her shoulder, tray aloft as she weaved between packed tables with the grace of a dancer; or someone who had worked there for a very long time.

'Oops, sorry,' I said to the man whose foot I'd just jerked my suitcase over, blinking idiotically when he looked up from his phone and gave me a dazzling smile.

'Would you like a hand?' he said in sexily accented English, a pair of strong eyebrows rising up his tanned forehead.

'Er, no, thanks. I'm fine, but thanks.' My banter needed work. 'Thank you.'

'No problem.'

'Thank you.' A *lot* of work.

His meltingly dark eyes lingered on mine, until the woman sat opposite gave a light laugh and tapped the back of his hand, saying something in French. I caught the word *Henri* as I moved past, dragging my suitcase like an unwilling toddler, trying to take in my surroundings, but the hubbub was overwhelming, with nearly everyone calling a greeting to the woman (she was definitely Dolly) and casting me curious looks.

My bags kept getting in the way, and apart from a delicious smell of baking mingled with coffee beans, I barely registered a thing until we entered the kitchen, where a tray of freshly made pastries was laid out, and then I was in a pretty courtyard enclosed by a vine-covered wall.

'Can't hear myself think in there,' said Dolly and gestured for me to sit at a picnic-style table, shaded by a red-and-white striped umbrella. She'd dispensed with her tray without me noticing, and picked up two glasses of fresh orange juice, glistening with condensation. 'You look like you could use a drink.'

I decided I liked – possibly loved – her. 'Thank you,' I said, relinquishing my suitcase as I gratefully took the glass and sat on the bench seat, aware of an ache in my shoulders from lugging my bags – and maybe from being knocked over. And the tension, which had accompanied me from home.

My temperature dropped as I drank the cold juice quickly, aware of Dolly's slightly distracted scrutiny. She was perched on the edge of the bench opposite and kept glancing at the doorway, as if the café was a beloved but demanding child, requiring every second of her attention.

'I'm Elle Matheson,' I said when I'd finished, placing my empty glass on the table, resisting the urge to wipe my mouth on the back of my hand like a child.

'Elle, I'm afraid there's no accommodation here.' Dolly eyed my array of baggage as though it might transform into a pack of braying dogs. 'The apartment upstairs is family only,' she said.

'Oh, no, it's fine, I've booked somewhere to stay.' I was horrified that she thought I expected her to house me. *Why was I even here?* I mean, obviously I knew why I was in Chamillon, but why, when I'd got out of the taxi less than half an hour ago, was I sitting in front of a woman the right age to be my birth mother (*Dolly*, so definitely not a contender, unless it wasn't her real name, and her real name began with M and she'd been born in Chamillon, which, by anyone's reasoning, was a stretch of the imagination) pretending to apply for a job I couldn't accept and wasn't qualified for?

'Well, that's good,' Dolly approved. She had an unremarkable face until she smiled, which she was doing now to great effect, her nut-brown eyes radiating warmth, and I could see she was the sort of woman people instinctively trusted – and if the heap of golden-topped pastries the young man I'd seen earlier was bringing out were anything to go by, a spectacular baker too.

'Thanks, Stefan,' she said to the man, who was almost black-eyed, with curly dark hair that bounced upwards and a shy but friendly smile. 'Help yourself,' she said, when he'd gone, and although I had the impression she was eager to get the 'interview' underway, I couldn't resist taking a pain au chocolat and biting into it, closing my eyes as the chocolatey, buttery flavours melted on my tongue.

'Do you make them yourself?' I asked when I'd swallowed, wiping my fingers on the accompanying napkin, battling the temptation to scoff the lot.

'I do,' she said matter-of-factly, as if it was no big deal. 'My grandmother was French and very keen on baking. She taught me everything she knew.'

'She was French?' For some reason, my heart gave a kick. 'Were… were you born here?'

Dolly shook her head, eyes darting once more to the door. 'I've only been here six years,' she said. 'The café was an impulse buy after my divorce, but the best thing I ever did.' Her eyes sought mine again. 'I can't imagine ever leaving now.'

My heart bumped up a gear. 'Did you know the café's previous owner?'

If she found my question strange and annoying she didn't show it. 'I didn't *know* them as such. It was a family business that the wife didn't want to continue with after her husband died. She still comes in every week to bake. Taught me how to make perfect macarons.'

I had no idea whether or not the café itself was significant, or just happened to be one of many postcards my birth mother could have picked up, but found myself asking, 'What's her name?'

This time, a frown creased Dolly's forehead. 'Do you know Mathilde?'

Mathilde! The name seemed to swirl in slow motion around my head. It couldn't possibly be that simple. Surely the odds of finding my birth mother the day I arrived were slim to none?

'No, I, erm… definitely don't know her, but the thing is… the reason I'm here—'

'You're not here about the job?'

Her tone prompted a rush of guilt. 'Sorry if I misled you,' I said quickly. 'I'm only here for a week.'

'On holiday?'

'N-*ooooo*.' I stretched the word out, as if my intentions weren't clear-cut, and Dolly's eyes narrowed, trying to work me out. 'I'm hoping to track someone down while I'm here,' I said as the silence lengthened. 'An old friend of my father's.'

Dolly's expression sharpened with interest. 'What's his name?'

'It's a woman, and I don't know her name, only that it begins with M.'

Dolly's neat fingertips started drumming the table in time with my heartbeat. 'Not much to go on.'

'I know,' I agreed. 'I found a postcard from her after he died, but she'd only signed it with her initial.'

'Was there an address?'

My cheeks felt broiled. 'No address,' I said. 'It had been given to him in person.'

Sudden understanding swept over Dolly's face. 'You want to reunite them!' She pressed a hand to her heart with a mushy smile. 'It might be hard to believe, considering my husband left me for a younger woman, but I have a romantic soul,' she said, while I tried to unfreeze my lips and tell her it wasn't that at all. 'I *never* gave up on meeting my true love, and when Frank walked in here last summer, I knew he was the one before he'd even asked me to dance.'

'He... asked you to dance?'

Her head bounced up and down. 'He said he could tell by looking that he'd met someone who'd perfectly fit into his arms, but he wanted to double-check.'

A smile rose to my lips. 'That's quite a chat-up line.'

'He was right,' she said. 'We were a perfect fit.'

'That's lovely, but...' My smile faded. 'That's not what this is about.'

'It's not?'

'My father passed away, eighteen months ago.' I couldn't believe in the space of an hour I'd told this to two different people – both complete strangers.

'Oh, I'm so sorry.' Dolly reached across the table and clamped a warm hand over mine in a gesture of comfort that felt surprisingly natural. 'That's terribly tough,' she said gently. 'I lost my parents too young, so I have some idea how it feels.' She squeezed my hand. 'You still have your mum?'

An image rose, of me climbing into Mum and Dad's bed each Saturday morning, snuggling between their warm bodies, and how she'd kiss my hair and call me her cuddle-bunny. I swallowed and shook my head. 'She died, twelve years ago.' *What was wrong with me?* At this rate, I'd be telling Dolly the real reason I was here. 'It's fine though,' I said. 'I mean, it's not fine, but you get used to it.'

Dolly's face was wreathed in sympathy. 'Your heart's taken a real battering,' she said, releasing my hand, but keeping her eyes bolted to mine. 'So, you're not in Chamillon to reunite your father with a long-lost love?'

'No,' I said, and perhaps because I was in a different country, where no one knew me, breathing different air – or because Dolly had secretly hypnotised me – I found myself telling her most of what I'd imagined saying as I crossed to the café, but without the exclamation marks. She didn't look shocked or outraged, or even very surprised, as if she'd heard much worse.

'So, you're looking for ladies of a certain age with dark hair and eyes, whose names begin with M and who were born in Chamillon?' she said when I'd finished.

'That's right.' I felt a bit floaty, as if I'd handed over a burden. 'But I'm not sure where to start, to be honest.'

'It's lucky you happened to be passing, then.' An odd light entered Dolly's eyes. 'Maybe we can help each other.'

'How do you mean?'

She pushed her fringe aside, revealing a pair of neat eyebrows. 'Someone left a few months ago, who turned out to be… well, something of a disappointment, shall we say, and the girl who replaced her kept throwing herself at Charlie and walked out when he told her he wasn't interested, so we're desperately short-staffed at the moment.'

My spinning mind changed direction. 'Charlie?'

'My son.' Dolly seemed to swell with pride, a smile lifting her tanned cheeks. 'He runs the café with me.'

'Charlie Croft?' It had to be the same man who'd bumped into me.

'That's right.' She paused, as if giving me time to let the information settle. 'Anyway, like I said, I think we can help each other.' She leaned forward, a penetrating glow in her eyes. 'August is our busiest month, and much as I live and breathe my job, I've only got one pair of hands.'

'O-*kay*.'

'I have a friend who works at the town hall.' *Town hall?* 'If you could help me out here for the week, I'll ask Francine to check Chamillon's birth records for anyone who could be a match for your birth mother.'

'Birth records?' There was a buzzing in my ears, and the sun felt too warm across my shoulders. 'I... I don't know when she was born.'

'But you have a rough idea?'

Dad had confessed that he hadn't known her exact age, but when he'd admired a bracelet she was wearing (the one now in my possession), she'd told him it had been a gift for her twenty-first birthday, and he'd had the impression she wasn't much older than that. Mum had lifted an eyebrow, and I'd wondered later whether it was the first time she'd heard it. It couldn't have been easy, listening to him relive that night, however accepting and non-judgemental she'd been. 'She'd be in her early fifties, I think.'

'Well, that's something.' Dolly slapped the table. 'So, what do you think?'

I wavered. There was nothing to stop me from going to the town hall myself – but I didn't speak French, and didn't know anyone there.

They might not even let me – a stranger to the island – look at the birth records. 'Don't you want to know whether I've any experience?'

'Have you?' Dolly's eyebrows rose, but I had the sense she wasn't really bothered, which was just as well, considering how much crockery I'd broken the summer I'd waitressed at a café called the Cup and Saucer, aged sixteen.

'Not recent,' I admitted.

'Well, it won't take long to show you the ropes.'

Oh God. Me, working in a café. Still, it would be perfect for investigating the locals without seeming too obvious, depending what the town hall search turned up – it looked like the whole of Chamillon frequented the Café Belle Vie, and Dolly probably knew them all. 'I'm a fast learner,' I said, which I wasn't sure was true. It was ages since I'd learned a new skill. Even so, excitement started fizzing through my veins. I was closer to finding answers than I could have imagined twenty-four hours ago, and it was all thanks to Dolly. Helping her out at the café seemed like a fair trade.

'I'd rather no one else knows why I'm here.' Excitement dimmed and was replaced by apprehension. 'I want to be discreet, because I don't think…' I hesitated. 'I don't think she ever wanted to be found,' I admitted. 'She might have a family of her own now, who know nothing about me, and I don't want to scare her off.'

Dolly nodded. 'You can trust me.'

'I can't just come out and say, *are you my birth mother?*' I persisted. 'The shock might be too much.'

'Let's take it one step at a time,' said Dolly in a sensible voice, and the sense of someone being on my side, of understanding – a stranger, who already felt familiar – made my eyes well up. Twice, I'd been brought to the edge of tears for different reasons, by members of the same family.

I could hardly compute the strangeness of it all.

'OK then.' I felt as if I was emerging from under the sea – or about to dive into it – trying to imagine what Toni would make of this surreal diversion. 'We can help each other.'

Dolly rose, smoothing her hands down her little black apron, a baby-pink flush on her cheeks. 'Welcome to the Café Belle Vie.'

I got to my feet, as wobbly-legged as a foal. 'I won't let you down.'

'I know you won't.' The strength of Dolly's beam induced a fresh wave of guilt. I'd been sacked from the Cup and Saucer when replacing my breakages began to cost more than my wages. 'When can you start?' she said.

Panic kicked in. 'Oh, I… I'll need to drop off my things at the house where I'm staying.' I adjusted my camera bag, which seemed to have grown heavier while I was sitting down.

'Fair enough.' Dolly chuckled warmly. 'I wasn't expecting you to jump in right away,' she added, though I had the impression if I'd offered, she'd have said yes. 'How about tomorrow?'

'That sounds good.'

'And I'll have a good think about your *situation*, see if I can't come up with a few names myself.' She tapped the side of her nose and winked. 'Come in early and meet a few people,' she said. 'We're like a happy family here, with more regulars than visitors, even at this time of year.'

'Are you open in the evenings too?'

'Yes, but you won't need to help out then.' Dolly couldn't seem to stop smiling. 'Frank, that's my man-friend – he's visiting family in England at the moment – helps me cook for the tourists,' she said. 'Nothing complicated, but they like eating by the harbour and watching the sun go down.'

'Sounds lovely.' I felt a pang of envy, recalling the last time I'd eaten out with Dad and Jess – our final meal as a family before my sister moved to Borneo.

As if on cue, my phone vibrated and the heat drained from my face. I'd already called Toni, after landing in La Rochelle, which could only mean one thing.

Jess had somehow discovered what I was up to.

Chapter Three

'Hello?' I said cautiously into my phone, once Dolly had ushered me through the courtyard gate and into the lane beyond, before vanishing with a wave. 'Jess?'

'Where *are* you?' My sister's voice was practically a whisper. I guessed there must be a poorly baboon, or a sleepy alligator nearby that she didn't want to disturb. Jess was living in a protected rainforest area on the banks of the Kinabatangan River in Borneo, helping out at an orangutan orphanage – 'a little pocket of paradise' according to the website I'd scoured two years ago, when she had announced her intention to move there after reading about its dwindling habitats. She was a conservationist and had been keen to extend her skills beyond estimating our local barn owl population. 'I tried calling earlier, but you didn't answer,' she went on, 'so I rang the studio and Toni said you'd gone on holiday.'

'What were you calling about?' I sent a silent *thank you* to Toni for agreeing not to tell Jess where I was. My sister didn't generally dig for details, unless the topic of conversation had four legs and a tail, and maybe a trunk, or two legs and a snout, or scales and a horn and feathers, or—

'You never said you were going on holiday when we Skyped last week.'

Bugger. 'It must have slipped my mind!' I made my voice bright and sparkly as I trotted down the lane, hauling my suitcase behind me. I had no idea where I was heading, but could see a strip of twinkling sea ahead.

'You never go on holiday.'

'Exactly!' My voice shot up the scale. 'That's why I forgot to mention it! Plus, it was only six thirty in the morning over there and nearly bedtime here, so I wasn't quite with it when we spoke, and then you had to rush off and breastfeed an orangutan.'

'*Bottle feed*, not breastfeed, Elle.'

'That's what I said.'

'You didn't, you said breastfeed.'

'Well, you know what I meant.' I was walking faster, camera-bag bumping my hip, suitcase clattering the cobbles, as if I could somehow outrun our conversation.

I hadn't set out to deceive Jess. It had been a subconscious decision, based on the fact that she now lived thousands of miles away, helping monitor local wildlife, in between feeding primates (she'd always preferred animals to humans) and, more importantly, wouldn't understand my sudden need to trace my biological mother. As far as Jess was concerned, we'd had a lovely mum who'd treated us equally and been everything a mother should be. I was sure she'd be hurt and appalled if she knew what I was doing. She had no inkling about the contents of the bag I'd found and I wanted to keep it that way – at least for now.

'I was ringing to say that Owen proposed this morning.' Jess's words delivered me back to the moment.

'What?' Owen – a burly, curly-haired Welshman, who helped plant trees to regenerate the jungle – had fallen for Jess on their flight to

Borneo, drawn by her passion for the project, he told me, when they came over for Dad's funeral. I liked him a lot. He was good for Jess, who was inclined to treat humans the way some people treated animals – as if they didn't have feelings – and she'd looked relaxed and happy in his company, despite the sombre occasion. 'What did you say?'

'I said, Owen proposed to me—'

'No, I meant, how did you reply?'

'I said yes.' The way she spoke, as if it had required no more thought than breathing, brought me close to tears.

'That's brilliant,' I said, voice wobbling a little. 'I'm so happy for you, Jess.' It was true. Happy – and envious. The closest I'd come to thinking about marriage in the past ten years was with Andrew, and only because he'd forced me to. 'Have you set a date?' Words I never thought I'd say to my little sister, whose only long-term relationship prior to Owen had been with the boy next door, who'd had a pet snake called Slinky.

'It won't be until next year, when the orangutan rehabilitation centre's finished, but we've decided on 11 October, Mum's birthday, at the church in Wishbourne where she and Dad were married.'

Of course. Jess never needed to think too deeply about what she wanted to do; she simply made a decision and followed it through. 'Animals have an inherent instinct they're born with, and so do I,' she'd said, when I asked once how she knew that going to Borneo was right for her (I was terrified she'd get murdered). 'Most people do too, but they tend to ignore it.'

'Mum and Dad would have loved that,' I said, blinking away tears. My hurried steps had led me to a stretch of golden sand, busy with holidaymakers sunning already bronzed flesh, and strolling barefoot at the water's edge. I longed to be floating on my back in the glittering water, gazing up at the holiday-blue sky where seagulls swooped around. 'They'd be so proud of you, Jess, and not just because you're getting married.'

'I know.'

There was a pause, and I knew we were acknowledging all the things our parents had missed, and would continue to miss, and how unfair it was that they hadn't lived long enough to enjoy their retirement, or become in-laws and grandparents – although Jess had long ago decided that she wouldn't be adding more humans to the overpopulated planet, and I didn't even have a boyfriend.

'Have you gone away because of your break-up?' she said unexpectedly, and my mind flashed back six months to Andrew, pressing me on how soon I'd be ready to marry him and have his babies (plural). We hadn't been seeing each other long but he was almost ten years older and keen to settle down. His question had brought home that I wasn't ready for either.

'Something like that.' I bit the inside of my cheek to stop myself blurting out the truth.

'I thought you'd be over it by now,' said Jess. 'It's not like he was the love of your life, or anything.'

'Yes, but... I suppose it made me think about things. Like whether I'll ever meet someone who's right for me.'

'I never thought Andrew was right for you. It was really hard, laughing at his terrible puns.'

'I think he could tell.' Andrew had somehow sensed Jess's ambivalence, and used to go out of his way to try and impress her. 'And I know you thought he was wrong for me, because you said so.'

'He was too old for you, and you only date men like him because they're so different to Declan-couldn't-keep-it-in-his-pants.'

Declan Jones was the handsome Irishman I'd fallen for aged eighteen, not long after Mum died. He'd chatted me up in a pub with the line, 'If I had to rate you from one to ten, I'd rate you a nine because I'm the *one* you're missing.' It was a line he couldn't resist using on other women, once the novelty of having a steady girlfriend had worn thin, but he'd reel me back in with his smiling eyes, and his clever words, until I forgave him. Eventually, Dad had become so worried, he'd left a magazine out with an article highlighted about how when we meet someone we like, dopamine tricks the brain into ignoring anything that makes us uncomfortable, and mumbled over dinner one night that Mum wouldn't have wanted me to be with someone like Declan.

'You sound just like Toni,' I said.

'That's because I was quoting her.'

'Ah.' I felt a momentary yearning to share my secret, but couldn't bear the thought of upsetting Jess, especially when she was so far away, with vulnerable primates (and Owen) requiring her loving attention. 'I suppose I just needed a change of scenery.'

'You could have come here.'

Jess's accommodation was basic at best, and I knew I'd be hopeless at coping with the conditions. 'Thanks,' I said, a lump forming in my throat as it hit me how much I missed her. 'But I'd only get in the way.'

'Probably,' she joked. At least, I thought she was joking. 'You will do our wedding photos, won't you?'

My heart plunged. I'd rather be a guest at my sister's wedding and simply enjoy it – like I had Toni's – without the pressure of wondering whether something might go wrong. Like the time I'd snapped a candid shot of the best man kissing a bridesmaid, only for it to turn out to be the groom. I hadn't realised until the bride had a look through the pictures and burst into tears, and ended up blaming *me* for spoiling her day. Or the time the bride's cousin turned up in an almost-identical white dress and tried to sneak into all the photos. My diplomacy skills had been tested to the limit that day.

'Elle?'

'I… of course I will, I'd love to,' I said, wanting to make her happy. 'What's that awful noise?'

A whooping sound had erupted down the phone, and I pictured a fanged creature crashing through the undergrowth towards my sister, who, despite being tougher than she looked, barely scraped five feet.

'Oh, that's the supper siren,' she said. 'I'd better go.'

I was both relieved and disappointed. Jess rarely called out of the blue just to 'chat', it wasn't her style, and our Skype sessions were few and far between, so if I stayed on the line much longer, she might sense something was up. 'Thanks for calling,' I said. 'And congratulations.'

'For what?'

'Er, the wedding?'

'Oh, that! Yeah, thanks.'

I rolled my eyes. 'Take care, OK?' I always said that, though she'd once given me a virtual tour of the area she lived in and it looked idyllic.

'Enjoy your holiday,' she said, as if she'd just remembered. 'Where did you say you are?'

I didn't. 'Greece.' It shot out before I could stop it. Although Jess had always known I hadn't 'come out of Mummy's tummy' like she had, and that 'the lady who grew Elle in her womb' was French, it was doubtful she'd make the connection, but I wasn't taking any chances.

'Greece?' She sounded understandably perplexed. My last trip had been hiking in Scotland with Andrew, who'd been keen on activity breaks and didn't like flying, and I hadn't visited anywhere hot since a family trip to Spain in the nineties had ended with Dad getting sunstroke, Jess being bitten by an insect she'd tried to nurture, and Mum and me falling ill after eating some dodgy ice cream.

'Yep,' I said casually. 'Sunny Greece.'

'Which part?'

I closed my eyes and tried to think. 'Crete?'

'Near the mountains?'

She sounded so excited, I said, 'Yes, definitely close to the mountainy bit.'

'Oh, lucky you!' Her voice was shot with jealousy. 'You might get to see the kri-kri.'

'Hmm?'

'It's a rare, wild species of goat that inhabits the mountainous regions.' *Of course it was.* 'Try and get a picture, Elle. I'd *love* to see one in its natural habitat.' She sounded more enthused than she had about her wedding.

'I'll do my best,' I said, patting my camera bag as if to reinforce my lie. Luckily, the line cut off before I could dig myself in deeper, and feeling as if I'd been given a reprieve, I quickly tapped 21 les rue de Forages into Google Maps. It was time to find *my* habitat for the week.

Chapter Four

Ten minutes later, after stopping to ask for directions in basic French with lots of miming – I was as rubbish at following maps as I was at speaking the language – I found myself on a long narrow street, lined with whitewashed houses topped with orange-tiled roofs. They all had shutters framing the windows in varying shades of green, and hollyhocks sprouting along the fronts, adding splashes of colour that dazzled my eyes.

Pausing to look around, I felt a tug of recognition and wondered whether I was experiencing an unconscious link to the area – then remembered, I'd roamed around using street view after booking my stay online, so it was bound to look familiar. Even so, the quality of light seemed different, almost luminous; the sort that preceded a transformative experience. Or maybe I was close to fainting from the heat, exhaustion and hunger. Apart from the pain au chocolat at the café, I hadn't eaten since the night before, too nervous to ingest more than a cup of tea before the taxi arrived at six thirty to take me to the airport.

Trembling slightly, wishing my suitcase would transform into something tiny I could slip in my pocket, I wandered down the street. It was quiet after the hubbub of the harbour, café and beach, and empty apart from a child, riding a tricycle outside a house further down.

Number twenty-one came into view, hot-pink geraniums in tubs outside, and apple-green shutters that matched the shiny front door. Alongside it was the guest house where I'd been instructed to pick up the keys, an old-fashioned, black-framed bicycle with a basket on the front propped against the wall. It was a photograph waiting to happen, but I resisted getting my camera out and made do with snapping a picture on my phone to send to Toni.

A mouth-watering smell of cooking was wafting out of the guest house, and my stomach gurgled in response. The owner was obviously home and preparing dinner.

As I raised my hand to knock, the door swung open to reveal a petite, fifty-something woman with thick dark hair pulled back off a smiling face. 'Mademoiselle Matheson?'

With a thud of relief that she'd been expecting me, I said, '*Oui, je suis Elle*,' and held out a sticky hand, aware I was dishevelled and sweaty with a whiff of aeroplane about me. '*Bonjour*.' Even when I managed some French it sounded wrong. *Bonjewer.* Having French blood in my veins clearly hadn't given me an aptitude for the language.

'I am Madame Girard.' The woman spoke in softly-accented English as she shook my hand with surprising assurance, and I felt another pull of familiarity, perhaps because she looked how I'd imagined a Frenchwoman her age to look: classy and well-coiffed, but homely, in a denim-blue linen dress and lightweight shoes. I peered past her into a hallway that was small and rather dark, the only light coming off the street behind me, my gaze landing on a cluster of heavily-framed paintings on the wall, of ballerinas in various poses.

'I love your pictures,' I gushed, reminded of the ballet lessons I'd taken as a child, when Mum had believed it was something girls should do – only Jess had preferred getting grubby in the garden and I'd had two left feet.

'*Merci.*' Madame Girard dipped her head in acknowledgement and pulled a small bunch of keys from the pocket of her dress. 'The house where you are staying, it belongs to my friends, Marty Bright and his daughter, Natalie,' she said, stepping outside and taking hold of my suitcase before I could protest (not that I wanted to). 'They are in England for now.'

She sounded sad and when I glanced at her face, I saw that her smile hadn't quite made it to her eyes, which were large and dark. 'You are their very first guest.'

'I'm honoured,' I said, which sounded over-the-top, yet somehow appropriate.

Madame Girard's smile reached its full potential – though I fancied there was still an air of melancholy about her. 'I think you will find it very comfortable.'

'I'm sure I will.' I hoped there was food in the house. I'd passed a boulangerie and a small food store on the way, but hadn't thought to go in and buy anything. 'There weren't many places left that weren't already booked,' I said, realising too late that my admission of desperation was hardly a compliment.

Madame Girard's smile stayed put. 'The Île de Ré, it is very popular.' She said it with pride, as though the island was a clever teenager. 'People, they all want to come here, even the film stars.'

'So I've heard.'

Her cheeks flushed a girlish pink as she tugged my suitcase next door, before I could wrest it from her (not that I tried). 'My good friend, Jeanne, she works at a hotel in Saint-Martin, where they come to stay.' She threw me an unreadable look. 'You have heard of Jay Merino?'

I nodded. 'I saw him announce his retirement on the news,' I said. Toni had been devastated. She was a massive fan of his *Maximum Force* movies. 'He was filming here, I believe?'

Madame Girard paused in the act of opening the door, and I had a feeling there was a lot she wanted to say, but she settled for, 'He seems to be a nice man,' which left me wondering whether she'd actually met him. 'You have not visited the island before?'

I shook my head, finally getting a grip on my suitcase and humping it over the doorstep, careful not to mark the parquet floor inside. 'It's my first time,' I said over my shoulder, mindful of the real reason I was there, aware of the postcard in my bag as though it was flashing like a beacon.

'When visitors come, they want to stay a long time.' Still smiling slightly in the doorway, Madame Girard enquired gently, 'You are alone?'

'I am,' I said, wishing it didn't sound so pathetic. Lots of people went away on their own, and after Andrew, I'd decided it was better to be single than with the wrong person, but at that moment, I wished that Toni was here – the single, child-free Toni, who'd been good at making me have fun, which was something I'd apparently forgotten how to do.

'What brings you here, Mademoiselle Matheson?'

'Please, call me Elle.' I had the feeling I was going to be seeing more of Madame Girard, especially if we were going to be neighbours. 'I, er… actually, I have a job,' I said. 'At the Café Belle Vie.'

'You are not here on holiday?' She seemed as surprised as I was to hear I was going to be working during my stay. 'I thought perhaps you take pictures.' She gestured to my camera bag, which had started to feel as though it was full of rocks. 'A lot of visitors, they come here for the views and the wildlife.'

I thought of Jess, asking me to get a picture of the kri-kri goat, and didn't know whether to laugh or cry. 'I *do* take pictures, but I wanted some work experience while I was here, something…' I was struggling for words. 'Something *rustic* and local, and the café was looking for staff.'

Madame Girard nodded, as if my logic was sound. Either that, or she'd sensed I was suddenly close to tears and thought it best to back off. 'It is a good place to work,' she said. 'The owners, they are lovely people.'

I thought of Dolly, who now knew more about this trip than my own sister. 'Yes, they do seem nice.'

After a little pause, during which she seemed to be weighing me up, she said, 'Every day, I cook for my guests and you are welcome to join us.' Perhaps I looked as hungry as I felt. 'It would be my pleasure,' she went on. 'I often cooked supper for Marty and Natalie.' She said 'supper' as though it was a word she relished.

'That's incredibly kind of you.'

She hooked a drifting strand of hair behind her ear. In the sunlight, grey strands were visible among the brown, but the effect was elegant rather than let-yourself-go. 'Are you an actress?' she said, out of the blue. 'I feel, maybe I have seen you before.'

Here we go. 'Some people say I look like a young Marilyn Monroe.' I pushed a hand through my short, blonde waves and gave an ironic smile. 'I can't see it myself.' Neither could she, judging by her knitted brow. 'Anyway, I'll let you go.' I switched my smile up a notch, before she could point out that I looked nothing like a fifties sex symbol.

She blinked twice and said, 'The keys.'

'Sorry?'

She held out three keys on a heart-shaped keyring. 'One for this door, one for the door to the garden, one for the… *cabanon*. The shed.' She pointed to each. 'You will keep these safe?'

She sounded a little anxious, and I guessed she must feel a weight of responsibility for her neighbour's home. 'Of course,' I said, taking them from her and curling my hand around them. 'I won't let them out of my sight.'

She began to move away, her forehead still lightly creased. 'Do not be a stranger,' she said, before slipping out of view.

'I won't!' I poked my head outside, but she'd already gone into her house and shut the door, and I wondered whether it would be rude to take her up on her offer of dinner, once I'd unpacked.

With a burst of renewed energy, I dropped the keys in a glass bowl on a plant-stand by the door, and spun round to take in my surroundings. I was in a low-ceilinged lounge, an open staircase leading up to the landing, sunshine pouring through a deep-set window and across the buttermilk walls. A pair of inviting armchairs were grouped on a patterned rug in front of an open fireplace, with a well-filled bookcase to one side, and a comfy-looking sofa under the window. There was a floor lamp nearby that I could imagine reading under, in front of a crackling fire on a winter's evening.

The place smelled faintly of pine, and looked clean and well-loved, but I guessed from the uncluttered surfaces that the owners had sensibly stashed their personal items away from prying eyes.

In the red-and-white farmhouse style kitchen, a handwritten note of welcome had been left on the wooden worktop.

Hi, Elle!

There's food in the fridge and cupboards so help yourself, but Marie next door is a fantastic cook and will probably invite you round – I advise you to accept! She also has a spare set of keys, just in case (I've locked myself out more than once). The Café Belle Vie

*is five minutes away and a brilliant place to hang out. My (British)
friend Charlie runs it with his mum, Dolly. They can tell you about
the best places to visit while you're here, and feel free to borrow my
bike (in the shed in the garden). I'm missing Chamillon already!*

Have a wonderful time,
Natalie Bright x

PS The bathroom door sticks at the bottom so give it a shove.
*PPS My dad says you're welcome to read his books if you get bored
– AS IF!!*

I smiled as I read the note again, which included simple directions underneath for using the cooker, television and washing machine. I'd booked the house through a holiday website so hadn't made direct contact with the owner, but had a feeling I'd like Natalie Bright, and wondered what had brought her to Chamillon – and what had taken her away.

There was fruit in a glass bowl on the kitchen table and I quickly ate a banana to take the edge off my hunger, while searching for teabags and milk. Finding both, I made a mug of tea and took it upstairs, where three plain doors led off a red-carpeted landing that reminded me a little of my grandparents' house in Cornwall.

The first was locked when I pushed down the handle and the second led into a blue-and-white tiled bathroom, containing a walk-in shower that looked brand new. The third door was ajar and I entered a shady room with a sloping ceiling, dominated by a brass-framed bed. It was covered with a puffy duvet, and there were several fat pillows that made me want to sink down and bury my head in them, and through the uncurtained window was a view of blue sky. There were four fat seagulls on the rooftops, squaring up for a fight.

Finally unhooking my camera bag, I dropped it on a raffia chair by a cream-painted wardrobe, catching a glimpse of myself in a full-length mirror on the wall. It was like seeing a stranger in new surroundings – one with hair that needed a wash, and cheeks too pink from the sun. My eyes looked bluer than usual, as though their brightness had been turned up, and there was a brown smudge on my top from the pain au chocolat I'd eaten, which Madame Girard must have spotted. Turning away, I sipped my tea, blushing when I remembered the look on her face when I'd mentioned my passing resemblance to Marilyn Monroe. More like Marilyn Manson – but less attractive.

I knew I should go and fetch my suitcase; unpack, have a shower and something proper to eat – I'd noticed a pack of bacon in the fridge, as well as chicken breasts, a wedge of cheese, eggs, ham and salad ingredients – but my eyelids felt heavy and the temptation to sit on the bed for a moment was irresistible.

I put my empty mug on the floor and removed my cross-body bag, taking out my phone and placing it on the glass-topped bedside table. Perhaps I should test the mattress. I wasn't relishing sleeping in a bed that wasn't my own, but as I lay down and stretched out, the tension in my body began to recede. I wriggled around with pleasure. The mattress felt just right – not too soft, not too hard – and the pillows were soft, yet supportive. It was like being cradled in air. Nicely fragranced air. I wondered what brand of detergent Natalie used. It smelled so good, reminding me of happy times. Cotton-wool clouds on a bright summer's day, as I played in the garden with Jess. My grandmother calling us into her cottage for scones and lemonade. The puppy they'd had, leaping unfeasibly high to catch a tennis ball.

My head swam, images from earlier circling round in my mind. I needed to close my eyes, just for a second. The images slowed… the café, Charlie, Dolly, the old man with the little black dog; Madame Girard shaking my hand and... seagulls. Seagulls, fighting and... the sea... the sea, washing the sand... someone snoring.

Must be me.

Chapter Five

I snapped awake with a snort, blinking at a kaleidoscope of colours on the ceiling. Why was there a crystal pendant light in my bedroom, making rainbow patterns across the paintwork? My lightshade was beige, I'd had it for years, and my duvet cover was patterned with owls, not soft and white like a cloud. More importantly, where the hell was my arm?

Twisting my head, I realised I was lying on it. I tugged it free and it flopped, completely numb, like something that didn't belong to me. In a flash, I remembered. I was in Chamillon, in a stranger's house, where I'd stretched out on the bed and must have drifted off.

With the arm that was working, I scrabbled my phone off the table and gasped when I saw the date had changed and it was seven thirty – *the following morning.* How had I slept for so long? Without eating dinner? I hadn't even been to the bathroom.

I sat up, my arm prickling painfully back to life, and registered a lack of the tension across my shoulders that had been present for the past few months. It had started when I found the bag in Dad's wardrobe, and had worsened to the point where I'd tried a yoga class to try and ease the stiffness, but was so inflexible I'd sprained my hip and walked with a limp for a week. Apparently, all I'd needed was fifteen hours' sleep in a different country. Or maybe it was because I was finally doing something, instead of endlessly talking things over with Toni.

Determined to hold onto my sense of well-being, I almost skipped to the bathroom – Natalie was right, the door needed a little shove – and emerged ten minutes later, swathed in a soft white towel, smelling of lemons and coconut and feeling impossibly serene. Through the window, the sky was a delicate blue, the sun already shining across the rooftops. I opened it wide and inhaled a draft of fresh air, certain I could detect a hint of salt.

I decided to let my hair dry naturally and hummed 'You Are My Sunshine' as I bounded down to fetch my suitcase, hoisting it up the stairs as though it contained nothing but feathers, instead of most of my wardrobe. I'd checked the weather in France before I packed, and ignored it. Forecasts were often wrong, and summer at home had been a washout, so I'd brought a bit of everything just in case. Still, it was unlikely I'd need my chunky black sweater and matching scarf, or the showerproof raincoat that had served me well on my trip to Scotland with Andrew, and I probably wouldn't need so many socks – or any. Four cardigans seemed excessive (what had I been thinking?) and the eye-catching, aquamarine midi-dress I'd bought in a sale, and hadn't been brave enough to wear, still seemed a bit too 'French Riviera' – even though I actually *was* in France. My jeans were more suited to longline jumpers and boots, but I'd packed some shorts and stripy wide-legged trousers, which, combined with a plain white T-shirt, would have to do, bearing in mind I had a job to go to. (*Really, Elle?* I imagined Toni saying. *You already have a job.*)

I'd intended to phone her with an update the night before, but realised it would have to wait now as my phone battery was about to die. I'd brought an adapter plug and put my phone on charge while I went downstairs in search of breakfast, eager to get the day going. As I scoured the open shelves, which were stuffed with packets and jars, telling myself it wasn't snooping as everything was on display, my eyes grazed the note on the worktop and the name Marie leapt out. *Marie.* I couldn't believe it hadn't registered before. *Marie next door is a fantastic cook...* Madame Girard was Marie – her name began with M!

I remembered the feeling I'd had when she shook my hand the previous day, as if I knew her from somewhere, and hadn't she thought I looked familiar too? Toni had pointed out that inheriting my father's looks might be the clincher once I arrived – that my birth mother might even recognise *me* before I knew who she was.

'Just hope she doesn't scream and slap you round the face,' she'd joked, though her face had been swathed with worry. 'If a dark-haired fifty-something takes one look at you, turns white and runs away, you'll know it's her.' There'd never been a happy outcome in Toni's scenarios, which had included my birth mother denying my very existence, or at least blaming me for ruining her life.

My legs suddenly felt like melting candles, and I dropped onto a chair at the kitchen table, my head a mishmash of thoughts. Marie was the right age to be a mother. *My* mother? And her hair was dark. Still, it wasn't much to go on. And how was I supposed to approach her? It properly sank in that blurting out *Did you sleep with a man in London thirty years ago and give him your baby to raise?* was reckless and borderline dangerous. Trying to imagine Madame Girard's reaction – a real, flesh-and-blood woman, who could have had all sorts of reasons for doing something so drastic; reasons that might bring back such painful memories, she'd hate me for reminding her – made me shiver, in spite of the sunshine flowing through the window onto my back.

I shakily rose and pulled a carton of pomegranate juice from the fridge, and after sinking a glassful, felt slightly calmer, though my heart was still beating too fast.

Maybe I was overreacting. I couldn't go around assuming every female I met with the initial M was the woman who'd given birth to me – but what else could I do until I'd ruled them out? I began to pace, as adrenaline flooded my veins once more. Or maybe it was sugar in the juice, powering me up.

I would take Marie up on her offer of dinner and try to talk to her then, and in the meantime, I could ask Dolly about her. As I wondered whether Dolly had contacted her friend at the town hall yet, I glanced at the clock on the wall and gave a start: almost eight thirty. Dolly had asked me to come in early, but how early was early? What if she'd meant half six? The café probably opened then to catch the breakfast crowd and would now be in full flow, while I was faffing about as though on holiday.

Forgetting about breakfast, and doing my best to push Marie to the back of my mind for now, I tore upstairs to fetch my bag, and, once I'd snatched up the keys, practically threw myself outside. As I was fumbling with the lock, a man's voice said in a French accent, 'Would you like some help with that?'

I jerked so hard with fright, the key dropped from my fingers into a pot of geraniums, and I turned to see the dark-haired man from the café, whose foot I'd run over with my suitcase, coming out of Madame Girard's front door (I found it was better if I didn't think of her as 'Marie' just yet).

'I'm sorry,' he said, raising his hands as if staving off an attack. 'I didn't mean to startle you.'

'It's OK,' I mumbled, bending to retrieve the keys. *Great.* Now I had damp soil underneath my nails. Someone – probably Madame Girard – had watered the plants, which were almost indecently perky and green-leaved.

'Shall I look too?'

'It's fine, I've got them,' I said, holding up the keyring. He was tall, his hair tousled, as though he'd had an athletic night, and had what Toni would call (OK, what *I* would call) 'bedroom eyes'. They were currently narrowed as a smile stretched over what Toni (and I) would call a 'ruggedly handsome' face that I hadn't properly appreciated the day before.

'You ran over my foot,' he said, wagging a finger in recognition. 'With your luggage.'

'I'm sorry about that,' I said breathlessly (why was I breathless?), finally locking the door. I didn't have time to stand around making conversation, however good-humoured he seemed to be, but felt obliged to add, 'I hope it didn't hurt too much.'

'It's OK, I have a spare one.' He grinned as he pointed to his feet, which were tanned and nicely shaped, and just a little bit hairy (but not unattractively so) in well-worn leather sandals. His lower legs were dusted with dark hairs too, and also nicely shaped beneath a pair of cargo shorts. 'You're staying here?'

Obviously. 'Yes,' I said, looking away and slotting the keys in my bag to show I meant business. I didn't have time for flirting with strange men – if that's what was happening, which it probably wasn't, only his smile indicated it might be. 'I'm just on my way to work.' That sounded so weird. Going to work meant heading to the studio to take client headshots, or shooting (not literally) families, often with a pet in the mix, not doling out coffee and pastries. I hadn't even unpacked my camera, and it hit me that I had no idea how to use a coffee machine. When I'd worked at the Cup and Saucer, tea had been the more popular beverage, and the coffee had come from a jar anyway.

No longer serene, I felt a prickle of annoyance with whoever he was, appraising me with his head cocked, as though trying to work something out.

'Where do you work?' His French accent made everything he said sound unsettlingly sensual, and I briefly wondered what he made of mine. Even to my own ears, I sounded strait-laced, like someone playing an English teacher in a film.

'It's my first day at the Café Belle Vie.' Saying it aloud reminded me of the postcard in my bag, and my heart did its customary bounce.

'Ah, my friend Charlie works there,' said the man, the creases around his eyes deepening as his smile grew. He looked to be around my age, maybe a year or two older, his tan suggesting he spent his days outdoors, probably doing manual work. Observing the firmness of his body, my face coloured and grew hotter when he caught me looking and folded his arms. It was either a protective gesture, or a way of emphasising the swell of muscles in his arms.

With an effort, I wrenched my eyes away. 'I met him yesterday,' I said, fiddling with the zip on my bag, not mentioning the circumstances of our meeting. 'He seemed very pleasant.'

'He is indeed *pleasant*, and you'll love working at the café.' He sounded amused as he added, 'I'm Henri Durand, by the way.'

I remembered the woman he'd been with the day before, saying his name in a chastising way. Probably his girlfriend. 'Elle Matheson,' I said, and was about to walk away – why was he still looking at me? – when a thought struck.

'You know Madame Girard?' I pointed to her front door, aware I could smell bacon cooking, wondering whether I would ever eat again.

Henri nodded, generous enough not to point out that he wouldn't have been in her house if he didn't – unless he was burgling the place.

'I was bringing her fresh fish to cook tonight for her guests,' he said. 'You've met her?'

It was my turn to nod. 'She gave me the keys for the house, she knows the owners.'

'Ah yes, she was friendly with the Brights when they lived here.' His gaze was speculative, and I decided it would be odd if I started asking more personal questions about Madame Girard.

'How come you're bringing fish to the house?' I glanced around for a supermarket delivery van, but there were no vehicles on the street other than a couple of bikes thrown down on the kerb nearby.

'We have an arrangement,' he said, and a horrible vision rose, of Madame Girard trading sexual favours for bunches of haddock (haddocks?) before Henri explained, 'I'm a fisherman. Customers pay well for the morning's catch.'

'Oh!' Surprised, I gave him a closer look, as if I'd missed something in his appearance that gave away what he did for a living, though what, I had no idea. Fish scales in his hair, perhaps; a fin sticking out of his pocket? He didn't even smell fishy, though there was a definite whiff of ozone about him. Realising I was almost sniffing the air by his shoulder, I quickly backed away. 'Well, it's nice to meet you, Henri, but I have to go.' I wanted to be alone now, to digest all the information rattling around in my head, and work out how to avoid getting fired before I'd even started work, but Henri fell into step beside me.

'You are going the wrong way,' he said, placing a hand on my elbow and gently steering me in the opposite direction.

My skin felt scorched where he'd touched me. 'Thanks,' I mumbled, blinking as the sun hit my eyes. Disorientated, I bumped against him and sprang away, stumbling a little.

He caught my arm to steady me, and once more I felt a strong reaction to the feel of his fingers on my flesh.

'Sorry,' I said, laughing a little. First Charlie, knocking me down and pulling me back to my feet, and now Henri saving me from falling. It felt like it meant something meaningful, and possibly unflattering.

'I'm going to the café for breakfast,' he said amiably, as if I wasn't acting like I'd never been outdoors. 'It's a good place to have a little break before I go back to work.'

'Go back?' Recovering, I picked up my pace, trying to project the sort of confidence I had in spades in my studio, coaxing out smiles and playing around with poses.

'For the visitors,' he said, espresso-dark eyes flashing in my direction. 'My family runs fishing trips around the island. Something they've done for years.'

'What about in the winter?'

'We make a good enough living in the spring and summer to see us through the quieter months.' He sounded guarded, and I realised it must seem as though I was digging for information about his income, which – as a fisherman – probably wasn't very much.

'Sorry,' I said, just in case. 'I wasn't prying.'

'You may pry all you want to, Elle.' His voice had dropped an octave, his gaze somehow inviting. 'I'm open to questions.'

Oh God, he was a womaniser. I should have known. The bedroom eyes, the tousled hair and – accent notwithstanding – his seductive way of speaking, as though we were on a steamy date, about to take it to the next level. Now I was picturing him without his shirt on, wondering whether his chest was hairy too. I felt a pinch of panic and started walking faster, barely taking in my surroundings. I must *not* get attracted to Henri. He was exactly the sort of man that Dad had warned me to stay away from – that *I'd* warned me to stay away from. The type I'd vowed never to fall for again, after Declan.

Not that I was planning to fall for anyone, at least while I was in France. Though a *fling* with someone like Henri wouldn't be the same as *falling* for them, and if I was on holiday I might… But I *wasn't* on holiday and I didn't have time for any distractions.

'Here we are.' Henri's voice derailed my dizzying thoughts, and I realised we'd reached the café, which was teeming, inside and out, with customers.

'I think I'm late,' I said, feeling even more breathless, as though we'd been sprinting. I looked over at the harbour, which was packed with multicoloured fishing boats, pitching gently in the glassy water. 'Is that where you work?' *Stop talking to him, Elle.*

Once more, I felt the weight of his assessing gaze and colour ran up my face, probably making all my freckles stand out.

'I work from Saint-Martin, the island's capital,' he said, leaning past to hold the door of the café open for me. 'How long are you here for? I could show you around sometime.'

'I'm going to be very busy,' I said, dipping under his arm to avoid his gaze. *He definitely didn't smell of fish.* 'Goodbye, Henri.'

I didn't look back as I hurried towards the counter, half-expecting Dolly to be angry that I hadn't arrived sooner, and was relieved when she looked up and broke into a welcoming smile.

'Elle, I'm so glad you're here,' she said, coming out to greet me. 'Now, let me find you an apron.'

Chapter Six

Within minutes, I'd stuffed my bag in a cupboard in the little staff room, washed the dirt from under my nails, and was back in the kitchen with an apron around my waist.

'Just to let you know,' said Dolly, in a confidential tone, 'I tried to contact Francine, but she's away today.' My heart dropped. 'But I've been having a think, and I already know of a couple of people who could be...' she looked round and lowered her voice 'the person you're looking for,' she said. 'One is Marie Girard—'

'I've met her,' I said. 'I'm staying in the house next door.'

'Oh, lucky you.' Dolly nodded her approval. 'Well, she's a wonderful woman, but doesn't talk about her past, and I actually don't know her that well, *soooo*...' She made a balancing gesture with her hands. 'You should definitely talk to her.'

'I will,' I said, not mentioning I'd already decided to.

'Another is one of our regulars, Margot.' Dolly peered behind her again, as if the kitchen might be filled with eavesdroppers. 'She should be in later. I'll give you a call when I see her and introduce you.'

'That's great,' I said, feeling nervy all of a sudden. Possibilities were taking shape, becoming tangible, and the thought of unleashing questions that might bring answers was as terrifying as it was exciting.

'Of course, there's a big chance your birth mother doesn't live in Chamillon any more,' Dolly continued, pulling on an oven glove and removing a tray of croissants from the oven. 'People born in villages often move away, but we can at least rule out anyone here I can think of, until I hear from Francine, and then you could widen the search on the internet.' *Widen the search sounded momentous.* 'Now, have one of these while I run you through what to do,' she added, nodding to the oven-fresh pastries, as if she suspected hunger had robbed me of the ability to speak. 'We don't want you passing out on the job.'

I helped myself to a croissant, my mind awash with confusion, and felt almost tearful with gratitude when a cup of milky coffee – the café's speciality, Dolly explained – was brought through by Stefan, as if she'd summoned him telepathically.

'We're a good little team,' she said as he smiled and disappeared, and the woman I'd seen serving customers the day before bustled in.

''Allo, I am Celeste.' Her voice was as warm as her smile, which was wide and genuine.

'Hi, I'm Elle,' I said, and Celeste fired off a few words in French to Dolly.

'Yes, I'm welcoming Elle to our family.' Dolly patted my arm, and I felt a ridiculous flush of pleasure.

'She seems nice,' I said as Celeste departed with a pile of trays and another smile.

'She's new, but the customers love her already.'

I decided I was going to enjoy helping out at the café. I liked being in Dolly's kind but efficient orbit, and it was nice not to be in charge for once. I was probably a much better waitress than I had been, and it couldn't be harder than photographing a wedding where the bride repeatedly accused me of 'lingering too long' on the groom because I 'fancied him' or trying to get a decent shot of a disgruntled newborn determined to fill his nappy.

I accepted another croissant, restored by carbohydrates, while Dolly ran through a list of health and safety rules I barely absorbed, before showing me where everything was, and how to operate the dishwasher.

'You'll be in charge of clearing tables and washing-up,' she said, patting the front of the shiny machine as though it was a pet. 'Although, Basil here will do most of the work on that score.' She gave me her eye-crinkling smile. 'It's not like you'll be up to your elbows in suds, like the old days.'

Basil? Washing-up? 'But… what about the coffee machine?' I said as Stefan returned with an armful of empty plates and placed them in the sink before hurrying out. 'Or, I can take customer orders and restock the pastries and… things.' I eyed the tray of goodies on the central island, wondering how the staff resisted helping themselves.

'Stefan and Celeste have that covered, and Mathilde will be in later to help with the lunchtime rush.' *Mathilde.* I'd almost forgotten about her. 'I'm afraid it's the washing and clearing up I need some help with.' Dolly surveyed me, hands on hips, a query in her eyes. She was wearing a palette of black and white that made me think of my dad's old chessboard, and her tanned forearms looked strong. 'Are you OK with that?'

'Of course,' I said, thinking that it served me right for agreeing to help without asking what that entailed, and feeling silly that I'd worried about what to wear, when it seemed I was going to be stuck in the kitchen for hours. Even though the kitchen was bright and modern, and clean enough to double as an operating theatre – apart from the sink, and the areas on either side, which were piled with unwashed crockery.

Eyeing it warily, I reminded myself it was a fair exchange for Dolly's help, even if it was less glamorous than I'd imagined. 'I'll make a start, shall I?' Aware of her expectant gaze, and keen to show that I wasn't the type that baulked at getting my hands dirty (even though I didn't want to get my hands dirty), I reached for a stack of plates. 'Should I rinse them first?'

As I turned, the top three slid off the pile and I watched with horror as they crashed to the floor, the sound of shattering china ricocheting through the building. 'Oh no!' I whispered, transported back to my disastrous stint at the Cup and Saucer, fourteen years ago. At least the sound hadn't prompted a cheer, like it had whenever I'd broken something back then. 'I'm *so* sorry.'

Stefan appeared and took in the mess with a smile. 'Now I am not the only one to break all the plates,' he said in passable English.

'He had butterfingers during his first week,' said Dolly fondly. She'd magicked a long-handled brush from somewhere and was sweeping the scattered shards into a neat pile. 'Maybe wear rubber gloves, it'll create a firmer grip.' She nodded to a pair on the side. 'And yes, give everything a rinse before loading Basil.'

Half-wishing I'd given the café a wide berth until I'd settled in, creating an alternative future where I didn't look like an idiot, I put down the remaining plates carefully and snapped on the yellow gloves. 'How much do I owe you?' I said, hot with embarrassment, hoping I'd got enough euros in my purse.

Dolly simply chuckled as she flipped open the bin and deposited the broken pieces inside. 'Let's put it down to first day nerves.'

First day nerves. Her words brought back my first day at Perfect Moments, fresh from college, shadowing and assisting middle-aged wedding photographer, Ivan, who took great pleasure in telling me I had the potential to ruin someone's day.

'There are no second chances to shoot a wedding,' he'd said grimly, confessing he'd learned the hard way after forgetting to load his camera with film (in the days before digital) until the wedding in question was nearly over.

'I could have been sued, if my assistant hadn't been taking photos too – though, naturally, they weren't as good as mine.'

'I would have given up,' I'd said, despite having previously decided weddings would be my speciality.

'You can't give up the first time something goes wrong, however would you learn?' he'd said sternly. 'I never made that mistake again.'

Nevertheless, I hadn't been able to help imagining a different outcome and never fully relaxed after that. Yet there I was, long after Ivan had retired and I'd taken over the studio, still doing weddings; still terrified every time.

'I'll be more careful,' I promised Dolly, realising I had the potential to ruin *her* day if I carried on like this.

She waved a dismissive hand. 'I'll leave you to it,' she said as Stefan popped back, saying someone called Gérard wanted to talk to her. 'I hope Hamish hasn't weed on the floor,' she added, following Stefan through to the café.

I wondered whether Hamish was Gérard's partner, and what was wrong with him.

'Hamish is a dog, in case you were wondering.'

I spun round to see Charlie filling the doorway to the courtyard, his eyes alight with amusement.

'Thank God for that!' I said. 'I was worried for a moment.'

'No lasting damage from yesterday?' Coming closer, he looked me over, as if checking my limbs were intact.

'Not even a bruise, and my wrist has stopped hurting.'

'You hurt your wrist?' Concern replaced his smile.

'Only a bit, and it's fine, I promise. I'm tougher than I look, see?' I flexed a weedy bicep.

'I'm glad to hear it,' he said, a little doubtfully. 'You got the job, then?'

'Well, only for a week, but your mum was desperate.' I waggled my rubber-gloved hands. 'Although this wasn't quite what I was expecting.'

'Oh?' Leaning against the worktop, he gave me a speculative look. 'What *were* you expecting?'

Realising I might have come across as petulant, I said quickly, 'I just meant, the last time I worked in a café, there wasn't a dishwasher.'

'Ah, well, we have all mod-cons here.' His smile reappeared. 'I take it Mum's introduced you to Basil?'

'Why Basil?'

'It's one of her quirks.' He moved over and opened the dishwasher, and a fog of steam billowed out. 'Mum thinks giving appliances names makes them more appealing.'

'Fair enough.'

'Want a hand?'

'No, no, you must have things to do.'

'Catching up with some admin this morning.' He pulled his mouth down at the corners. 'It's pretty boring, but someone has to do it, and that person happens to be me.'

'I'm not good with that side of things.' I started to unload Basil – Dolly was right, naming the machine *did* make it seem more appealing – taking care not to drop anything. 'My friend runs that side of my business.'

'You have a business?' He sounded surprised, as well he might, when I was doing a good impression of being so desperate for a job, I'd agreed to help out for a week.

'I'm a photographer,' I confessed. 'I have a studio, back home. In Camden. Though I don't live in London. Toni – that's my friend – does, with her husband Mark. He's a copywriter, they had a baby last year.' *What was I rattling on about?* 'I live in Hertfordshire, I grew up there, in a village called Wishbourne and commute to work every day, which is a bit of a pain, but I never fancied living in the city.'

Abruptly, I ran out of words.

'Well, that explains the camera,' Charlie said, taking a pair of clean cups from me and placing them on a tray by the door, ready to be made dirty again. 'If you have your own business, why are you in Chamillon, washing dishes in a café?'

Grateful he'd glossed over my landfill of information, I said, 'That's a great question,' and bent to grab a handful of spoons, while I tried to think of a convincing answer.

'Sorry, I was just being nosy.' His voice held a note of regret. 'My friend Natalie says I have a habit of asking too many questions.'

'Oh, she mentioned you in a note she left for me.' I straightened. 'You're her friend.'

'I am.' He grinned with obvious affection. 'She's great, you'd like her.'

I wondered if they were more than friends, but didn't like to ask. 'I suppose I'm having a bit of a crisis at the moment,' I said truthfully, handing him the spoons, which he put on the tray with the cups. 'I wasn't actually looking for a job, but when your mum said she was short-staffed—'

'Isn't that why you were here?' He pointed to where we were standing, his brows drawing together, and I felt a flash of relief that Dolly had been true to her word and not revealed my reason for being here. 'I thought… you were standing outside and I assumed…' Understanding worked its way across his face. 'You didn't even know about the vacancy, did you?' he said. 'You just wanted to sit down and have a drink?'

'Well, maybe, but I'm glad you mentioned it.' I pulled off the rubber gloves, which were making my fingers sweaty. 'You did me a favour really, the café's lovely, and so is Dolly.'

'I can't argue with either of those statements.' It was clear he was expecting more from the angle of his eyebrows.

'I… er, remembered my father once mentioning Chamillon and decided I wanted to see it for myself.'

He rubbed his beardy chin in a contemplative way. 'I always wanted to go to Egypt to see the pyramids after watching *The Mummy* when I was younger, but what a let-down.' His eyebrows crinkled. 'The Great Pyramid of Giza isn't even in the desert. I could see it from the Pizza Hut where we'd stopped for lunch.'

I couldn't help a splutter of laughter at his expression. 'I don't think Chamillon is going to be a disappointment,' I said. 'I love it already.'

'Good to know.' He grinned. 'Have you been to France before?'

I shook my head. 'This is my first time.'

'Not even on a school trip?'

I could hardly explain that my father hadn't wanted me to visit, presumably because of the connection to my birth mother – as if France was a street and I might bump into her. Just like he'd fretted for a while that she might have followed him home after handing me over, and would come back one day to reclaim me.

I'd thought about that for a while, after he told me the story that day on the sofa, trying to imagine a knock on the door and a dark-eyed stranger coming to whisk me away, and had felt violently glad it never happened.

'I haven't had much time for travelling,' I told Charlie, smearing my hands down my apron. 'But it's good to be here, though your mum might be regretting it. I've already smashed some plates.'

Charlie studied me for a moment longer, as if sensing there was more to my story, and just as my smile was beginning to hurt, he said, 'Yes, I heard, but it's a rite of passage to destroy at least three items of crockery, so I wouldn't feel too bad.'

Eager to change the subject, I returned my attention to the dishes in the sink, aware they weren't going to clean themselves. 'So, the café's a family affair?' Turning the tap on, I flinched as a jet of water hit the edge of a mug and sprayed up over my top.

'It is.' Charlie handed me a tea towel, biting his bottom lip as if to stop himself laughing. 'Well, when I say family, it's me and Mum. Dad's not been in the picture for a long time, and I don't have siblings, so…'

'I have a sister,' I said, dabbing at my T-shirt, now clinging wetly across my chest. 'But she lives in Borneo. For now, anyway.'

'Wow.' To his credit, he kept his eyes on my face, which felt swollen with heat. 'Sounds interesting.'

'She is.' For some reason, I added, 'She's just announced she's getting married next year.'

Pulling a face, he helped himself to a croissant. 'I know I should say congratulations, but marriage is one institution I hope never to enter,' he said, just as Dolly came in with yet more dirty plates.

'Charlie, don't say that,' she scolded, as if he'd announced he was taking up cliff diving. 'You just haven't met the right woman.'

As she spoke, her eyes skimmed mine, and I saw that light again – the one that hoped I might be a prospective girlfriend, and it crossed my mind that she might have had an ulterior motive for offering to help me out.

'Mum…' Charlie's voice held a friendly warning.

Dolly rattled the tray down. 'I tried to matchmake him with his friend Natalie and got a good telling-off,' she said to me. 'Quite rightly,' she jumped in, holding up a hand as Charlie began to speak. 'I've learnt my lesson.'

'Clearly you haven't.' He flicked me an apologetic look. 'I don't date staff,' he said. 'Plus, I'm already seeing someone.'

'Someone I've never even met.' Dolly did a dramatic eye-roll. 'I think he's made her up to get me off his back.'

'I told you, her name's Tegan, she's Australian, and I'm keeping her away from you for now, because I don't want her being scared off.'

'Charming,' Dolly said good-naturedly. 'You'd think it was a crime to want to see your son happily married.'

'Give it a rest, Mum.'

Stung by Charlie's assumption that I'd be interested in him in *that* way, as well as being referred to as staff (even though I was), I said, 'You don't need to worry, I'm not interested in marriage either.'

'I'm not worried,' he said kindly. 'But thanks for putting me straight.'

Dolly tutted. 'How are you getting on?' she said to me, eyeing the overflowing sink. 'Not very well, by the look of things.'

'I'm sorry,' I muttered. 'I'm on it.'

'My fault,' Charlie said. 'I kept her talking.'

I couldn't look at him after the turn the conversation had taken, and watched instead as Dolly's eyes sank to my chest. 'Do you want to borrow a dry T-shirt, love?' she said. 'I can see your nipples.'

Chapter Seven

Dolly found me a plain T-shirt a couple of sizes too big that she kept as a 'spare' and Charlie announced he was going to the bank, tactfully ignoring Dolly's observation and averting his eyes as he left. Once I'd got changed in the staff room – more flustered than I could ever remember being before – I returned to the kitchen, relieved to find it empty, and by lunchtime was in a routine of sorts, even managing to clear a couple of tables in the café without self-combusting. I told myself that no one was waiting for me to fail, and, if they were, I wouldn't notice anyway. I was too busy trying not to drop anything.

I looked for Henri the first time I entered the café, surprised to feel a twist of disappointment that he wasn't there. Probably back on his fishing boat, showing tourists how to cast off, or whatever the correct term was. My knowledge of fishing was scanty.

It was hard to keep my mind on work, and impossible to catch Dolly and continue our conversation about my search. If she wasn't talking to her family of customers, at one point dispensing advice to a couple tucked in a corner who looked like they'd had an argument, she was replenishing the display counter, baking baguettes – prepared the night before, she explained – or slicing fresh quiche into generous portions for customers who wanted something savoury to eat.

I was in the café clearing another table, face glowing from the heat of the dishwasher, when I heard her call out from the kitchen, 'Elle, come and meet Mathilde,' and almost let go of my tray. I was breathless and shaky when I got there, but when I saw a tiny, white-haired woman, tying her apron around her waist with weathered hands, I nearly burst out laughing. Mathilde was eighty, at least, and unless she'd been pushing fifty when she met Dad, I could definitely rule her out as a potential birth mother.

'Good to meet you, Mathilde,' I said, shoving the tray down, prepared to shake her hand. She eyed me with suspicion, and turned to drag a state-of-the-art food mixer across the worktop.

'She prefers to get on with her baking, but she's lovely when you get to know her,' Dolly said warmly. 'You have to shout though, because she's deaf.'

'LOVELY TO MEET YOU,' I yelled, tapping Mathilde's arm. She gave a forceful start, picked up a spatula and swatted me on the arm.

'Ow!'

'And even if she hears you, she won't understand. She doesn't speak much English,' Dolly explained, removing the utensil from Mathilde's hand and placing it out of harm's way. She looked at me, as something occurred to her. 'You didn't think…?' A mischievous smile lit up her face. 'You realise Mathilde is too old to be the M you're hoping to find?'

'I do now,' I said, feeling warm in a way that had nothing to do with the fact that Mathilde had whipped open the oven, releasing a blast of hot air.

'Apart from being eighty-five, I doubt she's ever set foot outside of France.'

'I know, it's just, when you mentioned her name…'

'You're on the alert for names starting with M, I get it.' Dolly gave me a wink. 'Her daughter Mattie's the right age, though,' she added, watching Mathilde tip out flour with abandon, spilling most of it on the worktop.

'Oh?' *Mattie.* It struck me as a childlike name that I couldn't associate with a fifty-something woman. Even so, my stomach flipped over.

'She lives in Spain with her husband and four children.'

'What… what does she look like?' I couldn't resist asking, but Dolly was already shaking her head, as if anticipating my question.

'Blonde and green-eyed, like her German father.'

'Ah.' So, that was two Ms ruled out, and I'd only been here a few hours.

Mathilde had taken some butter from the fridge and was pulling off pieces with her fingers and chucking them in with the flour.

'This kitchen was her life,' Dolly said, with obvious affection. 'She never mingled with the customers like I do, but was famous for her macarons.'

Turning, her currant-like eyes flashing with anger, Mathilde spouted a torrent of words in French, and slammed her palm down, sending up a cloud of flour.

'What's wrong with her?'

'Nothing.' Dolly's smile didn't waver. 'She wants her coffee, that's all.'

'Wow.' Glancing at Mathilde's profile, I couldn't help thinking how well she'd photograph, the lines and furrows of her face all telling a story (angry ones, by the look of things) and wished I'd brought my camera with me – until I imagined Mathilde's reaction to having a lens thrust anywhere near her frowning face.

'I'll be back in a moment.' Dolly vanished and returned seconds later with a tiny white espresso cup, filled with tar-coloured liquid, which Mathilde had knocked back before Dolly left the kitchen again.

Unnerved, I got on with reloading the dishwasher, casting occasional looks in Mathilde's direction. She seemed oblivious to my presence, adding sugar and glacé cherries to the mixture in her bowl, before turning on the mixer with a look of intense concentration. It made such a racket that, combined with the rumbling of Basil the dishwasher, there was no chance of making conversation – even if we'd wanted to, and she'd been able to hear me, and we spoke each other's language – and the next hour or so passed in a hot, steamy blur.

Just when I'd decided I never wanted to see a dirty plate again, Dolly came through and said, 'Take a break, Elle, and have something to eat.'

It felt like being back at school, or the early days at the studio, when Ivan would look at me disapprovingly if I said I was going to meet Toni on my lunchbreak, but Dolly was slicing some quiche, and added some salad to a plate, and told me to sit outside and 'recharge'.

'Got to keep your strength up,' she said, with another wink. I had the sense she was enjoying our little secret. It must make a change from her usual day-to-day routine.

The courtyard was flooded with sunlight, and once I'd finished every morsel of my lunch, I moved from the shade of the umbrella and rolled up my trouser-legs to bask in the warmth. The air smelt salty and warm, and had none of the humidity Jess would be experiencing in Borneo. Either that, or monsoon-like rain. Not that it bothered her either way. Jess took after Mum in that respect; accepting of her circumstances and making the best of them – we both did. People had often remarked how like Mum I was; not just our colouring, but our shared sense of humour, and the way we laughed – a scattergun giggle that made people around us join in – but since Dad's death, and discovering the postcard, I'd found myself wondering for the first time in years whether I was anything like my birth mother. Had she been creative? Was that why I'd been drawn to photography? Or was it because Dad had bought me a camera for my fourteenth birthday, keen for me to have a hobby like Jess, who'd joined a birdwatch scheme and spent hours looking for rare woodpeckers through her binoculars, and I'd wanted to please him?

Toni's verdict, that it took more than biology to be a parent – *Look at Paula, she never treated you any differently to Jess* – hadn't helped much. Some things *were* inherited, like genetic illnesses. What if she'd passed one to me? Maybe she was a drunk, or cruel – the way she'd picked Dad up and dropped him suggested a selfish nature, and I could hardly ignore the fact that she'd given me away. It hadn't properly hit me that way until I'd found the postcard, because I'd grown up feeling nothing but loved and wanted, but seeing her handwriting and deciphering the quote (thank goodness for Google) had brought her into focus.

Give the girl the right shoes and she can conquer the world.

She'd obviously wanted me to have a good life, but hadn't felt able to give it. Dad had been clueless about why, but surmised there might have been parental disapproval and I'd wished – reading the postcard for the umpteenth time – I'd pressed him for more details (surely they'd talked about *something* that night?). I hadn't felt the need to while Mum was around, and it hadn't occurred to me to bring it up after she died.

'You look miles away,' Dolly said, what felt like minutes later, and I realised I'd been in the sun long enough for my shins to have turned bright pink. 'Come and say hello to a few of our regulars, now that things have calmed down.' Her eyes were sparkling. 'There's someone here you might want to talk to.'

My heart gave a bump as I stood up. 'Where's Charlie?' I asked as I followed her back through the kitchen, surprised to see several neat rows of glazed madeleines cooling on a rack, and no sign of Mathilde

– just a pile of utensils heaped in the sink, and enough detritus on the worktops to suggest there'd been a small explosion.

'He's walking Mathilde home.' Turning, Dolly threw me a radiant smile. 'She's become his honorary grandmother.'

'That's nice,' I said, unable to imagine Mathilde as anything but the wolf-grandma in *Little Red Riding Hood*. 'Does he have a real one?'

'Actually, yes, his father's parents are still alive, living in Brighton, but we haven't seen them in years.'

'Right.'

'They're nudists,' she went on. 'Very embarrassing if we went to visit, them wandering about with their bits hanging out, not to mention dangerous.'

I bit back a laugh, imagining a geriatric couple gardening in the nude, with strategically placed plants protecting their modesty. Poor Charlie must have been mortified. My grandparents had been strait-laced by comparison, though Mum's mum had an on-off affair with her neighbour for years that Granddad knew nothing about.

The café was still half-full, and my attention was immediately drawn to a woman sitting by the window in front of an open laptop, her chin propped on her hand as she stared at the view.

'That's our resident writer,' said Dolly, following my gaze. 'Come and say hello to *Margot*.' She placed great emphasis on the name, and as I weaved behind her to where Margot was sitting, I scanned her for clues. She was in the right age group, with a faded beauty that made you look twice. Her piled-up hair was a muted shade of blonde, but her roots were dark, like her eyes, which had swivelled in our direction. She was wearing a billowing top that flowed from a delicate frame, and her fingers – one toying with a strand of hair, the other reaching absently for a pastel-coloured macaron – were long and elegant.

Dolly stopped suddenly and said in a clandestine fashion, 'It might be better not to ask outright whether she has children.'

'Why not?'

'When I asked once, she got tearful and said she couldn't talk about it, and didn't come back for a week.'

My stomach leapt into an anxious flutter. 'So, she could be…?'

'Well, yes,' said Dolly, picking up my thread. 'But you'll have to tread carefully, love, that's all I'm saying.'

My hands felt suddenly damp. 'I will,' I promised, and by the time we'd reached Margot's table, Dolly was all smiles again.

'This is our temporary staff member, Elle, from England.' She flashed me a look of anticipation, mingled with a warning. 'Margot knows England quite well.'

As I focused my gaze on Margot's face, her eyes widened with shock.

'*C'est incroyable*,' she said, a hand fluttering to her throat. 'You look exactly like her.'

Chapter Eight

'What... what do you mean?' So many conflicting thoughts were swarming my brain (who was '*her*'? My birth mother? I looked like my dad, so it wasn't possible (unless she'd been a blue-eyed blonde in disguise) that it took a moment to compute Margot's response.

'My Brigitte.' Margot's gaze bounced to her laptop and back to my face, still wide with wonder. 'You are exactly how I have imagined my sweet Brigitte to look.' Reaching out, she touched my hand as if checking I was real, her coral nails lightly scraping my skin. 'It is as if she has jumped out of the page and come alive,' she murmured, and it finally sank in that Margot was talking about a character in her novel. *Not* a long-lost daughter she'd pictured growing up in the image of her father.

'I look like someone in your *book*?' My voice was too loud and in my peripheral vision, Dolly's head jerked back.

'*Exactement.*' Margot spoke in the same, awestruck tone. 'It is unbelievable.'

As my brain recalibrated, I couldn't help feeling a tiny bit flattered. 'Well, that's... thank you,' I said, not sure how else to respond.

She continued to gaze in amazement, as if I was the living embodiment of all her dreams, speaking in a husky voice. 'The hair, though, on Brigitte, it is longer, to her shoulders, and the *eyes*, so blue and bright, and the *taches de rousseur.*' Freckles, I guessed, from the way her eyes darted over my face, as though attempting to count them. 'They are so cute. And the perfect nose, just like hers, and you are also the correct height.' Rising with poise, she placed a gentle hand on top of my head. She was taller than me and smelt of raspberries. 'If my book is made into a film, you would be the actress to play her.'

'Oh, I'm not an actress.' My voice sounded uber-British again; exactly like an actress playing a part.

'That is a great pity.' She sounded genuinely regretful, and I became hopeful once more that Margot may have unconsciously written her character as the daughter she'd given away. But why blonde-haired and blue-eyed, and not in her own image? Unless she'd instinctively based Brigitte on a distant memory of my father. 'Look,' she said, suddenly animated. 'You will see I am telling the truth.' Sitting down, she brought her laptop to life with a tap of her fingers and scrolled up several pages of densely typed text. After highlighting a couple of paragraphs, she prodded the screen, but it was written in French and I couldn't make it out.

Dolly leaned over, blocking my view with her head, and read a few words aloud under her breath.

'She's right,' she said, turning to me. 'She could be describing you, even down to your…' Her eyes ducked to my chest, which was getting more attention than it had in months. '*Petits seins mous.*'

'Let me guess,' I said. 'Small boobs?'

She nodded. 'In a nutshell.'

Great.

Now they were both staring at me, but where Margot looked beguiled, a smile of wonder playing over her pink-tinted lips, Dolly's expression was mildly sceptical. 'Pure coincidence,' she said, resting a hand on Margot's shoulder. 'More macarons?'

'Have you ever been to London?' I said, attempting to sound casual, while Dolly straightened with a sideways swipe of her fringe.

'Once, a long time ago.' Margot cocked her head, as if she could hear the past rushing in. 'I found it to be a fascinating city, but my heart was broken and I never went back.'

My heart lurched. 'Was this in the eighties?'

Something flickered over her face. 'I do not wish to talk about that time,' she said, a sad smile crossing her lips. 'It is in the past.'

Resisting the impulse to grab her shoulders and ask, *Are you referring to the time you chatted up a man with an impressive moustache in a pub in Covent Garden and then seduced him?* I said instead, 'I was wondering, whether you might have met a man there—'

'I told you, I do not wish to talk about that time.'

To my horror, her eyes had glazed with tears and her lower lip was trembling. Dolly laid a hand on my arm and gave me a *back-off* look. 'Sorry, Margot,' she said gently. 'Elle's looking for someone who might have known her father.'

Margot blinked, and a tear spilled over and slid gracefully down her cheek. 'I cannot help you,' she said, her voice becoming distant. 'That time, it has become…' She rubbed a hand in front of her face. 'It is like a very bad dream.'

Did she mean getting pregnant and giving up her baby? 'There was a pub,' I said, a little desperately. 'In Covent Garden.'

Something flickered over her face. 'I have to get on with my work,' she said.

Dolly and I locked widened eyes. It was obvious Margot was hiding something, but her gaze had slid back to her laptop.

'What sort of thing do you write?' I said, trying to hold her attention. Perhaps I could get hold of her books and look for clues in her stories.

Obviously, I'd need a translator, unless there were English versions. 'Don't they say a lot of fiction is autobiographical?'

'My novels, they are fantasy romances, set on a spaceship.'

OK, so that was unexpected. Even so, personal experiences were bound to have shaped her stories, even if they were in a different galaxy; each one featuring a version of Margot's troubled past. 'Are your books on Amazon?' I persevered. 'I could download a couple onto my Kindle.'

'Her books haven't found a publisher yet,' Dolly said kindly, squeezing Margot's shoulder. 'Only a matter of time, though.'

Margot's face grew pained. 'I have found a new agent,' she said. 'The last one, she was holding me back, but Louis, he is confident that *Tempêtes de Pluto* will be a very big hit.'

'Storms of Pluto,' Dolly translated, for my benefit. 'I'm sure he's right, Margot.'

Margot reached up and patted Dolly's hand, bestowing her with a beatific smile.

'You have such faith in me,' she said gently. 'How would I do it without you?'

'Oh, you'd be fine.' Dolly gave her another squeeze (Margot's shoulder must be feeling bruised) and said, 'We'll leave you to it, sweetheart. Are you sure you don't want any more macarons?'

Margot shook her head and patted her flat midriff. 'Just my usual coffee, *s'il vous plaît.*'

Stefan, passing with an order for a customer at a neighbouring table, offered to fetch it for her, and she blew him a kiss that made him blush.

Margot switched her gaze back to me, her smile deepening the lines around her eyes. 'It is wonderful to meet you, Brigitte,' she said, placing a hand on her heart. 'You do not mind if I call you Brigitte?'

I heard myself say, 'Of course not,' as though it was normal to be called something other than my birth name, because I couldn't shake the idea that there could be a connection between us that might become clear with a bit more digging, and I wanted to keep her on side. 'Lovely to meet you too.'

With a final, mystified shake of her head, Margot returned her attention to her laptop and started tapping the keys with an almost manic energy. It was clearly our cue to move on, and though I longed to ask more questions, I had no choice but to be led away.

'I think that's as much as you're going to get from her at the moment,' Dolly said apologetically, as though it was her fault that Margot wouldn't be drawn on her past. 'What do you think?'

'I don't know,' I said. 'There was a bit of a reaction when I mentioned Covent Garden.'

Dolly's face furrowed. 'Maybe she's rewritten history,' she said, almost to herself. 'That's what people do if there are things in their past they can't handle.'

'Maybe.' It was hard to imagine rewriting it to that extent, but then people handled things differently. But if it *was* the case, how was I going to draw her out in a week? *Less than a week*, I reminded myself.

'Come and meet some more people,' said Dolly, as if sensing my spirits had dipped, and introduced me to a big-busted woman in a wide straw hat, called Madame Bisset, who showed me a picture on her phone of a cat so furry, it was hard to see its features. The next photo revealed it looked like Chucky, the serial killer doll, and I stifled a gasp of fright.

'She's called Delphine,' Dolly said encouragingly. I didn't like to ask whether she meant Madame Bisset or her terrifying cat, so merely smiled and said, 'Wonderful to meet you both.'

As if she could tell I wasn't invested, Madame Bisset's richly lipsticked mouth tightened with disappointment, and she pushed her phone into the wicker basket on her lap.

'She comes here most days to get out from under her daughter's feet,' said Dolly as we moved away, leaving Madame Bisset to dab crumbs off her plate with a surprisingly dainty finger.

'Daughter?' I was behaving like someone hypnotised to react to the word, but Madame Bisset looked old enough to have a daughter who could have given birth, thirty years ago.

'Hélène,' obliged Dolly, with a knowing smile. 'She's head teacher at the primary school, and tends to treat her mother like one of the pupils. They clash terribly. Delphine is a great source of comfort to Madame Bisset.'

So, Delphine was the scary feline, and the daughter's name didn't begin with M. My shoulders dropped.

'Are you OK?' Dolly looked concerned.

'Fine, thank you.' My voice was strained, as if I'd been shouting all morning.

'Things aren't going to happen overnight.'

'I know.' I pushed a smile to my lips as she presented me to a couple more regulars, and managed to take in that Gérard was the elderly customer who owned Hamish the Scottie dog, and a dapper-looking man with a shock of white hair sweeping back from his forehead was Monsieur Moreau, a former violinist.

'*Enchanté*,' he said, standing up, his napkin sliding to the floor. Before I could react, he'd taken my fingers and pressed a courtly kiss on the back of my hand. 'Welcome to Café Belle Vie,' he said, with a twinkly-eyed smile '*Mon petit refuge*.' He flourished an arm, encompassing our surroundings. 'I think you would say, *little haven*.'

'I would,' I said, trying to look at the sheets of paper he'd been working on, covered with musical notes, but Dolly was ushering me away, a whisper of anxiety crossing her face.

'He's old-fashioned,' she said in a loud whisper. 'He doesn't see kissing a woman's hand as sexual assault.'

'Neither do I,' I said hastily.

'He doesn't mean any harm.'

'I know,' I said, nearly laughing. 'Honestly, Dolly, it's fine.'

Her face relaxed. 'He comes here to compose his music, bless him. It gets him out from under his wife's feet, and makes him feel part of the community.'

'Sounds like everyone's trying to escape someone.'

'Well,' said Dolly, swooping to grab some empty cups from a table as we passed, 'isn't it nice that they have somewhere to go to if they do?'

'It is,' I agreed, picking up some plates and following Dolly to the kitchen, before placing them on the worktop with extreme care. 'Everyone seems really nice.'

'Margot can be a bit intense.'

'She seems like an interesting person,' I said carefully. 'I actually wouldn't mind having a look at her writing.'

'Oh, she never lets anyone read it.'

'You talking about Mystic Margot?' Charlie was back, disturbing the air in the kitchen with his presence. 'You creatives should get together sometime.' He smiled at me, eyes crinkling at the edges.

'What do you mean, creatives?' Dolly queried.

'Elle's a photographer,' he said. 'She has a studio in England.'

'Really?' Dolly rounded on me with an excited grin. 'I don't suppose you do weddings, do you?'

'Mum!' Charlie sounded long-suffering, and I turned to see him making an apologetic face. His hair was dishevelled, as if he'd been caught in a breeze. It was the sort of hair that didn't stay tidy for long. 'I know what she's going to ask,' he said. 'Feel free to say no.'

'Well… I *do* do weddings.' I sounded as reluctant as I felt. 'Why?'

'This is fantastic news.'

I met her shining eyes with a sinking feeling in my stomach. 'It is?'

She nodded so hard, her fringe bounced. 'Did I tell you, I'm getting married at the end of the month?'

I shook my head, wordlessly.

'Well, I am.' Dolly clapped her hands. 'Will you photograph my wedding?'

Chapter Nine

'You're meant to be on holiday, yet you're washing dishes in a café, and you've agreed to return to Chamillon at the end of the month to photograph a *wedding*?' Toni sounded despairing. 'How the hell has this happened?'

'I'm *not* on holiday, and I didn't mean to do either,' I said, putting my phone on speaker and sinking down on the bed. 'The café job just happened, then Dolly was so excited I couldn't say no to the wedding.'

'Shouldn't she have booked a photographer already?'

'It's been a bit last minute, from what I can gather.' Dolly had explained that Frank asked her to marry him during a salsa night in Saint-Martin a month ago, and they'd decided they were too old to hang about. 'She was going to ask the guests to take pictures, but as soon as Charlie told her about the studio—'

'Charlie's the nice, good-looking son, and Henri's the sexy fisherman?'

Trust Toni to have homed in on those particular snippets. 'You make them sound like characters in a soap,' I said. 'But, yes, I suppose so.' I hadn't used those exact words, but she'd clearly deduced them from my description. 'Not that it's important.'

'It's very important, Elle. The fact you even mentioned them means something.'

'I've mentioned about fifty other people too, and Charlie's got a girlfriend.'

'I still can't believe you've got a job,' she said, starting to laugh. 'There was me, thinking you'd drowned, or been abducted.'

I'd got back to the house after finishing my shift at three o'clock – refusing to stay for coffee to punish myself for agreeing to photograph yet another wedding – and discovered a raft of missed calls and irate messages from Toni, demanding to know how I was, where I was, and whether she should start calling hospitals. After I'd thanked her for not telling Jess where I was, and explained the events of the past twenty-four hours, there'd been a stunned silence while Toni absorbed it all, broken by Mark in the background, asking where the toilet rolls were kept.

'If you don't know by now, there's no hope for our marriage,' she'd responded, before expressing her disbelief that I'd agreed to help out at the café – and not just because she remembered my short-lived stint at the Cup and Saucer.

'If Henri's single,' she said now, 'you should try to—'

'Don't say have a holiday fling,' I warned. 'I'm not on holiday, and I'm *not* into having flings.'

'I was going to say, get to know him, because he might be able to help you,' she said, in the innocent voice I knew from experience was the prelude to the real one. 'And if that leads to an *encounter*, even better.'

'An encounter?' My laugh turned into an ear-splitting yawn. Clearing tables and washing dishes, even in a machine as efficient as Basil, had proved more tiring than a normal working day. Lifting a camera hardly counted, and my exercise routine only extended as far as walking the fields near where I lived – providing it wasn't raining. Or windy. Or cold. Combined with meeting Margot, not to mention everyone else, the day had been exhausting.

'A *close* encounter,' Toni said, in case I hadn't understood her meaning. 'Providing he doesn't stink of mackerel.'

'He doesn't.' I pushed aside a vision of Henri's dark eyes and teasing smile. 'But even if he's single, which I doubt, I'm not interested.'

'You wouldn't have mentioned him if you weren't.'

'I mentioned Henri, because meeting him was part of what's happened since I got here.'

'I love how you pronounce it *Onree*,' she said, with a giggle. 'Your accent is terrible.'

'I know, it's embarrassing. I feel like a typical Brit abroad.'

'At least you've got this Dolly helping you out. It makes me feel better to know you're not on your own. And Henri, of course,' she said slyly.

I sighed. 'Jess is getting married.'

'WHAT?' I smiled as my diversion tactic worked. 'You're not doing her photos as well, are you?'

'I have to, she's my sister. I can't let her down.'

Toni tutted. She knew that weddings gave me a blinding headache, but had given up trying to persuade me to let Petra take over. Dad had been so proud when I'd told him I was going to be a wedding photographer, I couldn't bear to disappoint him – even if he was no longer around to mind. 'It's a shame your parents won't be there to see,' she said.

We were quiet for a moment. The sun had shifted, leaving the bedroom shadowy and cool. I stood up and walked around the bed. There was an ache across my shoulders, but it was the ache of physical exertion, rather than tension for once. My camera bag was on the chair where I'd left it the day before, the clothes I'd worn in a heap on the floor beside it. I wasn't this untidy at home.

'So, you think you've met a couple of women who could be her already?' said Toni, raising her voice over the sound of Freddie, shouting 'Dada, Dada!' at the top of his lungs.

'Well, Chamillon is very small.'

'Even so, it's pretty amazing. I mean, what are the chances of so many woman having names beginning with M?'

'That's weird, right?'

'Although… you've only mentioned three, now I think about it, and one of them was old enough to be your nan.'

'True.' I recalled Mathilde's beady eyes, and Dolly's words about her being Charlie's honorary grandmother. 'But considering I've only met a handful of locals, it's progress.'

'Isn't there a saying about there being no such thing as coincidence? That it's all to do with synchronicity and karma, and things being meant to be, and spirits aligning and the universe speaking in tongues?'

'That's a very long quote,' I said, pausing to check my reflection. I looked oddly elated, despite being tired to my bones. 'Really eloquent.'

Toni snorted. 'Quotes aren't really my thing.'

'You don't say.'

'You know the chances of her still living there are tiny.' Toni had turned serious, which couldn't be easy with the racket going on in the background. It sounded as if Mark was wrestling a feral cat into a sack, instead of changing his son's nappy. I knew that's what he was doing, because my last attempt had left me red-faced and weepy.

'Dolly said that too, but I don't see why,' I said. 'I still live in the area where *I* grew up.'

'Oh God, that's true.' Her voice grew distant. 'He can sense your weakness, Mark. Stop messing about and snap it on! You have to look like you're in charge. Sorry,' she said, switching back. 'You do still live in the same village, so I guess it's not that crazy.'

Her words gave me a quiver of apprehension. 'Exactly.'

'So, have you got a plan, Miss Marple?'

'No more than I've already told you. I'm playing things by ear.'

'Wow,' she said. 'Elle Matheson, acting on intuition.'

'I know it sounds a bit *Ghost Whisperer*, but I can't think of a better way.'

Toni chuckled fondly at the reference to one of our favourite TV shows. 'Whatever works, but, Elle, promise you'll keep me updated,' she said. 'You know I'm living vicariously through you, now I'm a married mother.'

'I will,' I promised. 'I'll send some photos of this place too, it's lovely.'

'The house?'

'All of it,' I said.

'What about Henri?'

'I'm not taking a picture of a man I've only just met.'

'Spoilsport.'

'I might go out and do some exploring.'

'You should, but, Elle—'

'I'll be careful,' I cut in, using the reassuring voice I deployed at work, when convincing a client her face didn't look fat. 'I'm a grown woman, Toni. I'll be fine.'

'It's not just that you've never gone away on your own, it's the whole finding your birth mother thing I'm worried about. Or rather, *not* finding her.'

'If I don't, it's OK,' I said. 'I'll have tried, and I've a feeling... I don't know, that I was meant to come here and explore my heritage, or something.'

'You're not in an episode of *Who Do You Think You Are?*'

'No, but it might be nice to discover a new branch of my family tree. Especially as I haven't much family left.'

'Now I'm really worried.' Freddie started wailing in earnest and Toni swore under her breath. 'I'd better go,' she said. 'Mark looks fit to burst into tears himself.'

After ringing off, I texted her the photo of the house I'd taken the day before, picturing them at home, cooing over Freddie. They were besotted with their eleven-month-old son, despite the sleepless nights and dirty nappies. It was Freddie's birth that had prompted Andrew to ask when we should have a baby.

'I don't know,' I'd said, feeling panicky. Cuddling newborn Freddie had been lovely, but I hadn't felt the maternal pull that Andrew assumed I had. 'Definitely not yet.'

Dad had died seven months earlier, and I'd put my reluctance down to that, but once I'd found the postcard, fears had risen to the surface like silt from a riverbed. *Maybe I wasn't cut out to be a mother.*

I crossed to my suitcase, surrounded by an explosion of clothes, and unzipped the compartment where I'd put the bag I'd found in the backpack in Dad's wardrobe. I'd never seen the backpack before, guessing afterwards it was the one he'd taken with him to London that day – the date of my conception. I'd thought of it like that, because it sounded less personal, more technical, and not as if it had much to do with me.

The carrier bag was nothing special, just plain white plastic – the sort shops charged for now – with no logo to suggest where it had come from. Dad could have placed the items in there himself to protect them, but a fuzzy image persisted, of a woman grabbing the bag in a panic and stuffing a few things inside, before rushing to the museum with a baby (me) in her arms.

I carefully removed the shawl and bracelet and laid them on the bed, just as I'd done when I'd found them, a faint trace of perfume rising from the shawl. That first time, I'd wondered if it was Mum's, somehow transferred by osmosis, but I didn't recognise her Body Shop fragrance and anyway, her wardrobe had been separate from Dad's, housing her collection of furry gilets, roll-neck sweaters, and the 'maybe one day' dresses she'd never been able to resist in John Lewis's sales.

The shawl was an ivory shade, warm and lightweight, with a delicate, scalloped edge, and despite the small, even stitches and intricate lacy pattern had a handmade appearance. *Made with love* was the first thing I'd thought. Had *she* made it? It seemed unlikely for a baby she wasn't planning to keep.

The gold bracelet was old and cluttered with charms: a heart-shaped padlock, an old-fashioned key, a cat, a lantern, a teddy bear and a pair of doves. Or maybe they were seagulls. It was hard to tell. Something of hers she'd wanted me to have? Yet Dad hadn't given it to me – or the shawl, or the postcard.

Toni said she thought he'd intended to one day, but died before he got the chance, but it was more likely he'd thought they might stir up questions he couldn't answer. So, why keep them at all?

'Perhaps she asked him to,' Toni had said. 'And then he forgot all about them.'

At first, I'd felt angry at him, for leaving me to discover the bag, and wished I hadn't opened it – then realised it was a link to my only other living relative, apart from Jess, and knew I had to find out more, before it was too late.

Now, as my tiredness eased, I left the shawl and bracelet on the bed and wandered downstairs to make some tea, then tried out the sofa, which was just as comfy as it looked. There was a newspaper on the coffee table called *An Expat's Guide to Living and Working in France* and I picked it up, idly flicking through, skim-reading a piece about visas and permits, before landing on a column about the intricacies of the French language, which had bamboozled the writer's father, leading to several misunderstandings. Smiling, I saw that the writer was Natalie Bright – the owner of the house. Charlie's friend Natalie, who Dolly had unsuccessfully tried to pair him up with. She was clearly more than the pretty face smiling from the photo accompanying her column and I wondered what she would do if she were in my position. Probably more than sitting around, waiting for something happen. Not for the first time, I wished Dad was here to talk to, then remembered, he'd never been great with emotional guidance, preferring to leave that side of things to Mum. Helping with homework had been his strength, along with a dry sense of humour, but he always had one eye on the past; keen to get back to his latest curation, or his office at the museum. Mum would have understood why I was here from an emotional perspective, and I hoped that Dad would too – even if only from an historical point of view.

Mum would tell me to get off my backside and start asking questions, which was easier said than done. I could start with Madame Girard, but when I checked the time, it was only five thirty; probably too early for dinner. She might not welcome a visitor if she had guests to cater for, especially one asking personal questions. But if I popped round with my camera, I could ask which local landmarks were worth photographing, and if she invited me in, we'd get chatting, and I could take it from there.

I was on my way upstairs to get my camera when a knock on the door made me jump. That was probably her now. Maybe she'd seen me return and had been waiting for the right moment to call round. I had the sense she felt as responsible for the guest staying in her neighbour's home as she did for the house itself. But when I pulled the door wide, a smile on my face, it wasn't Madame Girard outside.

It was Henri.

Chapter Ten

'I don't eat fish,' I said. I couldn't think of any other reason why Henri had knocked on my door, unless he'd mistaken it for Marie's. (For some reason, I couldn't keep thinking of her as Madame Girard.)

'That's good, because I don't have any on me.' He grinned, a sideways shaft of sunlight picking out hints of gold in his rumpled hair. His earlier outfit had been replaced by light-coloured jeans and a black T-shirt that somehow emphasised everything – eyes, hair, tan and teeth – and he smelt of something musky that made my head swim. 'See?' He pulled out his pocket flaps, as if to demonstrate his empty-handedness. 'No fish.'

I tried to speak, but my larynx had seized up.

'Though I'm sure if you tried my pan-fried sea bass, you would change your mind.'

Finding my voice, I said, 'I nearly choked on a bone once. It put me off for life.' I could still recall the sharpness in my throat and Dad slapping my back in the restaurant; Jess wide-eyed with shock and Mum asking if anyone knew the Heimlich manoeuvre, pronouncing it 'hemlock' in her panic. Thankfully, I'd coughed it up before the ambulance arrived.

'It's a common fear.' Henri's sympathetic grimace didn't detract from his overwhelming attractiveness. 'You would have to take a leap of faith, but I promise it would be worth it.'

'You're really passionate about fish,' I said, wishing I hadn't said *passionate*, and that I hadn't started talking about fish. 'Shame you can't leave them in the sea where they belong.'

He looked intrigued. 'You're against killing for food?'

'In principle,' I said, which was hardly the same thing. 'Look, what do you want?'

My ungracious tone, far from putting him off, brought a smile to his lips. *He was definitely one of those*, I decided. Probably bored, drawn to the stranger in town (or village), thrilled by the chase and challenged by rejection. I'd been down that road before, and had no intention of going down it again, even if my heart was pumping madly, and my nerve endings were tingling.

'I thought, if you weren't too tired, it might be nice to take a walk,' he said. 'I don't suppose you've had a chance to look around.'

Nice try, buster. 'No, I haven't.' I became aware that, once again, my appearance had fallen short. I was still wearing the baggy T-shirt Dolly had lent me and the coffee stains on my trousers weren't quite disguised by the stripes. I was pretty sure my face had a greasy sheen, and strands of hair were stuck to my neck. Not that I cared what Henri thought of my appearance, but I stepped behind the door and peered around it. 'I am pretty tired, though.'

'Oh?' A crease appeared between his eyebrows. *Not used to being turned down, are you, buddy?* I had no idea why I was thinking words my granddad would have used. 'The café is very popular,' he said in an empathetic voice. 'Although, it would be worse if it wasn't.'

'I didn't see you in there,' I said, as though I'd been searching for him (which I had, but only briefly), and flushed when his smile returned – a smile that said he knew only too well the effect he had on women (men too, probably).

'I couldn't stay long.' He adjusted his pockets and tucked his hands in. 'I had some boat trips booked.' Was he playing up his French accent to sound extra sexy? It was so different from listening to Andrew's smooth, educated vowels. Then I remembered how I'd been drawn in by Declan's appealing Irish lilt and strengthened my resolve when Henri said, 'Perhaps a relaxing walk will be good for both of us.'

'Don't you have a girlfriend?' I regretted the words as soon as they flew out – the presumption that he was inviting me out on a date, even though I was certain that's what he was doing. 'I saw you with a woman in the café.' Now it sounded as if I'd been taking notes.

Laughing, he swept a hand through his hair. 'I sometimes have coffee there with my bossy sister, who tries to tell me what to do,' he said. 'Don't you have a boyfriend?'

'None of your business,' I replied. 'I don't even know you.'

His laugh was a surprisingly joyful sound that made my mouth want to join in, but I resisted. 'That's why I suggested a walk,' he said, head tilted as though reassessing me. 'I would like to get to know you.'

Not that old chestnut. 'You've only met me once.'

His smile was joined by a mildly puzzled frown, 'Isn't that the point?'

'Of what?' I seemed to be losing control of the conversation.

'Meeting you once wasn't enough to get to know you, and that's why I wanted to see you again, to get to know you better.'

He was straightforward, I'd give him that. Nothing like the back and forth with Andrew, after his sister's wedding. The call to ask me to photograph a couple of houses for his property website, followed by an invitation to dinner to 'discuss future business opportunities' before he admitted he'd like us to see each other as boyfriend/girlfriend. We hadn't kissed until our third date, whereas it was frighteningly easy to imagine Henri cupping my face in his hands and thoroughly kissing me before we'd reached the end of the road, should I agree to go for a walk.

'I won't be here for long. In France, I mean.'

'It's just a walk.' Henri's gaze was quizzical, as though trying to grasp why I was making such a big deal of it. 'I'm not asking you to marry me, Elle. Not yet.'

No one had ever said my name like that – as if savouring a very fine wine. Not even Declan, who used to call me *babe*, probably to save him the trouble of remembering which of his girlfriends he was talking to. Obviously, it was the accent that made it sound so sexy. Henri could have said *cod fillets* and it would still have sounded alluring. 'Well, thank goodness for that,' I said in my most bracing voice. 'I'm not here to look for a husband.'

'That's good to know.' He looked to be fighting laughter. 'I promise I won't propose. Yet.'

It was the second time he'd said that. I narrowed my eyes. 'I really do need an early night.' Instantly, an image of the bed upstairs sprang into my head, with a naked Henri in it, a look in his eyes that made my knees feel rubbery.

'So, you *don't* want to go for a walk?' He shook his head, feigning bafflement. Or, maybe he really was baffled. 'You could have just said no.'

Reddening more than I already had, I said, 'I'm just…' *Just what? Out of my depth? Tired? Hungry?* Definitely hungry. 'This sort of thing wouldn't happen in England, that's all.'

'A man asking a beautiful woman to take a walk? That can't be true.' He looked around, as if seeking confirmation from someone, before returning his bedroom-gaze to mine.

Nice move. Call me beautiful and expect me to fall at your feet. I looked down, to see his feet were covered this time, in the sort of shoes designed to be worn on yachts. 'Thanks for asking,' I said as coolly as I could. 'Maybe tomorrow?' *What?*

I raised my eyes and the look in his raised my temperature a further few degrees.

'Tomorrow,' he said, his serious tone belied by a generous smile. 'Have a nice evening, Elle.'

He held my gaze a moment longer, before walking away, and I felt a tweak of disappointment as I closed the door. Had I *wanted* him to persuade me?

Then I remembered what Toni had said, about Henri helping with my search. But it was too late now. He wouldn't come back, I was certain of it. And anyway, I had Dolly.

I leaned against the door and let my breathing settle before rushing to the window, but Henri had gone, and the street was empty again.

'Elle, I am so glad you came,' said Marie, with a smile that looked genuine – either that, or she was a brilliant actress and secretly annoyed her temporary neighbour was already on her doorstep.

'I hope you don't mind,' I said, patting my camera, which I'd remembered to hang around my neck. 'I thought I'd pick your brains on some local landmarks.'

'Pick my brains?'

'Oh, sorry, it means I'd like you to share your knowledge of the area with me. Nice things I can take pictures of. With my camera.' I patted it again.

'Of course,' she said with a smile, standing aside to let me in. 'This is good because my guests, they are eating out this evening and there will be too much food for me.'

'You could probably freeze some,' I said, stepping past her into the hallway. 'That's what my mum used to do. She'd batch cook every Sunday.'

'Batch cook?' Marie looked captivated, as though I'd started singing her favourite song in a pure and melodic voice (being tone-deaf, this was one of my favourite fantasies). 'I have never heard of this.'

'It means preparing multiple portions of different meals, which she used to freeze so she didn't have to cook when she got home from work.' It was funny how we took our colloquialisms for granted.

'That is a good idea,' Marie said as I sniffed the air discreetly. I couldn't detect any food smells, only a floral scent from a spray of yellow flowers in a vase on a console table. 'I cook from scratch every day, but this is my job and I have the time.'

Deciding to present myself as someone who asked a lot of questions, so when they turned personal it wouldn't seem out of the blue, I said, 'How long have you been a landlady?'

'Landlady?'

Oh Lord. 'How long have you been doing… *this*?' I made an expansive gesture with my arms that I hoped was universal.

'I was only joking,' she said, a glint in her chocolatey eyes. 'Marty, my English friend, he asked me this too and explained what a landlady is.'

'Ah.' I grinned. 'Very good.'

Her smile widening, Marie led me into a bright living room, with blue and cream curtains at the window, and coordinating cushions on the sofa.

I glanced around, noting that the layout of the house was different from next door, despite looking almost identical from the outside. 'It's *très belle.*' It came out as 'trez bell' and I cringed. 'Lovely,' I added.

'*Merci.* It is very much the same as when my parents lived here,' Marie said, probably taking pity on me. 'Not the furniture, of course, except for the… um… *buffet.*' She gestured to a low sideboard, with a basket of fuchsia kitting wool on top, some thin needles poking out. 'But the rooms, they are how they used to be.'

My heart gave a flutter, as I realised what she was telling me. 'You grew up here? In this house?'

'I did.' She nodded. 'Not for many years. I lived in Paris when I was married, but after my parents died, I decided I would keep the house and take in visitors.'

'What did you do before that?'

She hesitated, perhaps unused to being bombarded with questions by virtual strangers. 'I… worked in hospitality for some years.' Her tone was more guarded. 'It was good practise for this.' She swept her hand slowly around. 'You could say, I found my vocation.'

Keen to keep the ball rolling, I said, 'It's small for a guest house.' *Nice one, Elle. Guest houses aren't meant to be massive.*

'My guests are very small.' A smile revealed she was joking, at ease again. 'I cannot take many guests at one time, but that is how I like it.' She ran a hand over the back of an upright armchair with a wooden frame. 'Many of them are like family now and return every year, sometimes twice.'

'That's nice,' I said, eyes scanning the surfaces for photos, or evidence of a family, of her husband, but there were just a lot of plants in ceramic pots, and a jug of purple flowers on the sideboard. 'Does Monsieur Girard help out?'

Marie's hand stilled on the armchair. 'I am not married any more.' Her tone grew strained. 'It is only me.' Turning, she bent to straighten the cushion in the armchair so I couldn't see her face. 'I have no children, in case you were going to ask.'

My heart started banging. 'No… I—'

'I was not able to.' She straightened, her face washed with sadness. 'A medical condition I did not know about until after I was married.'

Oh God. 'Madame Girard, I'm so sorry,' I said, aghast that I'd somehow forced the confidence from her.

'Please, call me Marie.' A ghost of a smile rose. 'Madame Girard was my mother.'

'Marie,' I said, the blood roaring in my ears. 'Forgive me, I get a bit nervous when I meet someone new and say the wrong things.' It wasn't true. In the years I'd been a photographer, I'd become adept at making small talk designed to put people at ease, but I needed an excuse for my horribly tactless questioning.

'There is nothing to forgive,' she said, with a little shrug. 'It is not a thing I usually tell people I do not know, but...' Her eyebrows puckered, as if she didn't quite understand it herself. 'I think perhaps, because we are neighbours for now, it is OK.'

'Thank you, Madame... Marie, that's very kind of you. I really do love your picture,' I said, desperate to make amends, pointing to a framed canvas on the wall of a ballet dancer in a white tutu, bending to tie her satin slipper. 'Did ballet originate in France, or is it just a French word?'

She turned to look and didn't answer for a moment. I had the sense I'd said the wrong thing once more and began to wish I'd gone for a walk with Henri.

At the point where I was thinking of slipping away, she said, 'It originated in the Italian Renaissance, but Paris is home to the world's oldest ballet company.'

A wistfulness in her voice prompted me to ask, 'Did you used to go there when you lived in Paris?'

'Yes.' She glanced at the slim gold watch on her wrist. 'Are you ready to eat?' she said politely. 'You cannot take photographs on an empty stomach.'

I'd almost forgotten my camera hanging around my neck. I gripped it like a talisman, the feel of it a comfort. 'I don't want to put you to any trouble,' I said.

'It is no trouble.' But in spite of her soft smile, I was certain I'd upset her with my questions and felt I should leave her alone.

'Thank you, but I have to go.' I backed out of the room, aware that I'd now turned down two invitations in the space of an hour.

'But you wanted me to tell you the good places where you can take pictures.'

Her puzzled voice followed me as I opened the front door and squinted into the sun. Guessing she was just being polite, I turned and flashed a smile. 'I think I'll leave it for now,' I said, too dazzled to see her face clearly.

'But have you eaten?' It sounded as if she didn't want me to go, but the thought of sitting at a table, making stiff conversation, seemed suddenly impossible.

'I had something at the café,' I said. 'I'll have a light supper then head to bed. *Bonne nuit.*' It came out as 'bonnweet', but she responded in French, even though it was too early to say goodnight, and by the time I'd fled indoors, wrenching my camera over my head, and eaten a mushroom omelette out on the patio, I was too tired to do anything but watch the sun slip down, and rewind the day's events in my mind. At one point, voices floated across from next door as Marie's guests returned, and I imagined them clustered in her living room, reliving their excursion, her face focused politely as she listened.

Wondering what Jess was up to, I took a selfie with the house behind me and sent it to her phone. She wouldn't be able to tell I wasn't in Greece; probably wouldn't check her messages for days. Signal was patchy where she lived, and she was too absorbed by her work.

I couldn't face another conversation, so messaged Toni. *Busy day at the café (!) speak tomorrow, love you! X* After flicking through a couple of thrillers on the bookshelf, I decided I needed an early night after all and headed upstairs. At least I'd made progress of sorts. I could now rule out Marie as my potential birth mother.

Chapter Eleven

Once again, I woke refreshed and full of anticipation – almost as if I was on holiday, except I wasn't. I was just in a different country, where the air smelt great, the sun was shining, and the sky a shade of blue that made anything seem possible; made me want to rush out and explore the island.

That's a holiday, Elle, I imagined Toni saying. She'd replied to my message with a photo of her and Freddie, him red-faced and grumpy, her in her dressing gown, pulling a sad face, captioned 'wish we were there', adding to the sense that I was on a relaxing break.

I replied with a heart emoji and eleven kisses, and a quick enquiry that everything was OK at the studio – her mum looked after Freddie while she worked – and by eight o'clock, I was showered and dressed and out in the garden, admiring the flowers and sniffing the air, which I couldn't seem to get enough of.

Sunshine slanted across the neatly-trimmed grass to a shed with foliage growing up the walls, and I padded over and peered through the window. I could see a pair of bikes inside, and remembered Natalie had given me permission to use hers. Maybe I could take it out? Dolly had instructed me not to come in until eleven, claiming she could manage until then, but I could acquaint myself with the area, perhaps even head to the next village and have a look around, and maybe take some pictures.

In a rush of enthusiasm, I turned back to the house to get the key for the shed and started when I spotted Marie, looking out of an upstairs window next door. I returned her wave as I shot inside, embarrassed to have been caught snooping. Perhaps she was making a note of my movements, intending to report back to the Brights. I could hardly blame her. I'd read stories online about people letting their homes and returning to find they'd been trashed or – in one case – used as a pop-up brothel.

In the kitchen, I quickly cleared a scattering of crumbs on the worktop from where I'd made some toast, then washed up my mug and put it away. If Marie had a set of spare keys, she might pop in while I wasn't here and take incriminating pictures. I hurtled upstairs and straightened the duvet on the bed, thrust my exploding suitcase in the wardrobe, then placed the shawl and bracelet on the dressing table, and ran to the bathroom to replace the cap on the toothpaste.

'What are you doing?' I asked myself in the cabinet mirror as I polished the glass with a make-up wipe. Holidays were about letting go of normal routines, and as long as I left the house as I'd found it, I didn't need to act as if I was at home. I threw down the wipe in an act of defiance and took the cap off the toothpaste. Then remembered I wasn't on holiday, and put it back on again.

I needed to get out.

I hadn't ridden a bike since my first, catastrophic experience, aged seven. A late starter, it had taken me ages to get the hang of staying upright, and then I hadn't known how to stop, my legs pumping the pedals as I travelled at speed down the street. Mum and Dad's cheers had turned to panicked yells, and a neighbour had shot out of his garden to catch me, seconds before I reached the main road. The memory of being swung in the air as my brand-new bike was crumpled by a passing bus had never left me, and I'd been wary of bikes ever since. But I had the sense that here, in Chamillon, I'd somehow become a natural cyclist, gracefully riding the cobbled streets, hair lifting in the breeze, dinging the handlebar bell and smiling hello at passers-by.

Only, there wasn't a bell, and as soon as I clambered on the bike and placed a foot on the pedal, it tipped to one side, causing me to slam my foot down. I tried again, only for the bike to tip the other way. After several more attempts, I decided the garden must be too uneven and wheeled the bike round to the front of the house, where I swung my leg over the saddle once more. Again, the frame tilted before I could get both feet on the pedals, forcing one foot to the ground. I was starting to feel a bit sweaty. My high-necked T-shirt was clinging to my armpits, and the hems of my trousers flapped unhelpfully around my ankles. Realising they could catch in the chain, I bent awkwardly to roll them up one-handed. Straightening, I blew a lock of hair off my sticky forehead, and watched a female around my age ride elegantly towards me, her corn-coloured hair lifting gently in the breeze as she called a cheery, 'G'day!' in an Australian accent.

I nodded and smiled, stiff with envy at the sight of her long, toned legs – shown to perfection in a pair of denim shorts – powering the pedals with seemingly no effort, while maintaining a straight-backed posture.

Once she'd gone, I mounted the bike once more, and this time managed to get the pedals turning without falling off. Keeping a firm grip of the handlebars, I steered myself in the direction I'd walked with Henri the day before, glad he wasn't around to witness my wobbly progress. I'd practically stopped breathing, and my shoulders were hunched to my ears, but soon I was cutting a dash down the street and managed to turn the corner without mishap. I gave an inward whoop. *I was riding a bike!* OK, so I daren't take my eyes off the road, and I had a feeling my face was set in a grimace – and my hair definitely wasn't lifting in the breeze – but it was more than I'd done in years. Jess would be proud of me (she'd been proficient by the age of five) and Toni would be astonished. I wished I could take a selfie, but didn't want to risk lifting a hand to root for my phone, or cause an accident. I was just congratulating myself on taking another corner with minimum shaking, and considering a quick look at my surroundings, when a group of people emerged from a hotel and swarmed in front of me. Shrieking, I swerved around them, clipping the kerb with my tyre. I jolted forward, my bottom lifting off the saddle, and slumped over the handlebars as though I'd been shot in the back. As I hung there, gasping for breath, there was a babble of Japanese voices behind me and, not wanting to create even more of a scene, I quickly dismounted and gave a jaunty wave – as though I hadn't just cracked at least twenty ribs. I briefly considered leaving the bike where it was and walking off, but couldn't risk it being stolen. Instead, I pushed it, not daring to look back, and despite my intention to explore the town, and perhaps check out the medieval courtyard where a daily market was held, I found myself heading straight for the café instead, wincing every time I was overtaken by yet another person on a bike. I appeared to be the only human on the island without a cycling gene.

'Hey, are you OK?'

I looked up from my dispirited and painful trudge – my ribs were hurting, there were too many cobbles, and I was seriously considering shoving the bike in the water once I reached the harbour – to see Charlie approaching with a look of cheerful concern. *His* hair was lifting in the breeze, and he wasn't even riding a bike.

'Just discovered the hard way that I shouldn't have brought this,' I said, when he reached me, aiming for a self-deprecating tone. Instead, I sounded on the verge of tears and had to blink a few times to clear my vision.

'You should have brought Natalie's,' he said, looking at the bike with a puzzled frown. 'This one's way too big.'

He prised it gently from my hands and I stared as he flung his leg over the saddle.

'This isn't Natalie's bike?'

'It's her dad's.' He indicated the crossbar. 'The frame's bigger and heavier, and the seat's higher.' *No wonder I kept toppling over.* 'You must have really struggled,' he added, giving the brakes an experimental squeeze. 'Her dad's over six feet tall.'

I managed a weak giggle, in spite of my bruised torso and aching arms. 'I'm afraid I'm not much of a cyclist, in case you hadn't noticed.'

'That's a shame.' He planted his feet on the ground, either side of the pedals. 'You know this is the Île de Ré, where donkeys wear pantaloons and the bicycle is king?'

'What?'

'You must have noticed the bikes everywhere.'

'I meant the bit about donkeys.'

'Oh, that.' He grinned. 'It's a tradition dating back to when donkeys worked in the fields, and were given trousers to wear as protection from mosquitoes. It's a novelty now, in Saint-Martin. Trouser-wearing donkey-rides for kids.'

'Sounds… fun,' I said, wondering what Jess would make of donkeys in trousers. *Animal exploitation or harmless fun?* I made a mental note not to mention it the next time we spoke. Not when I was supposed to be in Greece.

'You know there are bike racks everywhere on the island, you could have left it and picked it up later,' Charlie said. 'It would have been totally safe.'

I was fed up of talking about bikes and no longer wanted to explore the town. I wanted a cold drink and to sit on something that didn't chafe my undercarriage. 'It's too late now,' I said, gingerly prodding my ribs.

'Are you hurt?'

'I might have had a small collision with the handlebars.'

He winced. 'You know you should be wearing a helmet?' he said. 'Natalie has one, didn't you see it?'

'Obviously not,' I said snappily. 'It was dark in the shed, hence me picking the wrong bike.' Desperate to change the subject now, I said, 'Aren't you working this morning?'

'Actually, yes, I was on my way to the bank, but I was hoping to swing by and see you,' he said, unexpectedly. 'I wanted to apologise for putting my foot in it about the photography yesterday, in front of Mum.'

That was a surprise. 'It wasn't your fault,' I said. 'It's just that I don't really enjoy photographing weddings.' It wasn't something I had ever admitted out loud, but something about Charlie made me want to tell the truth.

'Why didn't you just say so?' he said, with a laugh.

'Because… it would have sounded mean.' I grinned sheepishly. 'Your mum sounded really excited.'

'She is,' he said wryly. 'I never thought she'd get married again and I don't think she did either, but…' He shrugged. 'Now she's going overboard to make it a special day.' He had the friendliest face I'd ever seen on a man. It was almost impossible not to smile back. 'Maybe tell her sooner rather than later if you really don't want to take the photos.'

There was no judgement in his voice, but as I opened my mouth to explain that once I'd agreed to something, I went through with it, his gaze slid past me and brightened. As he raised a hand and waved, I turned to see the Australian who'd cycled past me earlier, heading towards us. She blew a kiss, presumably meant for Charlie, rather than me, and I realised this must be Tegan.

'Your girlfriend?' I said, even though it was obvious.

'Well… she's here for the summer, and we've been seeing each other for a bit.' For the first time, Charlie sounded hesitant. 'I know it must sound awful that I haven't introduced her to Mum yet, but she's so desperate for me to settle down, it might put Tegan off if Mum immediately starts planning our wedding.' He pulled a panicked face that made me laugh. 'We don't need that kind of pressure, and I don't want to get Mum's hopes up.'

'I get it,' I said, remembering Dolly asking about my relationship status, clearly sizing me up as potential girlfriend material. It couldn't be easy for Charlie, if that happened every time he so much as looked at an eligible female. 'What if she runs into you together?'

'I'm trying not to let that happen,' he said, with a rueful grin. 'I just want to see how things go, for now. Nothing much has happened between us, we're just hanging out when I can get away. It probably won't last,' he confessed, rather pessimistically. 'I wasn't lying when I said I'm not in the market for a relationship, but I kind of promised Natalie I'd give one a try the next time I met a woman I liked.'

'Was there never anything like that between you and her?'

'Natalie's like my sister,' he said, with conviction. 'She's with Max Weaver now and they're really happy together.'

He said it as though I should know who Max Weaver was – the name *did* ring a bell – but before I could ask, Tegan was by his side, pressing a kiss to his cheek. 'Hi, Charlie,' she said, and turned to me. 'Who's your friend?'

'This is Elle.' He leaned over and looped an arm around her shoulders. 'She's helping out at the café this week.'

'Hi, Elle, I'm Tegan.'

Not only was she strikingly attractive, her mouth constantly beaming, her eyes bright and warm, she seemed as relaxed and outgoing as Charlie. 'Nice to meet you,' I said, wishing I had the legs for tiny shorts, and bosoms that demanded attention. 'I'd better get on,' I added, leaning to grab the bike from Charlie.

'Hey, let me take it.' He glanced at Tegan as if to check it was fine with her, smiling when she nodded easily. He clearly liked her a lot. 'I'll leave it round the side of the house for you to put away when you get back.'

A clang of relief resounded inside me, that I didn't have to climb on it ever again. 'Thanks,' I said.

'See you later.'

I watched them ride away (why wasn't *he* wearing a helmet?) and as Tegan chatted animatedly, her golden hair tumbling almost to her waist, I couldn't help framing them in my mind as a couple and turned away with a feeling close to jealousy. So much for Charlie not being in the market for a relationship.

It looked like Dolly might be in for a nice surprise.

Chapter Twelve

The need to sit down with a drink outweighed any lingering desire to have a scout around, so I headed straight for the café, already feeling better.

It occurred to me that Margot might be there and I could strike up a conversation before I started work. I was curious to discover more, even though my conviction that she could be my birth mother had wavered overnight. Wouldn't I have felt a connection of some sort if she was? Some sixth sense would surely have quivered to life; even some tingling in my extremities. And I couldn't help returning to the point that if I looked like Dad, she would have seen something in me that reminded her of him. Unless she had, but had mistaken it for a resemblance to the heroine in her novel.

Then again, if she *was* the one, she might have buried the memories of the past so deeply they no longer felt real. In the weeks after Mum died, I'd had to lock myself in the present to get through it, and months had passed before I was able to unlock precious memories without crying. But I'd had Mum for eighteen years, whereas my birth mother had only known me for about a week (not counting those in her womb) so maybe it hadn't been that difficult to forget me. Also, it had been dark in the car park when she'd handed me over before fleeing, and if she'd been as tipsy as Dad was on the night of my creation, she might not have a clear recollection of what he looked like. Even though I'd been madly in love with Declan, it was hard now to recall his features – apart from his teeth, which had needed work.

'You're early,' Dolly greeted me, after I'd dodged past two tables of chattering women with toddlers on their laps. 'You've just missed Charlie, he's gone to the bank,' she said, as if that was the sole reason I'd turned up.

'I know, I just saw him,' I said, without thinking.

'You did?' She stopped wiping the counter and looked at me, clearly expecting more.

'He's, erm… he was…' I cleared my throat. 'I had a bit of a disaster with a bike and he offered to take it back to the house for me.' *With the gorgeous, blonde Aussie he might be in love with.*

'Did he now?' Dolly's smile became knowing. She'd clearly deduced from my stammered response that I fancied him after all. 'Well, that's my Charlie all over.' She nodded, her blonde waves bobbing around her cheeks. 'What would you like?' she said, sweeping a hand to the display cabinet, which was stuffed with banks of golden croissants, berry-muffins, cinnamon swirls, and the madeleines that Mathilde had baked the day before. 'Anything you want, on the house.'

'Oh no, I'll pay.' I checked I'd still got my bag, surprised it hadn't flown off when I crashed the bike. I opened it and pulled out my purse. 'I've got some notes,' I said.

'Absolutely not.' Dolly wagged a playful finger. 'Staff perks,' she insisted, but I had a sneaking suspicion she was already picturing me snuggled beside Charlie on the sofa upstairs, pregnant with her first grandchild. 'In or out?'

'Sorry?'

'Sitting inside or out?' She nodded towards the chattering women, one of whom was rocking her grizzling child so vigorously he was starting to look a bit pasty. 'We've mothers and toddlers in this morning, so it gets a bit lively,' she said. 'You might prefer sitting outside.'

Putting my purse away, I looked around the café. 'Is Margot here?' I said. 'I was hoping to chat to her some more about her books.'

Dolly shook her head, her fringe swaying. 'She doesn't come in every day, and never before eleven,' she said. 'Are you planning to talk to her again about you know what?'

'I just feel there's more to what she said yesterday.'

'I know, but we have to tread carefully, love.'

'When did you say your friend at the town hall is back?' I felt awful, as if I was pushing Dolly for information, when it had only been a day. 'Maybe I could go there myself.'

'Don't you worry,' she said. 'I've spoken to her this morning, and she's promised to get back to me with a list of names as soon as possible.' She paused as Stefan approached with a tray in each hand and slipped past into the kitchen. 'Now, why don't you pop outside and I'll bring us a drink?'

As there didn't seem to be anything more I could do, I scanned the menu on the wall. 'I'll have some lemonade and a madeleine, please.'

Beaming, Dolly sprang into action. 'Be with you in two minutes.'

Outside, the sun was so bright it took my eyes a second or two to adjust. I picked a table nearest the door so if Margot decided to break with routine and come in early, I'd spot her immediately.

The light around the café made everything look more vivid, and I felt bedazzled by the richness of shades around me as I sat down. From habit, I looked at the scenery as through a viewfinder, and realised with a start that I hadn't brought my camera out after all. It was still in the house, where I'd left it yesterday. I couldn't remember the last time it had been more than a few feet away from me, but strangely, didn't feel any desire to rush back and get it. Probably because I'd exerted myself enough already, and I still had several hours of washing-up and table clearing ahead. Even more strangely, I was looking forward to it, and found myself thinking fondly of Basil.

I quickly checked my phone to see that Jess had responded to the picture I'd sent her with a thumbs-up emoji and a photo of Owen cuddling a baby orangutan in a nappy. It made me think of Freddie – though my godson was a lot less hairy.

I looked up as Gérard approached the door, his little black dog peeping out from under his arm. He nodded and smiled as though we were old friends, and even the dog seemed to be grinning. Everyone was so friendly, each offering a cheerful *bonjour* as they passed, but I guessed I'd be cheerful too if I lived here, with a café and the harbour a short walk away, and coffee and cake on tap. I'd always thought I'd love to keep living forever in the house where I'd grown up, surrounded by hills and fields, a short distance from the church where Mum and Dad had been married – and were buried – but sometimes it could be a little... isolating. I'd even been toying with the idea of putting the house on the market. Jess, being a 'wherever I lay my hat' kind of person, had no objections, and I'd started to feel weighed down, rather than comforted, by the memories at home. Without my family filling the spaces, it felt too sad and empty, surrounded by their belongings – the furniture Mum had chosen, the photos and albums, Dad's books and pictures, his clothes still hanging in the wardrobe. Clearing out his bedroom had been the start of me packing up my old life, but instead, it had brought me here, feeling less sure of myself than I ever had.

Looking around, it struck me that Chamillon was similar to the village in Cornwall where Mum's parents had lived, and where we'd spent many happy summers until Granddad Brentwood died and Granny had come to live with us. Over the years, I'd forgotten how much I loved being near the sea and realised I was inhaling again, as though the air held some vital component for life.

'Here we are.' Dolly appeared with a clinking tray and set it down on the table, flicking a crumb off the gingham cloth with a tut. 'You don't mind if I join you?' she said, pulling out a chair and settling down before I could reply. 'I think Stefan and Celeste can manage without me for ten minutes.' She beamed at a latecomer to the mother and toddler group, rushing up with a red-faced tot in her arms. They exchanged a few words in French, and I was struck by how at home Dolly seemed, talking in both languages – though lacking as I was in that area, she could have been talking rubbish for all I knew.

I reached for my glass, and had swallowed half the zingy contents in several blissful swallows when I noticed Dolly had pulled something out of her apron pocket.

'Is this yours?' she said.

I almost choked as I recognised my postcard. 'Where did you find it?'

'By the counter,' she said, waggling it in my direction. 'You must have pulled it out of your bag with your purse.'

I slammed my glass down. How had I not noticed? 'Thanks,' I said, heart racing as I reached for it, but Dolly had pulled it close and was examining it with a smile.

'It's the café!' She was clearly tickled as her eyes flicked over the image. 'This is the postcard you were talking about,' she said. 'It hasn't changed much, has it?'

'That's what I thought,' I said, desperate to snatch it from her. I couldn't believe how possessive I felt; how much I didn't want anyone

– besides Toni – to have read the message meant only for Dad and me. 'Thanks for picking it up.'

'It's a little piece of history.' Dolly turned it over, eyes scrunched as they scanned the back, before returning her gaze to the picture on the front. 'The café's featured in lots of pictures over the years, what with it being in such a prime position. It looks so eye-catching with the awning, and the shutters and everything, and of course, there's the food.' She glanced up. 'Maybe you should show this to Margot?'

'I… I'd rather not show anyone,' I said. 'It might be too much, at this stage.'

Dolly nodded. 'Of course, you're right,' she said. 'Especially for Margot.'

I wondered what she meant by that – had a feeling she knew more than she was prepared to say – but I didn't like to ask when she'd been so helpful already.

There was a momentary silence, while Dolly studied the image of the café once more, a smile playing over her lips.

'I suppose it seems silly, me coming here because of a postcard?'

'No sillier than any other reason.' Dolly pointed to herself. 'Look at me,' she said, fanning herself with it. 'I was a well-paid marketing manager for a tech company, but gave it up to come here because my husband left me for a younger woman.'

'That sounds like a valid reason.' I tried to place the rosy-cheeked, apron-wearing woman beside me in a corporate role, but couldn't quite manage it.

As if reading my mind, she said, 'I wore a suit every day, my hair in a bun.' She swirled the hand that wasn't gripping the postcard above her head to demonstrate. 'I had an expense account, a team working under me, and regular holidays abroad, but I'm ten times happier here than I was then, especially having my Charlie with me.'

That was easy to see. 'I'm glad,' I said as I picked up the madeleine and pushed it in my mouth, momentarily distracted by the lightness of sponge and delicate almond flavour. Mathilde might make a terrible mess in the kitchen, but she really knew how to bake.

'And you have a *very* good reason to be here.' Dolly turned the postcard over once more and I froze. It was one thing for me to have read that my birth mother didn't want me, but for someone else to see it written in black and white made me feel somehow exposed – as if I must have been totally unlovable. 'I'm no good at written French.' Dolly quickly averted her gaze. 'I just can't get the hang of it.' She was obviously referring to the Marilyn Monroe quote, and gave no sign that she'd read the rest as she handed the postcard back. 'Now, did you talk to Marie?'

I nodded as I pushed the postcard back in my bag, heat blooming over my face as I recalled my clumsy questioning. 'It's not her,' I said.

Dolly's eyes were wide. 'You're sure?'

'She…' I paused, brushing crumbs off my top, aware it wasn't my story to tell – even to Dolly. 'I'm positive.'

'Well, at least you've ruled her out,' said Dolly, and I liked her more for not probing. 'Now, I've been going through my contacts and… Mimi!'

I glanced round to see a woman approaching, a sunflower-yellow sundress skimming her ankles, her face partly obscured by giant sunglasses. 'Who's that?'

'Mimi Carruthers,' said Dolly, round the side of her hand, as if the woman might be able to lip-read. 'She moved here a couple of years ago with her husband, but was born in Chamillon, believe it or not. Said she'd always wanted to come back and I thought… you know.'

She gave a significant nod. 'She's the right age, I think, but she wears a lot of make-up, so I can't be completely sure.'

Mimi. The last time I'd heard that name was when Annabel, who'd lived next door to us in Wishbourne for as long as I could remember, had been trying to coax one of the pigeons she insisted on naming and feeding into her conservatory. 'Does she have any children?' I felt ambivalent about the possibility of having half-siblings, but couldn't resist asking anyway.

'No,' said Dolly, in a way that suggested this was noteworthy. 'She said she never wanted them.' *Brilliant.* 'But she could be covering up,' Dolly rushed on, as if I might be offended. 'She's lovely, apart from that, if a little... full-on.'

'Right.' That sounded ominous.

'She's making my wedding dress, she's very talented.'

'Right.'

'I've invited her for a coffee this morning, and thought I could introduce you.' Dolly was speaking out of the side of her mouth now as Mimi reached the doorway. She was short and stout, her skin tanned and rather crepey, her smile showing a set of big white teeth.

'I hope you aren't eating cakes, or I'll have to let out your dress,' she said to Dolly, her northern English dialect a shock, and it struck me that, although my birth mother had been born in Chamillon, she might not even be French, or have a local accent. 'I'll see you inside, it's too warm out here for me,' she added, before heading into the café, leaving behind a fog of throat-clogging perfume.

'Come on!' Dolly jabbed her head towards the window like a TV cop spotting a criminal, as Mimi arranged herself at a single table, clicking her fingers to summon a member of staff. 'Once she starts chatting up Stefan, there'll be no talking to her.'

'I thought you said she was married.'

'She is, but she loves flirting with younger men.'

Young enough to be her son? 'Dolly, wait…' I began, but she'd already darted inside, and by the time I'd staggered to my feet, she was sitting opposite Mimi and their heads were together in conversation.

Chapter Thirteen

I hurried after Dolly, narrowly avoiding a collision with Celeste, who was transporting food to a couple in Lycra at a table crowded with cycling paraphernalia.

'Wait!' I called, as if about to make a citizen's arrest. Celeste jumped back in alarm, slopping coffee onto her tray. 'So sorry, I didn't mean you.' Grimacing my apology, I moved to let her pass and stepped on Stefan's foot.

'So sorry,' I said again, my face growing hotter and redder by the minute. '*Pardon.*' Why couldn't I do a French accent? Stefan smiled kindly and managed not to limp as he returned to the counter, clutching his order pad.

I was breathing hard, as though I'd run around the harbour a couple of times, and Dolly gave me a startled look as I reached the table.

'I'm sorry, love, I should have waited,' she said, patting my arm. 'I wanted to have a little catch-up with Mimi.'

'It's fine,' I said. 'I don't want to intrude.'

'Not at all,' said Mimi, who'd pushed her sunglasses up into her liquorice-black, chin-length bob. It was obviously dyed, but it suited her square-jawed face and dramatically outlined brown eyes, which were small and round and framed by spidery lashes.

'Elle's from England,' said Dolly.

'Hertfordshire,' I added, feeling as if a box of frogs was leaping about in my chest.

'Oh, I knew someone who lived in Hertfordshire!' Mimi's voice was loud enough for several people to look round.

'You did?'

'Did you?' said Dolly, flashing me a look of excitement.

'Well, he *worked* in Hertfordshire.' Mimi adjusted the neckline of her sundress, which was low enough to reveal her tea-coloured cleavage and a hint of lacy nude bra. 'I don't know if he *lived* there.'

Dolly's eyebrows jumped and she shot me an enquiring look.

'Did he work in a museum?' My voice, in contrast to Mimi's, had shrunk. 'He worked there for years. Curated exhibitions. Charted the history of the Hertfordshire regiment.' I was talking in bullet points. 'In the paper a couple of times. Well known, locally.' The turnout for his funeral had been bigger than I'd expected. The church had been packed, and the warmth I'd felt from everyone who'd known him had carried me through the day. 'Had a big moustache in the eighties.'

'Ooh, he *did* have a moustache, I remember I didn't like it tickling my thighs.'

Dolly made a small choking sound, and I focused on Mimi's chin mole and tried not to think at all.

'I can't remember that much about him,' she went on. Her richly drawn eyebrows beetled together, and her top lip concertinaed as she pursed her lips. 'We didn't do much talking, if you know what I mean,' she said. 'Too busy playing tonsil hockey.' She made a nudging motion with her elbow and dropped a lewd wink at Dolly. 'No names, no pack drill.'

It was exactly the sort of thing Dad might have said, and, as my legs turned rubbery, I grabbed the nearest chair and sat down. 'Did you meet in London?'

'Sorry?' Mimi looked from me to Dolly. 'What's this about?' she said, but before I could respond, Stefan appeared with a mug of creamy coffee, and a plump, chocolate-topped choux bun, oozing crème pâtissière. 'Hello, gorgeous!' She took the plate as he transferred it from the tray, her knuckles brushing his, and I couldn't tell whether she was talking to her bun, or Stefan. 'Don't you look delicious?' *Still couldn't tell.* 'I can't wait to sink my teeth into you.' *Nope.*

The tips of Stefan's ears glowed red as he put down her mug of coffee, and Mimi laid her ring-clad hand over his. 'Could I please have a fork?'

I'd never heard anyone refer to a piece of cutlery in such a lascivious fashion, and neither had Stefan, judging from his pained expression.

Was I related to a cougar?

'Stop teasing the poor fellow,' said Dolly, with just the right amount of insistence. 'You're too much woman for him.'

'Aye, I suppose I am.' Mimi sighed, her broad pronunciation at odds with the accents around us. 'If only that husband of mine had a bit more oomph in the bedroom department.' Without waiting for her fork, she popped a whole choux bun into her mouth and chewed, delicately dabbing cream from her lips with a napkin.

Dolly caught my eye, suppressing a smile, but I was too on edge to respond.

'Mmmmmm,' groaned Mimi, closing her eyes in apparent ecstasy as she washed down her bun with several gulps of coffee. '*Délicieux.*'

I tried to imagine being related to her – being cradled in her arms as a baby, growing up in Yorkshire – and failed. What if I'd found my birth mother, only to feel no kinship with her? I was prepared for her to reject me (after all, she'd done it before), but hadn't considered we might not have anything in common at all.

'What were we talking about?' she said finally, banging her mug down. 'Oh yes, my old lover from way back,' she answered herself.

Old lover? 'I wondered whether you'd met him in London.' I swiped my hand over the back of my neck. It was warm by the window with the sun blazing through. Mimi didn't seem to mind, despite the beads of perspiration that had broken out on her upper lip.

'London?' She shook her head so hard, her sunglasses dropped over her eyes. 'Oops!' Chortling, she took them off and laid them on the table. 'No, this was in Leeds,' she said. 'He'd just moved up that way and we got chatting on the bus on my way to work and he mentioned he was from Hertfordshire – or maybe it was Herefordshire, I can't remember. Somewhere beginning with aitch.'

A sigh rose up from my depths. *It wasn't her.*

'Do you know, I haven't thought about him in years, but I really liked the man, even if we didn't do much talking that night…' She snapped her fingers, making me jump. 'Bellamy, *that* was his name!' A delighted smile creased her face. 'Jason Bellamy.' Her little eyes grew wistful. 'I haven't thought about him in years,' she said. 'He really was something in the sack.'

'I knew three Jasons in the eighties,' said Dolly quickly, shooting me a look that was kind, worried and sorry, all at the same time.

I shot one back that probably said, *It's fine, I don't think I could cope with Mimi being my birth mother anyway*, and glanced at my watch. It was almost eleven o'clock.

'I'd better get to work,' I said, noticing the mums and toddlers had left and the café had quietened down. 'Nice to meet you, Mimi.'

'What was all that about?' I heard her ask Dolly as I hurried away, and hoped that Dolly would come up with a reason to explain my line of questioning.

At least I'd ruled out another M, I thought, as I stuffed my bag in the cupboard in the staff room. I wondered how many there were. It was more draining than I'd anticipated, my hopes see-sawing up and down – and I'd only been here a couple of days.

Keen to switch thoughts for a while by reacquainting myself with Basil, I entered the kitchen, to find Dolly drying her hands. 'I said you were looking for an old girlfriend of your dad's,' she said. 'She apologised for what she said about the moustache and said there was no wonder you turned white.'

'Did I?'

'As her plate.'

We giggled.

'I shouldn't have left you to explain,' I said. 'I'm sorry.'

'Don't be silly.' Dolly began rummaging in the freezer. 'It's the least I can do when you're helping me out here.'

Doing some washing-up hardly equated to helping someone track down their birth mother. 'Thank you, anyway.'

She pulled out an armful of baguettes. 'No need to thank me yet,' she said, arranging the baguettes on a tray like batons. 'But I have thought of someone else beginning with M.'

'Oh?' I stopped fiddling with my apron strings, tying them in a neat bow 'Who?'

She flourished one of the baguettes, looking pleased with herself. 'Stefan's mum!'

'What?'

'Manon,' she said. 'She's a butcher and I know she grew up in Chamillon with her brothers, so I'm assuming she was born here.'

My heart had picked up pace again. 'And she's in her fifties?'

Dolly slid the tray of baguettes into the oven. 'Probably,' she said. 'She's not one of those women who bothers with make-up – you wouldn't, I suppose, if you were surrounded by animal carcasses all day long – so she's very fresh-faced. Looks younger, if anything.'

I hadn't imagined my birth mother being a butcher. It wasn't very glamorous. Mum had worked at the same museum as Dad – it was where they'd met – and while that wasn't exactly glitzy, at least it hadn't involved working with dead animals. *Jess definitely wouldn't approve.* 'Is it likely she's visited London in the past?'

'Hmm, now that I don't know.' Dolly turned, her hand on her hip. 'Stefan, has your *maman* ever been to London?'

I swung round to see him in the doorway, and had the sudden, shocking thought that he could be my half-brother – this big-haired, wide-eyed, skinny young man with impeccable manners, and a smile that could melt the hardest of hearts. Jess was my sister, and I didn't want another, but Stefan was lovely. Even though we looked nothing alike, and I didn't speak his language, I could imagine getting to know him better – though that would mean acknowledging his mother was also mine.

My heartbeat grew faster. I gripped the edge of the worktop and took a deep breath. Stefan had asked Dolly to repeat her question and was shaking his head.

'No, no, *Maman* does not like to go on the plane or the boat, she has not been overseas,' he said, 'She wants to be…' He pointed to the black, pointy-toed shoes at the end of his skinny black jeans. 'On the floor.'

'Terra firma,' said Dolly. 'She prefers dry land.'

He shook his head again, his hair bouncing. 'She does not like to even go in the car. It makes her go vertigo.' He spun his eyes and did a wobbly twirl.

'Oh dear,' said Dolly, adding weightily, 'So, she's *never* been abroad in her *whole life?*'

'Never.' He sounded anxious now. 'This is bad?'

'No, of course not,' said Dolly and I, simultaneously, and when she winked at me, I felt like I'd entered a twilight zone, where nothing quite made sense. *Had I just considered Stefan might be my brother?*

'I can take my break now?' He looked at us both in turn, rubbing his hands together, and Dolly picked up an oven glove.

'Of *course* you can. I'll just get my baguettes out and take over.' She threw me a mischievous look. 'I've been badly neglecting my customers this morning,' she said, as Charlie came through, and for a moment there were four of us in the kitchen, and it felt as if all the air had been sucked out.

'It's not like you to neglect your "café family",' he said. He didn't look as happy as I'd have expected after spending some time with Tegan, but maybe he was trying to throw Dolly off the scent. 'What have you been up to?'

I caught Dolly's eye and she must have seen something in my expression because she reached up and patted his cheek and said, 'I've been getting to know this lovely girl better, that's all.'

Charlie's eyes fastened on mine for a moment. I wondered whether he was thinking how much less lovely than Tegan I was, with her longer-than-average legs and sunny nature – not to mention her cycling abilities – and felt a flush of envy at the way he'd smiled at her, and how easy he'd seemed in her company. 'The bike's back at the house,' he said, as though speaking in code, and I realised I'd forgotten all about it.

'Oh thanks, that was really nice…' I began, but he'd already turned to follow Dolly into the café, and I found myself left alone with Basil and a sink full of unwashed plates.

Chapter Fourteen

There wasn't much time to talk after that, as the café grew busy again, though Dolly kept sending Charlie to 'help' whenever I went through to clear a table. Each time, he was waylaid by a customer, so our only communication was with eyebrows, and some apologetic wincing on his part – though he did manage to mutter, 'How are the ribs?' at one point.

'Fine,' I said, surprised to find that they were.

As I refilled Basil for the third time, I realised I'd found a rhythm again, and began to relax as my attention fixed on the task in hand. Maybe this was what mindfulness was all about. I'd tried it after Dad died, when I was sleeping badly, working too hard (according to Toni) and had broken up with Andrew. I'd listened to a couple of guided podcasts, but failed miserably at concentrating on the 'succulent taste of a raisin' and focusing on my breathing had made me hyperventilate. I'd tried other things too, but essential oils had given me a headache, a 'white noise' app kept me awake, and ditching caffeine had made me twitchy. The only thing that had helped – apart from working – were jigsaw puzzles (Jess's idea), but clearly, all I'd needed was a ready supply of dirty kitchenware and a dishwasher.

The only thing that spoiled the flow was the appearance of Mathilde around lunchtime, her eyes almost black against the whiteness of her hair, which was fastened in a long, thin plait. I thought she'd come to bake, but it seemed she'd put in an appearance just to peer hard at me, before launching into a tirade in French that made me back away.

'Don't mind her,' Dolly advised, catching the tail end of Mathilde's outburst, and was treated to a spiteful stare. 'She's not fond of strangers, that's all.' Watching Mathilde sweep out, Dolly's smile was smaller than usual, as if she too was rattled.

'I thought she was going to spit at me, like a llama.'

'Oh, she doesn't do that any more.' Dolly picked up some cake tongs and vanished before I could ask her whether or not she was joking.

Once again, I ate lunch in the courtyard, sunning my shins and deliberately thinking of nothing in particular. Afterwards, on her lunchbreak, Celeste chatted to me in the kitchen in halting English, over her coffee, telling me about a planned trip to London in the autumn with her husband. It wasn't until she mentioned her friend had once seen the Queen in London in the eighties that my synapses snapped into overdrive.

'What's her name?' I said, swilling water around the sink, unable to think of a cleverer way of asking.

'It is Elizabeth.' Celeste sounded understandably puzzled. 'You do not know what the Queen is called?'

'Sorry, I meant your friend.'

She looked at me over her mug, brow furrowed. 'My friend? She is called Deborah.'

'Oh, my mum had a friend with that name,' I said, feeling silly and sounding too effusive. 'It's a lovely name, but it's pronounced a bit different in England: DEBra, not DebORah.'

'I like the English names.' Celeste's round face relaxed into a smile. 'My great-grandmother, she was from the Blackpool,' she said. 'I called my daughter the same name, to honour her.'

'That's nice.' I rattled a pair of cups into the dishwasher, swearing inwardly when one of the handles came off. 'What is it?'

'Beryl,' Celeste announced, rolling the *r*. 'She is the only girl in her school with such a name.'

In the whole of France, probably. 'How lovely,' I said, removing the broken cup, wondering whether I could glue the handle back on.

'My other daughter, she is named from your *Coronation Street*.'

I turned to stare. 'You get that over here?'

'*Non.*' She shook her head. 'DEBra, my friend, she lived in London for a year and brought back some of the tape recordings of your wonderful show for me. We watched it *so* many times. It is why my English is very good.'

'Wow,' I said, remembering how Mum had got hooked on the goings-on in Weatherfield for a while. 'I'm surprised you don't speak with a northern accent,' I said, but seeing her frown quickly, added, 'So, your other daughter is called…?'

'Rita.' Celeste's smile was full of pride. 'A *very* strong woman.'

I turned away so she couldn't see my face and managed a rather strangled-sounding, 'Lovely.'

Realising there was no way I could start grilling her on how many women she knew with names that started with M – without coming across as deranged – I asked instead if she knew where Dolly kept the glue.

'Glue?'

I mimed reattaching the cup handle, and Celeste put down her mug and clapped politely. 'Maybe more… practising you will be better,' she said, as if I'd tried to perform a magic trick, and returned to work with an air of relief.

Making a mental note to replace the cup, I dropped it in the bin, and jumped when Dolly returned. 'Margot's here,' she said, without preamble. 'I'll sort out Basil if you want to speak to her.'

I was suddenly plunged into doubt, 'Maybe this isn't the best time,' I said. 'I should ask to meet her somewhere private and discuss it then.'

'She'd likely say no.' Dolly spoke with some authority. 'She's a very private person and doesn't like company.'

'Wouldn't she be curious?'

'The thought of real life approaching would probably scare her off.' Dolly looked suddenly troubled. 'She feels less vulnerable here, with people she's used to around her.'

'Do you *know* why she's so… fragile?' It was the only word I could think of to sum up Margot. 'I won't repeat anything you tell me, if you do.'

Dolly puffed out a sigh, and seemed to make up her mind. 'It's not really my story to tell, but one thing I *do* know is that Margot's broken heart has more to do with her career than with a man. At least, that's what I thought.'

I slapped on a smile as Stefan came through and dumped more cups and plates in the sink. '*Pardon,*' he said with a bow as he hurried out, but I couldn't tell whether he was apologising for the plates, or for interrupting Dolly.

'What do you mean?' I said, when he'd gone.

Dolly double-checked we were alone – even pulling the oven open, as if someone could be hiding inside – then spoke in a low voice. 'Margot came to a wine-tasting session here one evening, and got a bit merry – most unusual – and when everyone had left, she told me she'd been an actress with a theatre company, but fell off the stage and broke her leg while performing in London one night, and it ended her career.'

'That's awful,' I said. 'But, obviously her leg healed.'

'The part she'd played was given to her understudy.' Dolly shook her head. 'She got rave reviews for her performance, and Margot lost her confidence and never really recovered.'

'It must have been devastating.'

'Like I said, it's not my story to tell,' said Dolly, even though she just had. 'But she stayed in London for a while after that, sharing a house with a couple of actresses. Maybe something else happened while she was there.'

Like having a baby.

The unspoken words hovered between us.

'You did say I mustn't ever mention children to her.'

'That's right, I did.' After a moment's hesitation, Dolly added, 'I don't know for sure, and you mustn't repeat this, but I heard a rumour after I took over the café that she'd had a son who lived with his dad after they were divorced, and she hasn't seen him since, but maybe that's an elaborate cover story.'

'If it's even true,' I said.

'If it is, and he chose to live with his dad, that must be very painful for a mother to accept.' Dolly looked briefly stricken, her fingers reaching for the gold chain around her neck. 'I'd have been broken if Charlie had picked his dad over me, not that he had much choice as the bastard didn't want him.' She said it without any venom, as if she'd long since made peace with the facts, and I fleetingly wondered whether Charlie had. 'I can remember the day he was born as though it was yesterday.' Her focus drifted. 'Mainly because he was massive and I needed an epidoodah, which didn't work.' She gave a little shudder. 'Anyway, like I said, the only time I asked Margot about it, she got very tearful and wouldn't discuss it.' Her expression changed. 'Maybe it was a story she'd told to hide the truth,' she added. 'Maybe *you're* the child who lived with his dad, and you're not a him, you're a *her*.'

'And now she's rewritten the past,' I said, caught up in Dolly's revelation. Poor Margot, no wonder she wanted to lose herself in her writing. Science fiction too. About as far removed from acting and motherhood as she could get. Assuming 'Brigitte' wasn't a former actress with a child she hadn't seen for years. *If* the story was true. It seemed Chamillon was just as susceptible to gossip and rumour as any English village; but rumours often held a kernel of truth. Apart from the fact that I couldn't picture Margot giving up a baby, however desperate the circumstances.

Whenever I'd thought about the reasons why my birth mother had given me to Dad – parental disapproval (which he'd had hinted at), post-natal depression, or simply a driving ambition to continue with a career – they'd felt like plot devices, rather than explanations I could relate to. The truth was, I couldn't *feel* her, or even picture her as a real person, and couldn't work out whether that was a good or a bad thing.

It means she's no more than a stranger, Toni had said, when I asked her. *No more real than a character in a film.*

Why aren't I more upset, or angry?

Maybe you would be, if you hadn't had Paula, and your dad and Jess. Would you rather be messed up about it?

I wouldn't. But I wanted to know why she'd given birth when she didn't want a baby.

When my shift ended, with only one more breakage (a teapot spout hit the edge of the counter and snapped off), I resisted Dolly's plea to join her and Charlie for something to eat upstairs. Charlie seemed on edge as he waited for my answer, and I guessed he was waiting to shoot off and meet Tegan again and didn't want the hassle of Dolly berating him for being unsociable in front of a 'guest' (a.k.a. 'possible future wife' – I hadn't ruled this out as her ulterior motive for helping me).

'I expect you'll want a rest before opening again this evening,' I said diplomatically. Something flashed cross Charlie's face that vanished before I could grasp it, and I felt oddly let down when he didn't reply. 'You must get tired, working so many hours.'

'Oh, not really, I love it.' Dolly refastened her apron and patted her hair. 'It's not like work at all, and while Frank's away, I've a rota of locals coming to help me cook,' she said. 'It's *so* much fun.' She spoke with such utter conviction, I wondered when I'd last felt as passionate about my job. *Had I ever?*

'You weren't saying that when it was Monsieur Moreau's turn.' Charlie's mouth curled up in amusement. 'He massively over-salted everything, remember?'

'Yes, but everyone bought more drinks, so it worked out rather well.' Dolly winked at me. I'd never been winked at so much in my life as I had in the past two days. 'We have a licence to serve wine and cocktails in the evenings,' she added. 'You should come by and sample Charlie's Downfall.'

I couldn't help laughing. 'That doesn't sound very appealing.'

'It's called a Pineapple Downfall,' he explained, with a grin. 'Pineapple, white rum and mint, and anyone could make it.'

'He's like Tom Cruise in that film.' Dolly flipped an imaginary cocktail shaker and caught it behind her back, gyrating her hips, while Charlie dropped his head in his hands.

'She means *Cocktail*, in case you weren't sure.' As his gaze met mine, I caught a hint of redness on his cheeks. 'And I promise you, I *don't* attempt to dance,' he said. 'That wouldn't be a pleasant experience for anyone.'

'Shame,' I said, smiling, and for a second was overpowered by the thought that it *would* be nice to join them upstairs, and to return to the café later on to watch Charlie make his cocktails. 'I admire anyone who can dance while making a drink,' I added. 'I can barely walk and carry two plates without dropping them.'

'Noted.' Charlie pretended to write it on his palm with his finger. 'Mind you, I dropped the cocktail shaker on my first attempt,' he said. 'It was like an oil spill.' He spread his hands with a look of comic dismay. 'It took so long to clear up, we had to delay opening.'

'*And* you'd mixed up the measurements and used *way* too much rum.' Dolly's face creased with mirth. 'This posh bloke kept saying loudly, can anyone else smell *butterscotch?*'

I joined in their laughter, a ripple of warmth spreading through me. I missed laughing with family; silly things setting us off that no one else would have understood, like singing 'Happy Birthday' as off-key as possible, until we were all doubled up. 'I like butterscotch,' I said, which set us off again.

'Well, I don't know about you two, but I'm going for a shower,' said Charlie, eventually, his face still bright with hilarity. His eyes skimmed mine as he turned, and when I heard the sound of his footsteps running upstairs, I rejected an image of him pulling his shirt off.

'Sure you won't stay?' Dolly's eyes probed mine, as if trying to reach my innermost thoughts. 'We can talk some more about… you know what.'

'I'm pretty tired,' I said, though I wasn't tired at all after sleeping so well the night before. It was almost as if the air in Chamillon had healing powers. Even my terrible attempt at cycling to the café felt like a distant memory. 'I think I'm just going to put my feet up.'

'You know, it would be a shame not to do some exploring while you're here.' Dolly tipped her head to one side in exaggerated concern. 'I could ask Charlie to show you round.'

It was a blatant attempt to get us together. 'I'm not on holiday, remember,' I said, with a little laugh. The last thing Charlie would want was to act as my tour guide, and Tegan would be less than thrilled to have me tagging along. 'Honestly, Dolly, I'm fine.'

She didn't look convinced. 'Well, thank you for today.'

I thought of the cup and teapot in the bin and knew I should own up. 'I think I'm getting the hang of it.'

'You'll get there,' she said, and I wondered if I'd imagined that her words felt double-edged, and that her gaze stayed on me as I went to retrieve my bag. 'See you tomorrow, Elle.'

Chapter Fifteen

Back at the house, I changed into comfy shorts and a stripy, cotton top and took my phone into the garden with a cup of tea. Jess had texted, which was unusual, but it wasn't normal for me to be away from home for any length of time, and I guessed she was checking up on me.

Any sign of the kri-kri?! Maybe not. *How close are you to the mountains?*

Not far I replied, glad she couldn't see me. I'd forgotten I was meant to be in Crete. I'd have to tell her the goats were hiding, or had been banished from the area. No, not banished, or she'd probably start a petition to get them reintroduced.

Brilliant! They come out when it starts to get dark, so you should be able to see them then. Have you got your long lens?

I was surprised she wasn't sleeping. It must be way after midnight in Borneo.

Didn't bring it, I said, which was true. *What are you doing up?*

Bobo can't sleep, so we're keeping him company.

A picture arrived of Owen, cradling the same baby orangutan as before (at least, it looked like the same one), sticking its tongue out like a naughty toddler. Owen was smiling, despite the heavy shadows under his eyes.

Practising for when you have a human baby? I wasn't sure why I said it, when Jess was adamant about not wanting babies, but she was so good with animals, it was easy to imagine her having a brood of children. She would be a brilliant mother, because she'd had a fantastic role model, proven by the photo albums at home, stuffed with photos of Mum with us as babies and toddlers, looking as if there was nothing she'd rather be doing than spending every second with her daughters. Obviously, she couldn't, because of her job as an administrator at the museum, but every day, she'd walked us to school and home again, and had been to every parents' evening and Christmas play. I'd once heard her say to her friend Deborah that being a mum was her 'dream job'. Of course, I'd had the same role model as Jess, but I didn't share Mum's DNA. For all I knew, I was like my birth mother: lacking a maternal gene.

A cartoon image pinged onto my phone, of a baby with a speech bubble coming out of its mouth that read, *I hate people too much to consider giving birth to one.*

Ha, ha! I replied. *That's not even true.* Not completely, anyway. Jess just didn't like what people were doing to her beloved planet.

I do love you X

I was so surprised, I nearly dropped my phone. Jess wasn't given to verbally expressing emotion (to humans) and I wondered whether she'd used predictive text and had meant to say something else.

Love you too X I wrote back, just in case, my eyes swimming with tears as I remembered how I'd kept her under close scrutiny in the days after Mum died, checking for signs that she wasn't coping, only for her to tell me, 'I'm fine, Elle. I've still got you and Dad.'

In a rush of emotion, I added, *I'll do my best to find a goat! X*

Back in the kitchen, I connected my phone to the Wi-Fi, brought up Google and typed in *Are there mountain goats in France?* The answer was no, unless I fancied travelling to a wild, undeveloped area of the Southern Alps, which I didn't. There was a wildlife park nearby though, with goats that looked similar, but the lack of mountains in the background was a giveaway.

Sighing, I closed down the website, and was trying to make up my mind whether to call Toni, or make something to eat, when someone knocked on the front door.

Hoping it was Marie, insisting I join her for dinner, I wondered whether I could get her chatting about long-term Chamillon residents – specifically females whose names began with M – and smoothed my hair before yanking the door open with a smile.

It was Henri.

'Hi!' I hadn't meant to sound quite so welcoming. 'What are you doing here?'

Grinning, he said, 'I told you I'd call again this evening.' His eyes were appreciative as they swept over my outfit. 'You're ready to go for a walk?'

It took all my willpower not to glance down and check I was still wearing clothes. 'I… I don't know.' *Really, Elle?* 'I haven't eaten yet.'

'Even better.' He pressed a hand over his heart, which was probably behaving more rationally than mine was. 'We can have something to eat and drink in Saint-Martin,' he said. 'I know a good restaurant there.'

'Hang on, I thought you were suggesting a walk, not a meal.' Why did I sound so flirty? I should be closing the door in his sexy French face. He'd shaved, I noticed, eyes fixing on a dimple in his chin. Combined with his sculpted cheekbones and white-toothed smile, he looked like he should be modelling tuxedos.

'If you don't want to walk, and you'd like to eat, I've come prepared.' His voice sounded as if it had been smoked in brandy, or dipped in chocolate, or rolled in honey and biscuits.

'Prepared?' Catching a glint of sunlight on metal, I peered behind him and saw a bike that looked as if it had been stretched, with an extra saddle and four pedals.

'It's a bicycle for two.' He turned to sweep his hand along its length, squeezing the extra saddle in a way that made blood rush to my cheeks.

'I don't really do cycling.' My tone was higher than normal. 'I'm used to four wheels, not two.'

'That's why I hired a tandem, just in case.' He mounted the front saddle with an athletic swing of his leg, and placed his foot on the pedal. 'You won't have to do all the hard work.' His jeans had pulled tight across his thighs and it was an effort to rip my gaze away.

'I don't think so?' I said, accidentally turning it into a question.

'It's very stable, and it's only fifteen minutes to Saint-Martin.' His smouldering look burned through me. 'No hills, just long, straight cycle paths.'

'I don't have a helmet.' *Sexy.* And untrue. There was a cycle helmet in the shed, according to Charlie.

'You won't need one,' said Henri, eyes lingering on my hair as if it was made of spun-gold. 'Come on.' His coaxing smile made my pulse throb. 'It's a beautiful evening, and you shouldn't be here on your own.'

'I'm sure there are plenty of females you could take out to dinner.'

He gave a quick laugh. 'Maybe.' His eyes latched onto mine again. 'But they're not you.'

OK, he was totally corny, but it *was* thoughtful to go to this much trouble, and I hadn't been out to dinner with a man since breaking up with Andrew. And it wasn't as if I was planning to fall into bed with him, or let him kiss me all over, or remove my clothes with his teeth, or... 'I don't want to be out too late, I've got work tomorrow,' I practically squeaked, cheeks pulsating with heat.

'Then you need to eat, to keep up your strength.' His persuasive voice and Marmite eyes had all but cracked my resolve. It *was* a beautiful evening. The sun was still warm, the sky a gauzy blue, and I'd barely seen anything of the island since arriving. *Because you're not on holiday*, I reminded myself. Even so, my plan to grill Marie about the locals in the hope she'd let slip a name that would lead to my birth mother was blatantly ridiculous, and the thought of spending the evening alone suddenly unappealing.

'It's not a date,' I said, even though he'd brought a bike for two and was proposing to wine and dine me.

'Did I say it was?'

'Just so you know.'

His smile made me catch my breath. 'Is that a yes?'

'It's yes to a bike ride and dinner, but I'll pay for my own meal.'

He held out his hands in a gesture of supplication. 'If you insist,' he said lazily. 'You'd better put some shoes on.'

I looked at my pink shins and bare feet, glad I'd let Toni talk me into having a pedicure before leaving, and that my toenails were coloured a shade called Bahama Mamma. 'I should get changed.'

'You look good as you are.'

I knew that couldn't be true, but as this wasn't a date, I told myself it didn't matter. I didn't need to make a huge effort to get dressed up. 'I'll be back in a minute,' I said.

'I'll wait.' He folded his arms, still straddling the bike, and the word *magnificent* sprang to mind. He looked like a modern-day knight in shining armour astride a white horse, only 'Frenchman wearing an olive-green shirt on a bike' didn't have quite the same ring.

Pushing the door almost shut – inviting him in wasn't an option – I ran around, gathering my bag, phone and keys, before pausing to check my reflection in a picture above the fireplace. I couldn't see clearly past the painted couple, who appeared to be drinking champagne on board a train. Still, this wasn't a date, I reminded myself again, so there was no need to worry about make-up and, luckily, my hair didn't require much maintenance.

What if the restaurant didn't allow customers in shorts? Surely Henri would have said so. But he was a fisherman, and might not understand about dress codes. Although he was dressed casually too, he somehow looked better put together than I did. I pictured my turquoise 'Riviera' dress, and had just dashed upstairs to pull it on, when Henri called through the front door.

'Do you need a hand with anything?'

I was glad he wasn't there to see me blush from head to toe. 'I won't be a minute!' I called back, praying he wouldn't come in. Apart from anything else, I wasn't sure Natalie would approve of me having visitors in the house. I tossed the dress on the bed (it was too much for a casual outing) and hastily shoved my feet into a pair of sandals that had escaped my suitcase, hoping they'd be suitable for pedalling – *oh God, more pedalling* – then headed downstairs, looking around to check the house wasn't a mess in case Marie came round to take pictures.

Anticipation fluttered in my stomach as I slung my bag across my body. Although loath to admit it – even to myself – I was looking forward to spending the evening with Henri.

Chapter Sixteen

Once I'd straddled the rear of the bike and my feet were on the pedals, Henri called, 'Tally-ho!' in a posh British accent, and I just had time to glimpse Marie's startled face in her doorway as we took off, and sensed her watching as we rode down the street.

At first, it was easy to keep up with the pedalling, which was so much easier with Henri bearing the brunt. I tried to wriggle myself more comfortable (why didn't saddles come with a cushion attached?), relaxed my grip on the handlebars and even managed to smile and wave at a woman cycling the opposite way, with a hamster-cheeked toddler in a buggy attached to her bike.

As we reached the cycle path, leading out of the village towards Saint-Martin, I stifled a scream as a pair of teenage boys sped by, creating a backdraught.

Henri half-turned, while keeping the bike pointing in the right direction. 'OK?'

'Fine!' I said, trying not to stare at his shoulder blades, moving beneath his shirt. There was a lock of dark hair trapped inside his collar, and I curbed the impulse to untuck it. Instead, I looked at the ribbon of sand and sparkling blue sea hugging the coastline that ran alongside the path, and Henri slowed to explain that wooden fencing was made of chestnut poles, joined together with wire, necessary to prevent access to the sand dunes. 'It's so the plants that grow there don't get trampled on,' he said, managing to make this fact sound compelling. 'The plants reduce the impact of wind and water,' he continued. 'And the fences act as a windbreak, to protect against erosion.'

'I didn't realise sand dunes were so complicated,' I said, and was rewarded with a burst of laughter before he agreed that they were.

'Useful, though. They help to protect against flooding.'

I tried to remember it all to tell Jess, knowing it was the sort of detail she'd appreciate, before remembering I couldn't because I was supposed to be in Greece.

Henri started saying something else, about bio-diversity and the land being affected by pollution, but the Atlantic breeze had picked up and snatched away his words, and so I stopped trying to listen and gave myself up to the ride.

'Nearly there,' he called over his shoulder about five minutes later, speeding up so my legs were forced to move more quickly, until they felt like cartoon legs, spinning round and round in a dizzying blur. Soon, my hair wasn't so much lifting gently as in danger of being torn from my scalp, my calf muscles burning with the effort of keeping up, and my top flapping like a sail in the breeze.

'Please can you slow down?' I called, as colours merged into a haze and my eyes began to water, but Henri didn't seem to hear, so I lifted my feet off the pedals and stuck them out to the side, and let him transport us the rest of the way to Saint-Martin on his own. By the time he stopped, I'd recovered my breath enough to smile brightly when asked if I'd enjoyed the journey.

'Lovely,' I said, letting him help me off, certain my legs weren't going to hold me up. I sagged against him for a moment, and felt a rumble of laughter deep in his chest.

'Are you sure you're OK, Elle?'

Why did he have to say my name like that? 'Positive,' I said, reluctantly pulling away and straightening my shorts, which had somehow twisted up around my crotch. 'I'm just not used to pedals.'

'Not used to pedals.' He laughed again, shaking his head. 'I still don't quite get the British sense of humour.'

Unsure how to respond, I flattened my hair with my hands, watching him attach the bike to some railings with a chain. With any luck it would get stolen and I could get a taxi back.

'So, what do you think of my home?' He straightened and looked around. 'Beautiful, isn't it?'

'You live here?'

'I do indeed, as you English would say.'

I spun around, and had to admit Saint-Martin-de-Ré was picturesque, with elegantly weathered buildings arranged around the star-shaped port, which I knew from reading up on the plane had been fortified in the seventeenth century to protect the island against invaders, and was centred around a marina, surrounded by boutiques, antique shops, restaurants and cafés. 'It's really lovely,' I said, watching the sunlight strike the buildings, thinking what a good photo it would make. 'Have you lived here long?'

'I was born over there.' Henri gestured towards a hill beyond the buildings, as if his mother had literally given birth there. 'I've travelled a lot since then,' he added, and I had a vision of him as a toddler, holding a small leather trunk like Paddington Bear. 'But I'm back for good now.' His smile was proprietorial. 'I love it here.'

'Where have you travelled to?'

'All over,' he said. 'I lived in England for a while.'

That explained why his English was so good. 'Whereabouts in England?' I was distracted by the feel of his hand, cupping my elbow. His palm felt warm against my skin, but his touch had brought me out in goosebumps.

'Let's talk over dinner,' he said, steering me along the quayside towards the restaurants, the tables outside already filling up with visitors. Music drifted on the air, accompanying the sound of fluttering masts in the port, and mingled food scents made my stomach rumble. As I picked up pace, my ankle turned on the cobbled pavement and I toppled hard against him.

'Ow,' I said, as his arm shot around my shoulders.

'Are you hurt?'

'I don't think so.' I straightened to see Charlie across the street, looking right at us, and blinked a couple of times, as if seeing an apparition. His sandy-blond hair was distinctive, and when he raised his hand in a wave, I knew I wasn't mistaken. He must be meeting Tegan here.

As I waved back, Henri turned, his arm still holding me. 'Who was that?' he queried, but a gaggle of people were passing the spot where Charlie had been, and when they'd gone, so had he.

'I thought I saw someone I recognised,' I said, easing out from under Henri's arm and testing out my foot. 'They've gone now.'

'Can you put your weight on it?' He looked down, endearingly concerned.

'It's fine,' I said, trying not to limp as I resumed walking. I really needed to eat now, my head was reeling. 'Where are we going?'

'Just over here.' Taking my arm once more, he guided me to a cosy-looking restaurant opposite the marina called L'Etoile de Mer. 'The Starfish,' he translated. 'Because the fish is the star of the show.'

In truth, I'd have preferred a juicy steak (had he forgotten I was scared of eating fish?) but it seemed churlish to say so, especially as he was a fisherman. 'I can't wait,' I said. 'To eat, I mean.' Hopefully, there would be something on the menu I'd enjoy.

The restaurant was low-lit and intimate, with maroon leather chairs and dark wood tables, separated by indoor trees hung with lanterns. Piano music tinkled in the background, competing with the swell of voices, clattering cutlery and chinking glasses, and I immediately felt underdressed in my stripy top and shorts. No one was wearing evening dress, but everyone looked well groomed with a subtle air of affluence, and I knew already the food was going to be out of my usual price range.

'It's very busy,' I said, feeling like a country mouse visiting the big city for the first time. 'Maybe we should try somewhere else,' I suggested, unwilling to hang about for half an hour. 'There seem to be plenty of places to choose from.'

'There's always a free table here for me,' said Henri, flashing me a smile.

I noticed a few people glance at him in apparent recognition. 'How so?'

He gave a casual shrug. 'I supply their fish.'

Although I couldn't quite see why that entitled him to wander in off the street, I followed him to a free table in the corner, set for two, as though we'd been expected.

'I don't mind eating outside,' I said, hovering as he pulled out a chair for me to sit down. 'It's a lovely evening.'

'It's nice in here too.' He gestured to the polished floor, smooth white walls and a wood-beamed ceiling fitted with copper pendant lights, and I had to agree that it was. At least sitting down, with a linen napkin spread across my lap, I was less visible. Despite Henri's flattery,

I felt out of my league with him now we were surrounded by attractive, well-dressed people. I wondered how he could afford to eat somewhere like this on his fisherman's salary – assuming fishermen weren't well paid. Maybe that's why he hadn't objected when I'd offered to pay my way. And maybe he was allowed to eat here at a discount, in return for supplying the restaurant with cod.

'Order anything you like,' he said as a waiter appeared out of nowhere and handed us each a menu with a deferential smile.

A glance inside confirmed my suspicions. Nothing was priced, and everything was written in French. I hadn't a clue what I wanted, or how much it would cost.

Maybe I could ease out my phone and bring up a translation app.

Flicking a look at the window, I wished for a second we had a view of the marina, and imagined Toni saying, *For God's sake, Elle, you're out with a gorgeous bloke who thinks you're beautiful, so why not just enjoy it?*

She was right. Plus, I could pick his brain. Although he hadn't been born in Chamillon, he clearly knew plenty of its residents. I doubted Marie's was the only guest house or hotel he supplied with fish, and if his parents had lived on the island for years, maybe they could help too.

I returned my attention to the menu, and thought I recognised the word aioli from watching *MasterChef*. Wasn't it garlic mayonnaise? I loved mayonnaise, especially with fries, which would go nicely with a piece of tuna. If only I knew what tuna was in French. I'd just worked up the nerve to ask Henri to decode the menu when he slapped his shut.

'Let's start with oysters,' he said. '*Les huitres*,' he instructed the waiter, who leapt to attention with some more reverential nodding. 'And a bottle of Chablis, *s'il vous plaît*.'

'*Oui, Monsieur Durand*.'

As the waiter scuttled away, I said, 'Aren't oysters supposed to be an aphrodisiac?' Heat spread through me as I imagined Henri feeding them to me – in bed. 'Didn't I tell you this isn't a date?' It came out like an invitation, and his delighted laughter drew an answering smile from a passing couple.

'I ordered oysters because the island is famous for them.' He rested his elbows on the table. 'Didn't you know?' he said. 'They're considered the best in the world.'

'Oh.' I reassembled my expression. 'Well, I haven't tried them before.' I'd never been tempted in the past, put off by their slimy appearance.

'What?' Henri mimed astonishment, slumping back in his chair before leaning forward again. 'There are farms all over the island, it's the perfect environment for them,' he said, with a surprising amount of passion. 'They taste so good, you have to eat at least one.'

'I didn't realise they were grown on farms.' A crazy image of a tractor, harvesting a field of oysters popped into my head.

Henri lowered his head, his shoulders quivering. '*Grown,*' he said, raising eyes spilling with mirth. 'You are funny, Elle.' Unexpectedly, he reached for my hand and turned it over, studying my palm as if clues to my personality were written there. '*Grown,*' he repeated with a chuckle, shaking his head.

I couldn't bring myself to tell him I hadn't been joking, and focused on the top of his head. His hair was so dark and thick – a lot like Declan's had been. Probably still was, though I couldn't help hoping he'd gone bald like his dad.

'What are you thinking about?' asked Henri, finally releasing my hand as the waiter returned with the wine and filled our glasses.

'Just how nice this is.' I could hardly admit to thinking about a past boyfriend. 'I've not had a night out in a while.'

I hadn't meant to sound wistful, but Henri smiled, seeming pleased by my admission. 'I'm glad you're here,' he said simply.

My stomach growled and I said, 'Thank you,' loudly to disguise the sound.

He raised his wine and said, 'Cheers, my dear,' in his British accent, and I laughed as we clinked glasses, and decided to put everything else out of my head and enjoy the evening.

Then the oysters arrived.

Chapter Seventeen

'Look how shiny they are,' said Henri, as the silver platter of oysters arranged like flower petals was placed on the table between us. 'That means they're fresh.'

The word *snot* sprang to mind, but guessing it would be crass to say so, I made an approving noise and drank most of my wine to disguise my nerves. The waiter shot me a look, as if he'd guessed my thoughts. 'It's very pretty,' I said, putting my glass down, meaning the arrangement more than the oysters, which I didn't want to look at properly.

'You can use this little fork to get them out,' said Henri, demonstrating with deft movements, and I immediately imagined his hands caressing my body. 'Then tip the whole thing into your mouth from the wide end, and chew once or twice to get the mineral flavour. Don't just swallow.'

Rapt, I nodded, admiring the angle of his jaw as he expertly tipped his head to slide the mollusc into his mouth. After swallowing with ease, he said, 'Don't worry that you're killing them, they're already dead when you eat them.'

My stomach clenched. 'Good to know.'

He grinned. 'Give it a try,' he encouraged, and although I wasn't keen, I felt an urge to impress him – and to try something new.

I finished my wine for courage then picked up a shell between thumb and forefinger and dug in the tiny fork, as Henri had done. The oyster seemed clingy, and there was quite a lot of liquid in the shell, which dribbled onto the table.

'Don't worry, that's just filtered seawater,' said Henri, when I looked at it nervously, half-expecting it to bubble and froth and burn a hole in the wood.

I rooted a bit more vigorously while Henri refilled my glass, and the oyster flew out and landed on his side plate. 'Whoops.' Red-faced, I reached to pick it up, but he laughingly waved my hand away.

'Try again,' he said.

I took a hefty swig of wine, and then another. Determined not to be beaten, I managed to wriggle the next oyster free and eyed it cautiously. 'It's bigger than I expected.'

'You won't notice,' Henri promised. 'They slip down so easily.'

I must have tilted my head too far back, or not opened my mouth wide enough, because the oyster missed my lips and plopped onto my chest and the briny-smelling liquid shot up my nostrils. 'Well, that was a disaster,' I said, blowing my nose on my napkin, feeling my cheeks glow crimson. 'I don't think oysters and me are going to get on.'

Henri looked fit to implode with merriment as I replaced the oyster in its shell, and when he said, with obvious difficulty, 'Third time lucky,' I found myself reaching tentatively for another.

This time, to my relief, the oyster came free right away and slithered easily into my mouth. Following Henri's lead, I chewed a couple of times to extract the flavour – it really wasn't too bad – and had just given him a thumbs up when my mouth flooded with a milky liquid that made my eyes bulge and my throat rebel. I loudly retched, and managed to whip the soggy napkin to my mouth in time to eject the whole disgusting mess.

'Not bad,' I said, eyes watering, and gagged again. 'Sorry,' I added, wiping my eyes with the back of my hand. 'Do you think anybody noticed?' Not daring to look round, I chugged some more wine to settle my stomach.

Henri brought his features under control as he topped up my glass again. 'No one's looking, don't worry.' I noticed his eyes were damp too, but with tears of laughter, and didn't know whether to be pleased or offended I'd been the source of his amusement. 'At least you tried,' he said, beckoning the waiter, who swooped in and removed the platter. 'Now, let me order you something I know you'll enjoy.'

Thankfully, the main course looked and smelled edible, and although I was a bit fanatical about checking my sea bass for bones, eating each mouthful slowly, the accompanying vegetables were perfectly cooked and delicious.

Henri seemed interested in my life in England, asking me to explain what I did for a living, and looked impressed when I told him.

'You have your own studio?' He refilled my glass for the second time without asking, and I hoped he wasn't trying to get me drunk. My defences came down if I had too much alcohol, which I didn't do very often – not since my days with Declan.

'I took over when the owner retired,' I explained. 'But yes, I suppose it's mine, though it doesn't make that much money once the staff and bills are paid.' I supposed it was the perfect topic for a non-date. I'd expected him to go into seduction mode, not grill me about my finances, and felt a tweak of frustration. 'Enough to keep me ticking over,' I added, in case he thought I was trying to get out of paying my share of the bill.

'You have staff?'

'I do,' I said proudly. 'Though I don't really think of them that way. My best friend, Toni – you'd like her, everyone does – she's great at the business side, and it works really well, because she can bring her baby to work if her mum can't look after him. Petra, my assistant, she came to us for work experience, just like I did back in the day, and I ended up keeping her on like Ivan did with me, so—'

'But the business doesn't make a lot of money,' Henri clarified, swirling wine around his glass. His gaze was intense, as if he was digesting my information along with his food, which he'd eaten quickly, laying his knife and fork neatly side by side when he'd finished.

'I do pay Toni well, but she has a mortgage and Petra is saving up to—'

'Don't *you* have a mortgage?'

Wow. He really was fixated on my finances. Still, I *had* made it clear that flirting with me would be a waste of time, and he might be at a loss for something else to talk about. 'Actually, no,' I said, laying my cutlery down. 'When my father died,' I swallowed quickly, 'he left the house to my sister and me, and I'd moved back there a few years ago anyway, so…' My words trailed off as I briefly thought of our former schoolhouse, standing empty and unloved – though Annabel, our neighbour, would pop in to water the plants, and have a root through the cupboards. She'd lived in her thickly carpeted bungalow next door with her rescue cats for decades, and probably knew the contents of our cupboards better than I did.

'It's good not to have a mortgage,' Henri said, pressing his napkin to his lips, and added with a twinkle, 'So, you don't have a boyfriend back home?'

Here we go. 'No boyfriend,' I said blithely, nodding when the waiter returned to clear our plates and then brought over dessert menus. *In for a penny, in for a pound*, as my grandfather would have said. Though I'd obviously be spending a lot more than a pound.

'So, you really are here to work?' Henri leaned back, his head cocked as though weighing me up.

'Mmmm… mostly.' I propped my chin on the leather-bound menu, feeling a little drifty, noting the bottle of Chablis was almost empty, and Henri's glass was still full.

'You're too lovely to be stuck in a kitchen all day, as much as I'm a fan of the café,' he said, resting his forearms on the table as the waiter melted away. They were lovely forearms: muscly, tanned and lightly sprinkled with hair.

'Feel nice?' Henri enquired.

I snatched my hand from his arm. 'I didn't mean to stroke you.'

'I liked it,' he said.

He was so handsome, it was hard to look directly at him. 'You're very hairy.'

'I'll take that as a compliment.'

As his gaze flickered between my eyes and lips, I reached for my wine and emptied the glass, then topped it up with what was left in the bottle. 'Actually, I'd like to ask you something,' I said, reaching for my bag. Better to move things along before I made an even bigger fool of myself than I already had. 'It's going to sound a bit strange, but I have this postcard of Chamillon taken in the eighties that someone gave to… someone in London. In the eighties.' *Brilliant description.* 'A woman, gave it to a man,' I continued, doggedly. 'She was born there. In Chamillon, I mean, not London. Her name begins with M, and I'm hoping to track her down while I'm here and talk to her about… about the postcard, among other things. Or maybe talk to someone who knew her. I wondered whether you—'

'Henri?'

A female voice interrupted my babbling before I'd fumbled the postcard out of my bag. A woman had appeared in a bosom-boosting dress, ice-blonde hair cascading over her shoulders as she bent to whisper in his ear.

His face darkened briefly, before his smile reappeared. 'Elle, this is my ex-wife, Bernice,' he said, in a tone of forced politeness.

Ex-wife? I tried to rearrange my facial muscles into a welcoming smile. 'Mice to neet you, Bernice.' I had a feeling I might have mixed up my words. 'The food here is delicious.'

'English?' Bernice's eyes swivelled to meet mine. They were the colour of a muddy puddle, and didn't join in with her smile, but I was envious of her slanting cheekbones – the sort I'd tried to achieve with make-up when I was younger – and her breasts, which looked in danger of pouring out of her dress. '*Bonne chance, fille anglaise. Parce qu'il ne t'aimera pas comme il m'a aimé.*'

'What did that mean?' I said as she turned with a flick of her hair, throwing Henri an unreadable look and leaving behind a trail of perfume so strong the waiter, returning to take our dessert order, pulled a face that made me giggle.

'Let's just say, she didn't want to eat in the same space where I was,' said Henri, recovering his composure with an apologetic wince. 'I'm sorry to say, it wasn't the most amicable divorce, but we're fine, most of the time.'

It looked like there was unfinished business on her part. I looked round to see her shapely bottom disappearing through the door. She was with a tall man, who looked a lot like Henri from behind, his hand resting possessively in the small of her back.

'What would you like to try next?'

I spun back to see Henri widen his eyes before he dropped them to the menu. It was obvious he was talking about more than food. 'I thought you were ordering for me,' I said, putting Bernice out of my mind, and admiring the length and thickness of his lashes.

'Mine never looked that nice,' I murmured. My head felt bigger than usual and I supported it in my hand. 'Even with mascara.'

'*Pardon?*' Henri glanced up.

'Nothing.'

'I'd recommend a *café gourmand*,' he said with a playful grin, clearly not bothered about his ex's appearance. 'It's an espresso with a selection of tiny desserts. *Café gourmand* means "gluttonous coffee", which is a pretty good description, don't you think?'

'Actually, I think I'm ready for bed.' I gave an exaggerated wink. 'I'd like to go home now.'

'Your wish is my command, young lady.' Henri's British accent was more Eton than *EastEnders*, but made me giggle again. *Oh no, I was at the giggling stage.* From past experience, giggling led to crying, and I didn't want to end the evening in tears. 'Let me sort out the bill,' he added, as I fingered my balled-up napkin, wondering whether I should take it home and wash it. 'Leave that for Raymond.'

'Raymond?'

The waiter had appeared and pointed to himself.

I waved. '*Bonjour*, Raymond! *Je m'appelle* Elle!'

'*Bonjour*, Elle,' he obliged with a smirk.

'*J'ai…*' I tried to remember what thirty was in French, counting on my fingers as though that would help. 'Urn, der, twah, katr, sank, sees, set, wheet… *trent*,' I said, clapping my hands as it came to me. Shame the pronunciation was a bit off, but Raymond would know what I meant.

Henri's eyes were dancing with enjoyment. 'You're practically fluent,' he teased.

I flourished my arms. 'Now, how much do I owe?' Assuming he was going to ask Raymond for the bill (*billet?* It sounded French), I tried to pull my purse out and remembered I hadn't shown Henri the postcard. It didn't feel right to bring it up again. The moment had passed, for now.

'The bill's been taken care of,' Henri said, just as my purse unjammed itself, spilling coins on the floor.

'Oops.'

I dropped to my knees to retrieve them as Henri was approached by an elderly pair wearing complementary shades of oatmeal, who greeted him in French and started chattering away. The waiter bobbed down to help me, and as he scooped up a handful of euros, he spoke in a low voice. 'She said, "He will never love you as much as he loved me".' He thrust the coins into my hand with a pitying smile, and was gone before I could respond.

Mustering my last shred of poise, I scrambled to my feet and stuffed my purse in my bag. It was understandable that Henri hadn't wanted to repeat his ex-wife's words for my benefit. They sounded desperate, and didn't exactly put her in a good light. I couldn't imagine storming up to an ex in a restaurant and saying something like that to his new partner. Apart from anything, I'd be happy if he'd found someone he loved.

Not that Henri loved me. And I *wasn't* his partner.

I hiccupped softly, wondering what his hands would feel like on my naked buttocks, and almost leapt out of my flesh when he said, 'Shall we go?'

He didn't introduce me to the elderly couple as he offered me his elbow, and when I lurched past, clinging to his arm, my bag slipping off my shoulder, I was aware of their curious glances, and wished I'd stopped at one glass of Chablis so I could at least introduce myself properly.

'I can return the bike tomorrow,' Henri said, to my relief, once we were outside. 'I think it's better if we get a taxi back.'

The word 'we' sent my head spinning and I thought I might hiccup again if I opened my mouth, so I let him lead me across the cobbles in silence, sucking in air as though I'd been locked in a basement for several weeks.

The sun had dipped towards the horizon, burnishing the buildings with a rose-tinted warmth, and in the marina the water rippled and shimmered like liquid gold. Even the attention-seeking seagulls looked more attractive.

'This would make such a nice photo,' I managed, allowing my head to sink against Henri's shoulder. He smelled so good, it should be bottled. Although, it already had been. I giggled softly and felt him drop a kiss on top of my head.

'This is romantic,' he said gently.

'Mm-hmm.' I pulled away, swaying slightly. 'Home please, young man.' I raised an arm, as if to flag down a taxi, and realised it probably didn't work like that in Saint-Martin.

'Hey, you should come fishing with me.' He smiled, taking hold of my hands and drawing me towards him. 'We could go now, if you like.'

'Now?' I pulled my chin back, feeling as if my eyeballs were vibrating. 'It's a bit late, isn't it?' My words were belied by the hordes of tanned holidaymakers spilling around us, filling the restaurants' courtyards. Their night out was just starting.

'Maybe another time,' he said. His eyes were expressive and I could see I'd disappointed him, though he tried to hide it.

I nodded. 'Maybe.'

'Promise?'

'OK, I promise.' I tried to cross my fingers because I hated going on boats, they made me feel ill, but my hands were clasped in his so I couldn't, then a car drew up – long and sleek – and Henri tipped me into the back and clambered in beside me, seeming to fill the whole vehicle with his maleness.

He gave the driver my address and, as we set off, started to tell me that Île de Ré meant 'isle of ferns' referring to the fenlands that separated each of the communities. His voice was soothing, like an old-fashioned storyteller's, and I relaxed against him once more.

'The further west you go, the less tourists there are,' he was saying. 'The landscape is more agricultural, with vineyards, and fields of potatoes and asparagus.'

'S'paragus makes your wee smell like rubber,' I said sleepily, and felt him shake with laughter.

'I've heard that.' He took my hand again. It felt nice, so I let it stay there, warmth sweeping up my arm to my face. Straightening, I discreetly checked his profile and felt a shaft of desire. I was sharing a ride with the best-looking man I'd met in ages, on an island a long way from home, and he seemed to like me. What were the chances of something like this happening again? A fling could be just what I needed – a stopgap affair between my old life and whatever I was going home to.

'Tell me about your family,' I said, wanting know more about him.

'What's to tell?' Letting go of my hand, he smoothed his hands up and down his strong thighs in a hypnotic gesture. 'Mother, father, one set of grandparents, younger brother, older sister—'

'The one who tells you what to do?' I said, tugging down the hem of my top.

He slid me a smile and nodded. 'She models swimwear.'

'Nice.' I tried to bring to mind the woman he'd been with in the café, but could only vaguely recall a cap of glossy black hair.

'She could have had a part in a film, but refused to take her top off.'

'Good for her,' I said. 'Is your father a fisherman too?' I guessed it was the kind of trade that was generational.

'Would you mind if he was?'

Even in my slightly inebriated state, I could tell my answer mattered. 'Why would I mind?' I said. 'My parents worked in a museum, we're hardly the Gettys.' I was quite proud of that – even if I was hazy on how the Gettys had earned their billionaire status. Something to do with petrol?

'A museum?' He turned to face me, his brow knotted. 'Tell me more.'

'Not much to tell,' I said, biting off a yawn. 'My father was the curator, my mother worked on the visitor side, organising school trips, overseeing the café and helping maintain the collections.'

'I didn't know such jobs existed.' He sounded fascinated. 'You didn't want to work there too?'

'Not really my thing,' I said. 'My father's speciality was the Second World War. He spent a lot of time researching it, stuck in the past, and to my sister and me, that was dull.' I felt a pang of disloyalty, as though Dad could overhear. 'He was good at it though, and his exhibitions were popular.'

'It's not a well-paid job?'

I wondered whether Henri had grown up poor and had a chip on his shoulder. 'Quite well paid,' I said. 'I mean, we didn't go without, but we had a healthy respect for money. We knew it didn't grow on trees, and didn't expect any handouts. My sister and I were happy to make our own way. She's a conservationist—'

'I admire that,' Henri cut in, his tone more serious than I'd heard so far.

'Me too,' I said. 'She always wanted to save the planet, even as a child.'

'That *is* admirable, but I meant that you didn't expect handouts.' His expression was sober. 'You wouldn't ever marry for money?'

'Of course not!' So *that* was the issue. His ex-wife had wanted a lifestyle he couldn't provide on his fisherman's salary, and he thought all women were the same. 'If I married at all, it would be for love.'

'I like that,' he said quietly. His hand reached out and lingered so close to my face I could feel the heat. 'No one should marry, unless it's for love.'

'We're here,' I said, feeling breathless, recognising the rue des Forages.

Henri withdrew his hand and looked through the window. 'That went quickly.' He sounded surprised.

'I'm not in the habit of inviting men in,' I said, when he joined me on the pavement.

'I should hope not. You've only been here a couple of days.'

I giggled more than his comment warranted, ending with some inelegant snorting.

He laughed softly. 'I think we both need some coffee.'

The car stayed where it was, its engine purring, as if the driver was waiting for further instructions, and doubt forced its way in. 'It's not my house,' I said, wishing he'd suggested going back to his.

'I'm sure Natalie would understand.'

Saying her name seemed to conjure her up, and it suddenly felt as if a third person was standing between us. 'Henri, I've had a lovely time, but…' I wanted to say, *although I find you physically attractive, I don't really know you that well*, but seemed to have forgotten my words. There was also the matter of my unshaven armpits, and although Toni had tried to talk me into having a bikini-wax – *men these days don't know what a muff looks like* – I'd declined. I hadn't even planned on wearing a bikini, never mind letting a man see my lady-area.

As the silence stretched, Henri took a step closer and spoke gently. 'Fishing boat, same time tomorrow?'

It took me a second to realise it wasn't a riddle. 'Maybe not tomorrow,' I said, regretfully. 'I've got dinner plans with Marie.'

It was gratifying to see the way his face fell. I'd never had such a powerful effect on such a good-looking man, and felt an urge to press my lips to his.

'The evening after?'

I nodded too much. Hopefully, I could persuade him to go for a walk on the beach, instead of whipping me out to sea. Maybe we'd find a sheltered spot where we could get to know each other better.

'Then I'll see you on Thursday evening, beautiful Elle.' As Henri came closer, a fifty-something couple strode past and stopped outside the guest house.

'Evening,' the woman greeted Henri, her voice politely British. The man with her unlocked the door, and raised a friendly hand as they disappeared inside.

'You know Marie's guests?' I said, wondering vaguely what time it was. The sun had vanished, and the sky had turned deep lilac, suggesting it was after ten. My eyelids were starting to feel heavy.

'That's Ted and Miranda, they visit every year,' said Henri, seeming reluctant to leave. I hoped the driver wasn't in a hurry to get home. 'Quite a sad story.'

'Oh?' I stifled another yawn and felt a queasy twist in my stomach. No more alcohol, I decided. Expensive or not, it didn't agree with me. A thought floated in. Had Henri said the bill had been taken care of? *How?* I needed to pay my share. I'd only eaten a main course, but I'd wasted three world-class oysters that probably cost more than my camera.

'… return every year in the hope of seeing her.'

I tuned back into Henri's words. 'Seeing who?'

He gave a soft laugh. 'I was saying, sleepyhead, that Miranda comes each year, hoping she'll see her long-lost daughter on the beach.'

Something about this struck a chord with me. 'That *is* sad,' I said. 'I wonder what happened to her.'

'Come here, you.' Henri's face drew closer, and my eyes fixed on his mouth, heart leaping, but just as we were about to kiss, something else occurred.

'Sorry,' I said, rearing away as though he'd grown fangs. 'I've just remembered, I… I've left the oven on.'

'I know what you're doing.' He stepped back, wagging a finger, eyes almost black with lust. 'It's fine, Elle,' he said. 'I've got all the time in the world.' His eyes lingered on mine. 'I'll wait.'

I should have been thrilled by his words (or at least clarified that I was leaving at the weekend) but as I turned to unlock the door, not even bothering to wave him off as the car pulled away, all I could think was, *there's a woman next door, searching for her daughter, and her name begins with M.*

Chapter Eighteen

The second my eyes pinged open the following morning, all I could think about was heading next door to talk to Marie's guest, Miranda. I'd wanted to go round the night before, but worried I'd had too much to drink and would say the wrong thing – start demanding explanations and upset Marie. Hearing voices from her garden, I'd shot through the house and outside and strained to listen from the patio, but the accents had been American, the conversation punctuated by gales of laughter, and I'd known it wasn't them – *Ted and Miranda*. Surmising they'd gone straight to bed, I'd done the same, and although I'd expected to lie awake thinking things over – as well as reliving my oyster shame and the almost-kiss with Henri – I'd immediately succumbed to sleep.

It wasn't until I was outside Marie's front door that I fully registered I had a hangover headache, and wished once more that I'd resisted the Chablis. The cup of tea I'd forced down after my shower had done nothing to relieve the metallic taste in my mouth.

The sun was too shiny, and as I fumbled putting a pair of sunglasses on, I wondered how Henri was feeling. We hadn't exchanged numbers, so I couldn't call or text him to ask. Maybe he'd turn up with some fishy delights for Marie. That reminded me that I'd agreed to go out on his fishing boat, and the thought set up a sickly surge in my stomach.

I knocked on Marie's door, hoping I'd got the timing right and her guests were having breakfast. I was keen to get it over with now, like a dental appointment, but was almost relieved when she didn't answer right away. Maybe I could try again later, and go back to bed for a bit. I was turning away when the door swung open, and Marie appeared in an off-white, short-sleeved blouse, and a denim skirt half-covered by a floral apron.

'Elle!' She sounded so startled, I wondered whether my top was on back to front, or I had lipstick on my teeth. In an effort to disguise my hangover pallor, I'd dug out a tube of Muted Coral that was supposed to complement freckles, and worried I might have piled it on too thickly.

'Morning,' I croaked, and cleared my throat. 'Hope you don't mind me calling.'

'Of course not,' she said, breaking into a smile. 'What a wonderful surprise.' She stepped back. 'Would you like some breakfast?'

I'd been relying on her to ask, unable to think of another reason for appearing at her door this early. 'That would be lovely.' Perhaps it would settle my churning insides.

'You had a good time with Henri?' she said as I removed my sunglasses and joined her in the hallway, grateful to escape the sunshine. 'I saw you on the big bike.'

I couldn't work out her tone, but her expression was pleasantly enquiring. 'I met him the morning he brought you some fish,' I said. 'He... seems nice?'

I hadn't meant to sound as if I was asking, but she nodded. 'He is a nice man,' she agreed, rather formally. 'Very handsome.'

'A bit *too* handsome.' I hadn't meant to say that either. I was saying a lot of things I wouldn't say at home. Not that I was in the habit of meeting handsome men at home, though I'd shot some pictures a couple of years ago for an aspiring actor, who'd ended up playing a heartthrob in a soap.

'He is popular,' Marie conceded, in a guarded way that made me wonder what she wasn't saying.

'We went for a meal, but it wasn't a date.' *But I did decide I'd like to sleep with him.* The recollection brought hotness to my cheeks. 'I met his ex-wife,' I said, in case Marie was concerned that I didn't know he'd been married. 'I don't think she liked me.'

Her smile was tinged with disapproval. Of me, or the ex-wife? 'Bernice, she was very…' Marie made a grabbing motion towards me.

'Possessive?'

She nodded, and I thought I heard her say, 'Be careful,' and was about to ask her to repeat it when she said, 'I am cooking the American-style breakfast this morning,' and I remembered why I was there.

'For your English guests?'

'For my English guests, and my Americans too, but they like it bigger.' She made a shape with her hands, demonstrating a large portion.

'But you have some English guests here at the moment?'

It wasn't exactly subtle, and Marie's expression was a little uncertain as she reached round and patted her chignon. 'I do,' she said cautiously. 'They are from London.'

OK, so none of it added up yet – was Miranda born in Chamillon? – but the words London and English were triggering my heartbeat. 'I'd love to meet them,' I said.

Her face grew tranquil. 'Of course.' Her tone was understanding. 'The English guests, they like to glue together.'

'Stick,' I said automatically.

'You will have some things in common to discuss, like your weather.'

'It's not always grey in the UK,' I said, attempting a joke as she beckoned me to follow her. 'Sometimes, it's a lighter shade of grey.'

She laughed, her face lighting up, as if it was the funniest thing she'd ever heard. 'I shall remember that one,' she said, moving down the hall. 'My London guests, they come here each year, so they can tell you nice places to visit.'

'I'm working at the café, so don't really have the time.' I wondered whether it was healthy for my heart to be beating so fast. Maybe it was no different to exercising, but without the toning benefits.

'Don't you want to take photographs?' Turning, Marie caught me unawares.

I stared at her blankly for a moment. 'Oh.' I remembered my invasion a couple of days ago with my camera and guilt swept through me. 'Listen, I'm sorry I asked you so many personal questions, I—'

'I told you, it is not a problem,' she interrupted kindly, leading me through an arched doorway into a dining room awash with light, filled with the sugary scent of roses. There was a long table in the middle of the room with high-backed chairs grouped around it, and a dresser along the wall that boasted an assortment of colourful china my grandmother would have loved.

The room was empty of visitors, but through the open French doors were a pair of tables on the terrace, set for breakfast, and sitting at one was the couple who'd greeted Henri the night before.

I felt a beat of panic. 'Shall I give you a hand in the kitchen?' I said. 'I can't just barge in and expect to eat without helping.'

'Marty, he used this word, barge.' Marie smiled as she crossed to the French doors. 'Always, he thought he was intruding, until I tell him that I love his company.'

I followed her, gripping my bag so hard I could feel the shape of the postcard inside. I was going to have to find a way into a conversation with Miranda that was going to be tricky at best, and an embarrassing disaster at worst. I thought about Mimi, and how my mind had rejected the idea of her being my birth mother, and wondered whether it was going to be the same story with Miranda.

She was looking in our direction, a tumbler of fruit juice raised to her mouth. She had grey hair, short and layered, and large eyes in a small round face – like an owl. Her eyes were brown, as far as I could tell, and her hair might have been dark when she was younger, but it was impossible to imagine her approaching an Englishman in a bar, with seduction on her mind. But that was thirty years ago. What had I expected? A siren in fishnets with glossy red lips, eyes ablaze with passion, beckoning with a sultry smile and curl of a scarlet-tipped finger? Actually, yes – if I'd thought about what she'd looked like then, that was the image I'd had.

'Can I use your loo?' Without thinking, I'd grabbed Marie's arm, which felt surprisingly solid. I had an urge to keep hold of it forever.

She glanced at my hand in surprise, but didn't move. 'Of course,' she said, probably too polite to question why I needed the toilet so soon after arriving. 'It is through the door upstairs, to the right.'

On my way up, I paused to look at a gallery of pictures to buy myself some time. There were more portraits of ballerinas in poses, and in one of the photos, a group of dancers smiled for the camera, looking as if they'd just finished a performance. I looked for Marie, but couldn't tell whether she was one of the pretty, dark-haired females. There *was* a picture of her, easily recognisable, standing with a man, both young, dressed in heavy coats as snow swirled down around them. He was probably her ex-husband, his features striking, his arm around her waist. Marie was smiling, one gloved hand outstretched as if to catch the falling flakes, and I could see I'd been right to think she'd been beautiful. She still was, though her eyes were sad now, even when she smiled. Curiosity nipped at me, as I hurried to the bathroom in case Marie was listening for my footsteps. It was tragic that her marriage had broken down because she couldn't have children, and I wondered whether that was the only source of her sadness – although bad enough, it felt like there was more. As I flushed the toilet and washed my hands for authenticity, it hit me how inappropriate it would be to start probing one of her guests under her roof. I'd have to find another way – perhaps wait for them to leave for the day, and waylay them.

Downstairs, I bypassed the dining room and slipped into the kitchen, which was surprisingly modern, with glossy units and a built-in double oven, the shiny worktops teeming with pots of herbs. 'Hi,' I said, feeling shy. 'Sorry about that.'

'There you are.' Smiling, Marie picked up a plate of golden pancakes topped with crispy bacon. 'I have kept it warm, so now you can have breakfast with Miranda and Ted,' she said.

Nooo! 'You really shouldn't have gone to all this trouble.'

'The British are so polite.' She nodded to the worktop. 'You may bring the maple syrup.'

As I picked up the little white jug, resigned to making small talk with the couple, I saw her hesitate. 'What is it?'

'Perhaps...' Her eyebrows drew together. 'I know you are very interested in people because of your job taking pictures,' she said carefully, 'but you should not ask Miranda if she has children.'

Heat flooded my face, and an awkward silence hovered in the air. 'I won't,' I said at last. 'I know it's a sensitive subject.'

'It's only that... she thinks she sees her ghost.'

I banged the jug down. 'A ghost?' It was the last thing I'd expected to hear.

'Of her daughter, the child she lost, twenty years ago.'

Twenty years. It wasn't her. 'That's awful,' I said, pushing aside the realisation. 'Poor woman.'

'Lost her before she was born, if you understand.'

'Ah.' *A miscarriage.* 'Yes, I understand.' Though, I wasn't sure I did. 'And… there's a ghost?'

'Maybe a spirit,' Marie amended. 'Ghost sounds like…' Her eyes met mine, a faint twinkle in their depths. 'You know.'

I nodded, feeling a bit off-balance. This wasn't the story I'd anticipated – the one that Henri had told. The one I'd interpreted wrongly.

'They were on the island, taking a holiday, when the baby was lost,' Marie continued, talking quickly, as if worried Miranda might appear. 'They were my guests here, five years later, and Miranda told me one day she had seen the spirit of her little girl on the beach.'

'Right.'

'It made her very happy.'

'Well, that's good,' I said. I sometimes felt that Mum was with me, and it made me happy too, and I knew that Jess had taken comfort from hearing Mum's voice in her dreams. Neither of us had seen her ghost, though.

'They return for two weeks each summer to be close to her, and the rest of the time, live a normal life in England with their family.'

'Well… thank you for letting me know,' I said, feeling bad that Marie had only given me the details to stop me making a blunder, but glad that she had, because now I knew I was barking up the wrong tree. Though, in my heart, I'd known Miranda wasn't the one.

'So, you are ready to eat now?' Marie held out the plate of cooling food, and I picked up the maple syrup once more.

'It smells great,' I said, and although I could feel my headache gathering pace, and knew I should go next door and take some tablets before heading to the café, I went out with Marie to the terrace, to talk about the weather with Ted and Miranda.

Chapter Nineteen

'It sounds like you had a lucky escape,' said Toni an hour later, after I'd broken away from a heated discussion about global warming, and made my excuses and left the guest house.

'All I did was make an innocent comment about the sun feeling hotter here than it does in the UK, and Marie explained the island has its own microclimate, and they were off,' I said, putting my phone on speaker as I walked to the café, so I didn't have to press it to my ear. My headache was clinging on, and I hoped the fresh air would help shift it. 'Thanks to my sister, I know that climate change isn't a myth, but I couldn't get a word in edgeways.'

It had shocked me that a couple with such opposing views were still happily married, but they'd seemed to thoroughly enjoy the argument, and I'd guessed it wasn't the first time they'd had it.

'Maybe it's a good thing she's not your birth mother, if she's the sort that likes a good fight,' said Toni. 'Imagine having to deal with that, on top of the ghost stuff.'

'I kind of understand the ghost stuff, and, to be honest, I don't really know what I'm expecting my birth mother to be like – if I find her.'

'I know,' said Toni. 'That's part of the problem, Elle. Imagine meeting her and it turns out she's a politician who hates animals, and chocolate, and cheese, and music and doesn't understand the internet, or she's a militant vegan and knits her own yoghurt, or plays golf and talks about it all the time—'

'Stop,' I pleaded, laughing. 'I'm a grown-up, I'll have to handle it.' Even so, the thought of us having nothing but some shared DNA in common was daunting. 'I'll be fine.'

'Hmm,' said Toni doubtfully. In the background I heard a sound I recognised as Freddie banging his spoon on the tray of his high chair. 'Mark, can you take Freddie's bowl off his head?' she bellowed.

'I went out with Henri last night.'

There was a sharp intake of breath at the end of the line. 'Is he the sexy fisherman?'

I rolled my eyes. 'Yes, he's the sexy fisherman.'

'That's the best thing I've heard all week!'

'It's only Wednesday.'

'Tell me you're going to have sex with him.'

'I will *not* tell you that.'

'Oh my God, you are!' she practically screamed. 'Elle's going to shag a fisherman,' she said, presumably to Mark.

'Good for her,' I heard him say. 'Have you seen my shampoo?'

'I used it in the washing machine,' she said. 'Didn't I tell you to go and get waxed *down there*?'

It took me a second to realise the last sentence was directed at me. 'I'll pretend I didn't hear that,' I said. 'He wants to take me fishing tomorrow evening.'

'*Fishing?*' She'd have been less shocked if I'd said he was taking me to church.

'Not with a rod, on his boat,' I said. 'When I said he's a fisherman, what did you expect?'

'Not for you to go to sea with him. Don't you get ill on water?' Toni knew me too well.

'The sea's really flat around here.' I glanced at the harbour as I approached, as if to prove my point. The water was glassy, reflecting the boats like a mirror.

'It's the Atlantic,' Toni pointed out. 'Remember you had to lie down the entire time on the ferry when we went to Belgium in Year Eleven?'

'That was a long time ago,' I said. 'And I'm going to suggest a walk on the beach, instead.'

She snorted. 'I doubt he'll go for that,' she said. 'He's probably got plans and wants to get you somewhere private.'

'You make it sound like he's going to kill me and throw me overboard.'

'Christ, I hadn't even thought of that!'

Neither had I, but somehow, I doubted that was Henri's intention. 'I'll get hold of some seasickness pills, just in case,' I said.

'Probably for the best.'

'How are things at the studio?'

'All good,' said Toni breezily, though I knew she'd have said that even if the studio had burnt down. It struck me how little I'd thought about my real job since being in Chamillon. Already it seemed like my old life belonged to someone else, but that wasn't surprising with all the distractions here. 'Petra's looking forward to doing the wedding on Saturday.'

'I'm glad somebody is.' I'd met the bride, and she'd had very specific ideas about what she wanted, including shots of people's feet. 'No one ever gets to see the footwear,' she'd said in an entitled voice. 'It cost a fortune to have our trainers customised and I want them in every picture.'

'She'll be great,' I added, jumping aside as a car meandered past; the first I'd seen in Chamillon since arriving. 'I'd better go,' I said as

I reached the café, glancing up at the shutter-framed windows above, certain I'd caught a flash of Charlie's hair. I felt a swoop in my stomach, but when I looked again, he'd gone. 'Give Freddie a kiss from his Auntie Elle.'

'Can she change his nappy and give him a feed while she's at it?'

'Sorry,' I said with a laugh, and then I was shot with guilt that I was here, while my friend was holding down a job as well as being a mum.

'Don't you dare,' she warned, as though my thoughts had transmitted through the phone. 'You know I love my job, I've got the best boss in the world—'

'I'm not your boss.'

'—and I get to be in charge while you're not here.'

'You're in charge when I am,' I joked.

'True, and now I'm ordering you to go and have a good time.'

Smiling, I said goodbye, promising to update her about 'the sexy fisherman' and brought up *how much are fisherman paid?* on Google as I entered the café, almost tripping over Hamish, who was lying by Gérard's leather moccasin-shod feet, the dog's beardy chin resting on a pastry he was probably saving for later.

I quickly read that a fisherman's earnings depended on the type of boat, and had got as far as *a trawler man can earn between £10,000 and...* when Dolly called my name.

'Quick!' she said, emerging from behind the counter as if she couldn't wait for me to get there, and I checked the time to make sure I wasn't late.

'It's only five-to,' I said, smiling hello at Gérard, who was clearly trying to catch Dolly's attention. 'I would have been here sooner, but...' I lowered my voice for some reason. 'I was checking out an "M".'

'Ooh, any luck?' Dolly's eyes were avid, but seeming to remember where she was, she turned to Gérard and said, inexplicably, 'Baker's dozen.'

'Ah, *bien sûr!*' Beaming so hard, his face collapsed into wrinkles as he wrote something down on his newspaper.

'He likes doing English crosswords,' Dolly explained. 'My sister sends them over for him.'

'Does Gérard know what a baker's dozen is?'

'I've tried explaining what things mean, but I think he just likes the sound of the words.'

'*Treize!*' he said suddenly, so loudly that Hamish jumped up and gulped down the pastry he'd been protecting. 'Baker's *dozern*, it eez thirteen!'

'Yay!' cheered Dolly, and watching them high-five made me smile and wish there was a café like this near where I worked, but somehow, even if there was, I knew it wouldn't be the same.

After turning to greet two smartly dressed women with knitting poking out of their bags, and instructing Stefan to bring them iced water with their coffees, Dolly ushered me out to the kitchen, and fished a small piece of paper from her apron pocket. 'I got a call from Francine first thing,' she said, pushing aside a rack of fragrant cinnamon swirls and smoothing the paper on the worktop. 'She emailed over some names, and I wrote them down.'

'Is that it?' I stared at the paper, trying to see what was on it.

'It's not a very long list,' she admitted.

I pressed my chest to make sure my heart was still beating. *This was it.* 'I suppose that's good,' I managed. 'At least it narrows things down.'

Dolly bristled with importance. 'Luckily, all the Ms that fit your birth mother's age are still alive,' she said. 'One now lives in Ireland – I'd forgotten about her – but the others live in Chamillon.'

'Really?'

'You've met most of them,' Dolly reminded me. 'Marie, Margot and Mimi.'

'Oh, right.' Of course I had.

'The only ones left that fit your criteria are Maud, who works at the lighthouse – I'd forgotten about her too – Mabelle, who lives in Ireland, but comes over every couple of months to visit her father, and Dee who runs the florist's on rue des Caillotières.'

'Dee?'

'Her birth name is Madeleine, but everyone calls her Dee.'

Staring at the names, I felt as if one should leap out, or start glowing neon, but Dolly's loopy handwriting didn't change. 'Do you know much about them?'

'Well, Maud has grown-up daughters, one in Australia, and she travelled a lot when she was younger. Mabelle's a lesbian. She's been with her partner a long time, and is very anti-men, so I doubt she's the one you're looking for.'

'So, that's a list of two?'

'Well, yes, I suppose so, but Dee's a strong contender.'

'Oh?'

'As soon as I saw her name, I remembered her coming to one of my monthly baking sessions and mentioning she'd had an affair with an Englishman, years ago. He told her he liked Jaffa Cakes, which she'd never heard of. She wanted us to make them and I managed to find a recipe.'

My mind scrolled back, trying to recall whether Dad had ever mentioned a fondness for Jaffa Cakes. 'Doesn't sound like a very good affair if they were talking about Jaffa Cakes,' I said, wondering whether Dee could be the one.

'But don't you think it's significant that she remembered, all those years later?' said Dolly. 'It obviously stuck with her.'

I remembered Dad's snack of choice had been salted peanuts, but maybe he'd thought Jaffa Cakes sounded more romantic – or he'd had a thing for them in the eighties.

'And Maud, who travelled when she was younger?'

'Well, we've kept in touch because she helped out here one summer to earn some extra money before moving to Ireland, so I called her—'

'Dolly!'

'It's fine, she's very laid-back,' she said, flapping a hand. 'I just asked if she'd been in London thirty years ago, and she said she went there with her parents when she was a child, and sometimes goes over to see a show – she loves musicals – but no, she wasn't there in the eighties.'

I let that settle for a moment. 'Didn't she want to know why you were asking?'

'I said it was a long story, nothing for her to worry about.'

I looked at the 'list'. 'So, why not cross her off?'

'I don't know,' said Dolly. 'It would have looked too sad.'

Suddenly, we couldn't stop laughing, and it felt like a nice release.

'Thank you,' I said, when we'd finally sobered up. 'I really do appreciate this.'

She leaned across the counter and laid her hand on my arm. 'I'm happy to help,' she said, warmly, and for a second, I wished that Dolly was the woman I'd come to find.

'So, there's only one person left to talk to.'

'And Margot.'

'And Margot,' I agreed.

'What were you two cackling about?' Charlie came in with a mug in one hand, a plate in the other, and deposited them in the dishwasher. 'Is Mum telling you one of her terrible jokes?'

'My jokes aren't terrible.' She straightened her face and aimed a slap at his shoulder as he pretended to cower. 'You're the only one who doesn't find them funny.'

'Well, let's see.' As he gripped his jaw, looking thoughtful, it struck me that he was all light compared to Henri; bright-haired and eyed, his smile somehow innocent. 'Why did the bald man paint rabbits on his head?'

Dolly was already chuckling.

'I… don't know,' I said, playing along.

Charlie did a drum roll on the edge of the worktop with his fingers. 'Because, from a distance, they looked like hares!'

I groaned. 'That's really bad, Dolly, sorry.'

She gave a mock-offended sniff. 'I like to keep it simple for the customers,' she said. 'They enjoy my sense of humour.'

'God help them.' Charlie widened his eyes. 'I don't know what they'd do if they actually heard something funny.'

'Humour's so subjective,' I said. 'My sister thinks *The Simpsons* is hilarious—'

'It is,' agreed Charlie. 'Your sister has great taste.'

'Well, it is, but I prefer *Parks and Recreation*, which she doesn't get at all.'

'I like that too.' Charlie gave me an appraising look. '*Brooklyn Nine-Nine*?'

'Love it,' I said. '*Modern Family*?'

'Not so keen.' We exchanged a smile.

'He has the boxset of *999*, if you want to come round and watch it,' said Dolly, and this time Charlie and I couldn't stop laughing, and every time we tried to stop, he said, 'Your laugh is so funny, it's like you've got hiccups' and set us off again, and by the time we'd recovered, Dolly had retreated from the kitchen, leaving us alone.

'I'll, erm, just get my apron,' I said, expecting Charlie to have gone by the time I returned, but he was leaning against the sink, arms folded, a contemplative expression on his face.

'I saw you in Saint-Martin,' I said redundantly. He knew I had, because we'd waved at each other. 'Were you there,' I looked round, checking Dolly was out of earshot, 'to meet Tegan?'

'Supposed to be.' He rubbed his earlobe, dropping his gaze to the floor. 'She didn't turn up, actually.'

'Oh, I'm sorry,' I said. 'Did she say why?'

'Just that something cropped up, but I'm meant to be seeing her this evening.'

'That's good?' He didn't sound very excited.

'I don't know.' He shrugged, lifting his eyes. Although they were brown, they weren't as dark as Henri's – more amber than bitter chocolate. 'I'm not sure it's going anywhere.'

'Isn't that why you're keeping it quiet,' I said, 'to see what happens?'

'I guess.' We paused as Celeste came through with a crockery-laden tray, passing us both a smile as she put it down and left, and I began to unload the dishwasher, glad to have something to do with my hands.

'I didn't realise you were going out with Henri.' Charlie's tone was light.

'It wasn't a date,' I said quickly. 'He called round to the house and invited me out for a meal on the spur of the moment.' I didn't mention he'd called the evening before.

'That sounds like Henri.'

I looked round, knocking a cup with my elbow, and managed to catch it before it hit the floor. 'Meaning?'

'He can't resist a newcomer.' Charlie was smiling, but not in a way that suggested he approved.

'I thought you were friends,' I said. 'He spoke very highly of you.'

'We are, but...' He ran a hand through his hair, and looked as if he was wondering whether to continue.

'I met his ex-wife,' I said, as I had to Marie, in case that was the issue. 'I know he's been married, not that it matters, we weren't on a *date*.' I stressed the last word for effect. 'Like I said, I'm not here looking for a relationship.'

'Well, I'm glad he told you about Bernice.' Henri hadn't told me, actually – not until she appeared at the table, but he might have been about to. For some reason, I didn't want to tell Charlie this. 'I hope he told you he owns that restaurant too, and that his family are one of the oldest and richest on the island.'

'What?' I spun round, and the glass I'd been holding slipped from my fingers and shattered. 'Oh, hell,' I said, squatting to gather up the nearest pieces. Toppling slightly, I slammed my hand on top of the broken glass, and blood started spurting out.

'Let me see.' Charlie dropped down and took my hand, turning to look at the palm, as Henri had last night. After plucking out the lethal shard, he wound a tea towel tightly around my hand. 'Raise your arm,' he ordered, as I dropped back on my haunches, light-headed and nauseous. I'd never been good with blood. As a child, I'd hated losing my baby teeth, and nosebleeds had brought me to the edge of fainting.

'Blood and water...' I murmured weakly.

'I think I've seen that series.' Charlie held up my arm with gentle fingers. 'Canadian, I think.'

'No, I mean blood and water make me feel ill.'

'Ah.' His face loomed in front of mine, so close I could see dark flecks around his pupils. 'If it's any consolation, I can't bear the sight of needles.'

Footsteps approached. 'Oh dear,' said Dolly, taking in the scene. 'What on earth happened here?'

'It was my fault,' Charlie said quickly. 'I made her jump.'

'I'll clear this glass, you get her upstairs.'

'No, no, I'm fine.' I stood up and everything went swimmy. My headache was back, my hand was throbbing, and blood was spreading on the cloth.

'You might need stitches,' said Charlie, unwrapping the tea towel to look while I closed my eyes.

'I don't want to go to hospital.' I felt close to tears all of a sudden. 'I just need to sit down for a minute.'

'Let's give it a while, and see what happens.' I felt his breath, warm on my wrist. 'I'll get the first aid kit and do my Doctor Charlie bit.'

'He's very good,' Dolly assured me, resting her hand on my shoulder. 'Let my boy take care of you.'

'Mum, I'm not an *actual* doctor.' But he didn't sound annoyed, even though Dolly was obviously relishing this opportunity to pitch us together.

'What about the washing-up?' I said.

'We'll manage.' I couldn't be sure, but thought I felt her shove me gently towards the door. 'Off you go,' she said. 'Make her some tea with plenty of sugar,' she instructed Charlie. 'At least three.'

'I'm sure that's an old wives' tale,' he said. 'Some brandy would be better.'

I hadn't the strength to argue, and was only vaguely aware of being guided out of the kitchen, up a flight of stairs, and into a room with a sofa that looked so inviting, all I wanted to do was lie on it.

Chapter Twenty

'You've had a shock,' said Charlie, what felt like minutes later. 'I kept an eye on you, made sure you didn't bleed out.'

'Thanks for that visual.' I struggled upright, wincing as my hand throbbed a protest. 'How long have I been sleeping?'

'Not long,' he said, perching on the table in front of the sofa. 'Don't get up.'

'What about work?' I swung my legs over the edge of the sofa and planted my feet on the floor. 'I should go.'

'Celeste's sister pitched in. She happened to be here, and wasn't busy today, so…' He made a pressing motion with his hands. 'Stay right where you are.'

I was used to being the one deciding everything, but it felt nice to be told what to do; to have an adult in charge. I sank gratefully against the cushions.

'Your unnaturally sweet tea went cold,' he said, nodding at the mug beside him on the table. 'I can make you some more.'

'That would be nice.' I'd meant to say *no, don't be silly, I really should leave*, but I liked it up here, and really didn't want to move. The room was cluttered, but cosy, with books and newspapers and photographs everywhere, and the colours around me were soothing. Lots of blue and green – apart from the sofa, which was orange, but like a sunset, not a clementine.

Aware my thoughts were wandering, I prodded my temple. 'My headache's gone,' I observed.

'You had a headache, too?' Charlie winced in sympathy.

'Too much wine last night.' As soon as I said it, his words came crashing back, propelling me upright once more. 'What did you mean, Henri owns that restaurant we went to, and how did you know we were there?'

'Why wouldn't he take you to a restaurant he owns?' Charlie shrugged. 'He was testing you.'

'*Testing* me?'

'To see how you reacted to it all.'

My mind sped back, sifting in snapshots through the meal; the way everyone had seemed to recognise him, the fact the bill had 'been taken care of' and the waiter's deference around Henri. It all made sense. 'He told me he was a fisherman.'

'Well, he is, but from choice. He goes out every morning as a way of feeling…' Charlie thought for a second '… feeling more normal. Like an everyday guy, except he doesn't *have* to do it, not like the real fishermen. Not that I'm saying he's not a real fisherman, he is, and a good one, but he could give it up and never work again.'

I could barely take it in. 'And what you said about his family?'

He nodded, hands curled beside him around the edge of the table. 'One of the oldest and wealthiest on the island. In France, actually. Their fishing company supplies all the restaurants, not just here, all over the country, and they own loads of land and property.'

I stared at him, open-mouthed. Toni would *love* this. Not just a sexy fisherman, but a *rich* sexy fisherman. 'Why didn't he tell me?' But it was obvious, even before Charlie started to explain.

'He's had some bad experiences with women wanting him for his money,' he said. 'His ex-wife being a case in point – she got half the restaurant in the divorce, by the way – so now he does this thing where he pretends to be from a humble background, so he knows if he's liked for himself and not his status.'

'Like Ryan Reynolds in *The Proposal*,' I said. 'Only I don't think Ryan was deliberately hiding that his family was wealthy.'

'Oh yeah, Margaret notices nearly every shop in town has the name Paxton.'

'You've seen it?'

'I like a good romcom.'

'No wonder Henri was cagey when I questioned him about his family and his job,' I said. 'What happens when the women find out?'

'Things don't normally get that far, to be honest.' Charlie scratched his head. 'He's a bit of a player at heart, and I think he likes the game.' *I knew it!* 'Not that I'm trying to put you off him,' he went on. 'And he must be keen, because he hasn't taken anyone to the restaurant for a long time, and I've never known him hire a tandem before.' I was a teeny bit flattered, even as I was absorbing Charlie's words. 'Did you wear a helmet?' he said.

'*What?*'

'You didn't appear to be wearing a helmet.'

'How long were you spying on us?' I felt annoyed, because he was right. I *should* have been wearing a helmet.

'I wasn't spying, I was across the quay, waiting for Tegan, and happened to see the pair of you getting off the bike. I noticed you weren't wearing a helmet.'

'Stop saying helmet!'

'It's important, especially when you're not used to bikes,' Charlie persisted. 'Henri could have hired one for you.'

'*You* don't wear a helmet.'

'Only because I'm used to cycling around the island. If it was anywhere else, I would.'

'It was a tandem and perfectly safe, and why are we even talking about bikes?' I shot back. 'Why are you telling me about Henri, anyway?'

But again, it was easy to guess why. Charlie was a straightforward person. He wouldn't deceive people like his friend, whatever Henri's motives. 'I don't like the thought of you being misled,' he said. 'Henri knows how I feel.'

'Will he be mad that you've told me?'

'I don't know.' A crease appeared between his eyebrows. 'I guess I'll find out.'

'You don't normally hand out warnings?'

'I haven't been introduced to any of his women.'

'He does this a lot?' The thought of being another female Henri had duped wasn't very appealing, however much I wanted to believe he liked me.

'Less often, lately.' Charlie sounded vaguely surprised. 'Like I said, I think he's really taken with you, the glamorous Brit on the island.' He mimed flicking his hair and pouted his lips. 'You've caused a bit of a stir.'

A reluctant smile tugged at my mouth. 'Hardly glamorous,' I said, holding out my hand, still bandaged in the blood-soaked tea towel.

'We should get that off.' Charlie edged closer. 'I was going to do it while you were asleep, but didn't want to disturb you.'

I shuffled forward until our knees were almost touching, thinking about him watching me sleep. 'Did I snore?'

'Only for the first hour.' He grinned. 'No, I left you in peace, just popped up every ten minutes to check you were OK.'

'Well… thanks,' I said, grinning back. 'Sorry I snapped at you, just now.'

'I get it,' he said. 'The messenger gets shot at.'

'Do you think he's planning to tell me?'

'I don't know,' he said, honestly. 'But at least now you know what you're up against.'

I think I already did. I didn't say it, because now the shock had worn off a bit, I thought I understood. I was an unknown quantity, and Henri had already been badly stung by his ex-wife. I could hardly blame him for wanting to keep that side of his life hidden until he got to know someone better. I got why Charlie had put me in the picture – he clearly saw things in a black and white fashion – but I wasn't sure it made any difference when I wasn't planning to embark on a full-blown relationship with Henri.

'I sicked up an oyster,' I said.

'What?' Charlie, who'd been carefully unwrapping my hand as if it was a gift, raised his head.

'I tried to eat an oyster and it was disgusting,' I said. 'I coughed it into a napkin.'

A spasm of laughter crossed his face. 'Poor you,' he said. 'Why didn't you just say you didn't like them?'

'I didn't know until I tried.' I sighed. 'And then I dropped money all over the floor, so God knows what Henri must have thought of me.'

'He'd have loved it,' Charlie said, peeling back the tea towel. 'You're different.'

'You mean unsophisticated?'

His eyes darted up to meet mine. 'I definitely didn't mean that.'

'I expect he's used to women like... well, like Bernice.'

'Cold and money-obsessed?'

I laughed. 'OK, when you put it like that...' I paused. 'He's invited me on his fishing boat tomorrow evening.'

'Well, that's a first.' I couldn't make out whether he sounded impressed, or slightly annoyed. 'I hope you have a better time.'

'I probably won't go. I get horribly seasick.'

'I doubt he'll take no for an answer.' He dropped the tea towel and brought my hand closer to his face, like a palm reader. 'The bleeding has stopped, and the cut doesn't look too deep,' he said. I couldn't bear to look, so focused on the green medical box beside him. 'My trusty first aid kit.' He gave it a pat, before releasing my hand into my lap. 'Let's see what Doctor Charlie can find.'

'It's a bit creepy when people refer to themselves in the third person.'

'I only do it when I'm being Doctor Charlie.' He jigged his eyebrows.

'Is that a regular role?'

'Nah, you're my first – apart from Monsieur Moreau a couple of years ago. He had a heart attack in the café.'

'Oh my God,' I said, recalling the gentleman who'd kissed the back of my hand. 'Did you have to do CPR?'

Charlie looked sheepish. 'I just called the ambulance,' he admitted. 'Mum did CPR until they got here, she's brilliant in a crisis.'

'You're very close,' I said, as he chose a plaster from the first aid kit. 'You like working together?'

He nodded. 'We're a pretty good team, but we know when to give each other space.' He met my eyes and smilingly said, 'OK, *I* know when it's time to put some space between us. Obviously, she'd prefer me not to be out of her sight, at least until I'm married.'

'My parents worked together,' I said. 'Somehow, they still enjoyed each other's company at home, though Mum used to despair that all Dad talked about was his job.'

'Which was?'

'They worked in a museum.'

Charlie glanced up. 'That sounds interesting.'

'They loved it, but Mum was always happiest at home.'

He gestured for me to hold out my hand. 'Was?'

'Sorry?'

'You said she *was* happiest at home.'

'She died, a long time ago.'

His hands froze above mine. 'You're telling me you've lost *both* your parents?'

'Yep… I'm an orphan.' I'd almost got used to saying it in a light-hearted way, because when it came up in conversation people never knew what to say and I couldn't handle their clumsy attempts at sympathy, however well-meaning.

'That really sucks, Elle. I'm sorry.' He said it without a trace of awkwardness.

'To lose one parent is sad, to lose both is downright careless.' I gestured at him to stick the plaster on my hand, and stop looking at me so candidly – as if trying to read how I really felt.

'My dad's a waste of space, but at least he's alive,' he said, patting the plaster over my cut before lightly resting his hand on top. 'I can't imagine Mum not being around.'

'Mine died ages ago,' I said. 'Nearly twelve years.'

'Even so, do you ever really get over something like that?'

A ball of emotion rose in my throat and cut off my breath. I remembered after Mum's death, how the days had become seamless for a while, rolling into one, before I'd gradually begun to take notice of my surroundings, and of myself again. Then, the chest-wrenching sobs in my bedroom after Dad's funeral, when it all caught up with me – the realisation that the one person left who'd loved me unconditionally was gone forever.

'You don't get over it, you get through it,' I said. 'And I do have my sister, and... well, I'm not alone.'

Charlie curled my fingers over the plaster and gave them a gentle squeeze, which hurt so much, I squealed.

'God, I'm sorry!' he said, dropping my hand. 'That was a stupid thing to do.'

'No, it's...' I looked down, blinking hard, not sure whether it was my pulsating hand, or the effect of Charlie's kindness making me want to cry. 'Thank you,' I said.

'You're very welcome.'

'Natalie's lucky to have you as a friend.'

'She knows it.' He grinned. 'Right,' he said, slapping his thighs as he leapt up, and I felt a wrench of disappointment that my extended break was over, until he said, 'I'm going to make some more tea, and then you can tell me your sister's name and why she lives in Borneo.'

In the end, we had two cups of tea, and shared a plate of apricot croissants he must have brought up from the café while I was sleeping, and I told him all about the work that Jess was doing abroad.

'She was always into saving animals and plant life, even when we were kids,' I said. 'I think she always knew what she wanted to do.'

'She was lucky,' said Charlie. 'It took me a long time to figure out what I wanted to be when I grew up.' He was sprawled in an armchair, his leg flung over the arm. The sun streamed through the window, creating a halo effect around his hair. 'I did a degree in precision engineering, because Emma, my girlfriend at the time, thought it would lead to a good career, and it wasn't until after she cleared off with my cousin Ben that I realised I hated precision engineering with a passion.'

'Sorry about that,' I said. 'Your girlfriend going off with your cousin, I mean.'

'Old news.' He balanced his mug on his chest. 'I'm over it now, though I don't really talk to Ben any more, which makes family gatherings a bit awkward.'

'I don't have much family to gather,' I said, without self-pity. 'Mum and Dad were only children, so there aren't any cousins, or aunts and uncles.'

'I've got a few on my father's side I've never even met.' Charlie's brow scrunched up. 'Then again, I haven't seen him in years, either.'

'Aren't you in touch at all?'

Charlie shook his head. 'It was obvious early on that responsibility wasn't really his thing,' he said. He spoke with the same lack of bitterness that Dolly had displayed. 'He wasn't a terrible person, just easily distracted,' he went on. 'He worked in construction and was away a lot, so I didn't see him that much. He was often abroad – having affairs, as it turned out.'

'I'm sorry.' I was thinking of Mum and Dad, with their well-worn routines, and the open displays of affection that Jess and I had taken for granted. 'That must have been tough.'

'Not so much for me,' he said candidly. 'My best friend Ryan's dad treated me like a son, so in some ways, I didn't miss out. It was worse for Mum, to be honest. She'd fallen for Dad's "charms",' Charlie's fingers made quote marks, 'and forgave him a lot, until he fell for a younger woman and finally left for good.'

'And he lives abroad?'

'Managing an olive grove in Spain, the last I heard. He calls occasion-ally, but I don't feel much of a connection, so it's always a bit awkward.'

'Well, your mum's made quite a comeback,' I said, filled with admiration for Dolly – and the way that Charlie didn't condemn his poor excuse for a father. 'She seems really happy here.'

Charlie gave a quick smile. 'We both are.'

I could hardly believe I was chatting to him as though I'd known him for years. I was starting to think of it as the Chamillon Effect. Or maybe it was the Café Effect. Or even the Charlie Effect. Either way, I appeared to have forgiven him for his comment about not dating staff. 'No wonder you're not interested in marriage,' I said.

'I just remember how horrible it felt to be cheated on.' Charlie wrinkled his brow. 'I used to worry that I might turn out like my dad, but I know I'd never treat a woman like that.'

His words ignited a flame of warmth inside me. 'You just need to find the right woman,' I said.

'I'm coming round to the idea.'

'Good.' I shoved aside an image of him down on one knee, proposing to Tegan. 'Someone was unfaithful to me too, but I ended up with someone nice after that.' I didn't mention the years before meeting Andrew, which were littered with dates that never went very far, as I tried to recreate what I'd had with Declan – without the cheating.

'Someone so nice, you're not with him any more?'

'OK, he was nice, but Toni – the friend I told you about – thought I was playing it safe because he was the opposite of my ex and ten years older.'

'Were you?'

'Maybe,' I said, admitting it for the first time. 'I didn't realise until he asked me to marry him that I didn't want to.' I suddenly remembered

Henri, asking whether I'd marry for money, and it struck me as such a Regency thing to say, I smiled.

As if he'd guessed what I was thinking, Charlie said, 'Well, you won't get safe with Henri, so maybe you're on to something there.'

I searched for some condemnation in his voice, but it was mildly teasing as he vigorously stirred his tea. I liked that he accepted his friend for who he was – even if he didn't approve of his behaviour.

The familiar sound of a text notification made me jump. 'Is that mine?'

'Oh, I brought your bag up, in case you needed anything.'

The flame inside grew warmer. 'Would you mind passing me my phone?'

'Sure.' Charlie put down his mug and reached to the side of the sofa, and I uncurled my legs from beneath me and leaned across to take it. He'd produced some painkillers with my tea, and they'd dulled the pain in my palm, but I felt clumsy handling my phone with my other hand. 'It's from Jess,' I said, reading her message. *If you haven't got your long lens, maybe borrow some binoculars. If it doesn't have a dark band around its neck, it's not a kri-kri.* 'She's obsessed with these goats.'

'Goats?'

When I explained I'd told her I was on holiday in Crete where the mountain goats lived, Charlie gave me a funny look.

'Why did you tell her you were there?'

Shit. My defences must have come down because of the tablets. 'It's a bit of a long story…' I shifted, suddenly awkward. There were blood spatters on my trousers and I quickly looked away. 'It's hard to explain.'

'She doesn't approve of France?'

I laughed, but knew my cheeks were a tell-tale red. 'I actually think she'd love it here.'

'So…?' He was leaning forward, elbows on his knees, and I knew he wasn't being nosy, just genuinely curious.

'So, she wants photos of these goats,' I said, deliberately misunderstanding. 'And I told her I would get some.'

Taking my cue, he nodded. 'Could be tricky, but there's a wildlife park not far from here. I'm pretty sure they have goats there.'

It was so close to my own far-fetched idea, I couldn't help laughing.

'You don't look alike,' he said, and for a second, I was tempted to say – for probably only the third time in my life – that she wasn't my biological sister, even though we both had blonde hair and blue eyes, then I remembered Jess had a picture of a barn owl as her profile picture and laughed. 'I can't go to a wildlife park, I'm supposed to be helping in the café.' *And I have to talk to a couple of women, one of whom might be my birth mother.*

'You can't work with that hand,' he said.

'Of course I can, if I'm careful.'

'Well, I'm due a few hours off tomorrow afternoon, and I'm sure Celeste's sister wouldn't mind attending to Basil again.'

'You're really proposing a trip to the wildlife park?' The word *proposing* sent heat to my face for some reason.

'I'm sure we can improvise some goat photos if we try.' He made a funny face. 'Not a sentence I ever thought I'd say.'

I laughed, the idea oddly appealing. 'Jess would be cross. She's against animals being kept in any kind of captivity, unless there's a strong conservation policy.'

'We can check that out.'

'What about Tegan?'

He looked at me blankly, as if he'd forgotten who she was. 'You want me to ask her to join us?'

'Well…' *No*. 'If you'd like to,' I said gamely.

'I doubt wildlife parks are her thing.' He rubbed the back of his head. 'She's more into water sports, like sea-kayaking and stand-up paddle-boarding.'

'Interesting.'

He hunched his shoulders. 'I'm not that adventurous,' he admitted. 'Swimming, yes, scuba-diving, maybe, but white-water rafting, big-wave surfing…' He shuddered. 'No, thanks.'

'She's into all that?'

He nodded. 'A self-confessed adrenaline junkie.'

'How come she's here?'

He blew out his cheeks, thinking for a moment. 'Her family's funding two years of travel and she wound up here in July, and decided to stay for the summer because she likes it.'

She likes Charlie. 'Cool,' I said, for the second time in my life. 'She sounds…' *Annoyingly perfect.* 'Great.'

'So, we're going to see the animals?' He rubbed his hands together, as if he'd had enough of talking about Tegan, and I wasn't disappointed. Apart from the pang of jealousy I experienced whenever her name came up, I felt horribly inadequate by comparison.

'I guess we are,' I said, caving in with a laugh. It might be fun, and Toni would approve of that – and I would still have time to talk to Dee and Margot.

'Not a date,' Charlie said, with a trace of anxiety, as if I might get ideas.

'Obviously.' It was supposed to be *my* line. 'I know you don't date *staff*.'

He grinned. 'That's settled then?'

I grinned back. 'It's settled.'

'Great.'

We carried on smiling, and for a moment I had the oddest feeling that all was right with the world (the Chamillon Effect) – then Charlie's gaze shifted.

'What's that?' he said, while I checked my plaster was still in place, and wondered whether it would be rude to eat the last apricot croissant, and when I looked up, he was studying my postcard, a smile playing over his lips. 'It's the café,' he said, sounding tickled. 'I wonder where Mum found this.'

And before I could find my voice, he'd flipped it over to look at the back.

Chapter Twenty-One

'That's mine!' I dived forward and plucked the postcard from Charlie's hand as Dolly came in, eyes gleaming.

'Ah, here you are.' She beamed at Charlie, as if he was exactly where she'd hoped he'd be, before turning to me. 'How's your hand, love?' she enquired with more kindness than I probably deserved, considering I'd smashed a glass, covered her kitchen floor in blood, and left her with a pile of washing-up. 'Has he been looking after you?'

'Very well,' I said, sounding a bit breathy with shock.

Her gaze sharpened when she spotted the postcard dangling from my fingers. 'Oh, you've told him.' Her beam stretched wider than ever. 'You can't think of any other women between fifty and sixty whose names begin with M, who grew up in the village, can you?' She'd switched her attention back to Charlie and as I struggled for words, I caught his puzzled look. *Had he read the postcard?* Hopefully, like Dolly, he couldn't read French.

'Is that what you were discussing, earlier?' he said, still looking at me. 'I thought I heard you mention Dee.'

'We've been trying to work out who M is and have gradually narrowed it down.'

'Right,' said Charlie, keeping his eyes on mine.

As Dolly's gaze flipped between us, horror flashed over her face. 'You *didn't* tell him,' she said, slapping her hands to her cheeks. 'Oh, me and my big mouth!'

'He thought the postcard was yours.' Moving quickly, as if breaking out of a trance, I picked my bag off the floor and pushed the postcard inside. 'I was just about to explain.'

'I'm sorry,' said Charlie, sounding genuinely remorseful. 'I wouldn't have looked if I'd known.'

'I'm sorry too,' said Dolly, but there was a layer of relief in her voice too, and I guessed it was because she didn't like keeping things from her son, and would have loved nothing more than to talk to him about it.

'Look, it's fine,' I said, feeling guilty on two counts. 'It's a silly quest anyway, and I feel like I've taken up far too much of your time.'

'Don't be ridiculous,' Dolly burst out, as though I'd accused her of theft. 'Like I said, we all love a good mystery.'

'I take it you've asked Margot?' Charlie was sitting forward, hands steepled under his chin, his brow furrowed. 'And Marie?'

'It's neither of them,' I said, softening. He was trying to help, without even knowing the full story.

'The only real candidate is Dee, the florist,' said Dolly.

'I'm going to go and see her.'

'It's a pity Natalie isn't here.' A light jumped into Charlie's eyes. 'She could have put together an article for the local paper, asking people to come forward if they have information.' He stood up. 'I could message her if you like.'

'It's fine, your mum got a list of names from her friend at the town hall, and we've covered everyone born here,' I said, and he gave Dolly an odd look – as if he was wondering why she'd gone to such lengths, but was also impressed.

'But there must be hundreds.'

'Not during this particular time frame,' I said.

'How do you know how old she is?'

'I don't… exactly.'

'Francine covered a few years either side, just in case,' said Dolly. 'But we could put something on the café's Facebook page, or Twitter, just in case.' Her face brightened. 'Someone might know somebody we haven't thought of.'

'Good idea,' said Charlie. He was fiddling with the laptop, shaking it like the old Etch A Sketch that Dad had kept from his childhood, and used to demonstrate to Jess and me how children had entertained themselves in the seventies.

'How should we word it?' said Dolly, pulling an order pad from her apron pocket and sitting with her pen poised and her legs crossed, like an old-fashioned secretary ready to take down a letter for her (sexist) boss.

'I'd rather not go online yet,' I said, the enormity of it hitting home. 'I'll talk to Dee first, and speak to Margot again.' My headache was creeping back, and it felt as if someone was stabbing a knife in my palm. 'What if it goes viral?' I added. 'We could end up with all kinds of people coming forward.'

'That's a good point.' Dolly jabbed the pad with her pen. 'I've heard of cap-fishing.'

'Catfishing,' Charlie corrected with a smile. 'It's not quite the same thing, but I know what you mean.' He put the laptop down. 'I think it needs a new battery, it's playing up,' he said.

Dolly's head flew round. 'What about the accounts?' Her voice sharpened in alarm. 'We can't do the accounts if the laptop's not working.'

'Don't worry, Mum, it'll be fine,' said Charlie. 'Did someone just call you?'

I hadn't heard anything, and wondered whether Charlie was attempting to distract her. If so, it worked. Dolly shot to her feet, slipping the pad and pen back into her pocket, along with a tube of mints she'd spotted on the table. 'You'd better come too,' she said to Charlie. 'Elle can put her feet up and join us for dinner later.' She held up a hand to stall my protest. 'You shouldn't be on your own when you've lost a lot of blood.'

'She's right.' Humour shone from Charlie's eyes. 'You did lose an awful lot of blood.'

Dolly tutted. 'It'll be nice to have you for dinner,' she said, as though planning to eat me. 'You can be our guest of honour.'

I glanced at Charlie, to see if he looked annoyed, but he was smiling – probably out of politeness. 'The house is only five minutes away,' I said. 'And it's only a little cut.'

'You might go into delayed shock,' insisted Dolly. 'We'd never forgive ourselves if you woke up dead.'

It was the sort of thing Mum used to say, and I had to admit it felt nice to be fussed over. 'I look a mess.' I indicated my crumpled, bloodstained trousers.

'You don't,' said Charlie and Dolly together, almost as if they meant it.

'Fine.' I couldn't keep up a protest. 'If you're sure I won't be in the way.'

'You won't be.' Dolly nodded with the air of a job well done, and when Charlie and I traded smiles, my cheeks pulsed with colour.

'Now, have a little rest,' she advised.

After Dolly and Charlie had departed, I tried to relax. I didn't want to dwell on Dee or Margot when there was nothing I could do, so I read through a few past issues of *An Expat's Guide to Living and Working in France*, smiling through some of Natalie's columns, and learning more about the area. I made a mental note to tell Jess that the south of the island was a pit stop for avian migrants between northern Europe and Africa, and a reserve there boasted three hundred and twenty species of bird – then remembered I couldn't, because I was supposed to be in Greece.

Eventually, I plumped a cushion under my head and lay back, worn out by the last few hours, and soothed by the sounds from the café and occasional cry of a seagull, let my mind drift about until I floated into sleep.

When I opened my eyes, the sun had shifted and the room was filled with an almost celestial light. I half-expected to see an angel hovering, which made me think of Miranda and her ghost child, then remembered where I was and sat up with a start. It was almost seven and quiet downstairs – the lull before the evening's trade began – and I realised with a shock that I'd been at the café all day.

My headache had eased, but I must have knocked my hand as some blood had seeped through the plaster. Trying not to look, I reached for the first aid kit, still open on the table, and managed to replace it without taking my eyes off a photo on the wall, of Dolly posing in the café with a customer who looked like the actor Jay Merino, and I remembered he'd been filming recently on the island.

Trying to locate the bathroom, I stumbled into Dolly's bedroom by mistake. It was surprisingly sumptuous, with peacock blue walls and silk curtains, and purple velvet cushions scattered across the bed. There was a Hollywood-style mirror above the dressing table, and a chunky-framed photo sat on the nightstand of a much-younger Charlie, his hair almost vertical as he dived to catch a football.

Further down was a room that could only be Charlie's. Dominated by a neatly made bed, it was smaller than Dolly's, but reasonably tidy with a fresh, soapy scent. His clothes hung neatly on a rail, and there was a wide-screen TV fixed to the wall, opposite a giant poster of Max Weaver from the *Maximum Force* films. I remembered what Charlie had said, about Natalie being with Max Weaver, and I suddenly understood what he'd meant – Natalie was dating Jay Merino! Smiling, I glanced towards a shower room through a half-open door, but resisted the temptation to go and peer at Charlie's toiletries, making do with scanning the pile of books by his bed, beneath an arching lamp: an eclectic mix of literary fiction, biographies and volumes on business management.

Finally, in the bathroom – another surprise, with its petrol blue tiles and black marble washbasin – I freshened up, amazed to see my face looked smooth and well-rested, despite what felt like the longest day of my life (since yesterday). As though I'd been on holiday.

I couldn't do much about my outfit, apart from rub the bloodstains out with damp toilet paper, but after checking myself in the mirror, decided I'd pass muster.

When I went downstairs, Charlie was in the kitchen preparing food, and there was no sign of Dolly.

'Hi,' he said, with a grin. 'Feeling better?'

'Much,' I said, feeling shy again. 'Thanks for letting me rest and… you know, for looking after me.'

'No worries.' He sliced a tomato and threw it into a frying pan on the hob with some chopped up courgette. 'You hungry?' he said. 'It's just *ratatouille*.'

'Starving.' I looked into the café, which was empty. 'Where's Dolly?'

'Apparently, Frank's getting an earlier flight back because he's missing her too much, so she's gone to pick him up from the airport. She'll be back soon.' He brandished the knife he was holding. 'You'll have to make do with me a bit longer.'

'You cook?'

'I'm getting better,' he said. 'It's Mum's domain really, but I won't poison anyone.' He looked at me, hovering in the doorway. 'She's left us here alone on purpose,' he said. 'Frank could have got a taxi.'

'You think?' I moved over and picked up a sliver of tomato and chewed it. 'You should just tell her about Tegan.'

'I will when there's something to tell.'

'What if you end up going away with her?'

His expression suggested he hadn't considered that. 'I wouldn't leave this place.' He sounded very certain. 'She'd have to stay here.'

'Move in with you and your mum?' I raised my eyebrows. 'No girl wants to do that, however lovely the mum.'

'Well, I hadn't planned on living here forever,' he said, slinging some diced onions into the pan. 'But, as it happens, Mum's moving in with Frank after they're married, so this can be my love nest.'

I groaned. '*Love* nest?'

'Shag-pad?'

'Gross!'

He laughed, then looked at me through his lashes. 'What are you planning to do when… when your time here's up?'

I noticed the hesitation – as if he'd been going to say something else, but before I could work up a reply, there was a sharp rap on the door, and when Mathilde poked her head round, I gave an involuntary gasp.

Charlie looked round and grinned a welcome.

'She's here to help with the food this evening.' He waved her in with a smile and I instinctively backed away as she entered like a storm cloud. Mathilde ignored me as though I was invisible, but her weathered face transformed into a web of smiles for Charlie.

Twisting the knife out of his hand, she made a shooing gesture and spoke in rapid French.

'She wants us to go outside while she cooks,' he said, and I was only too happy to oblige, seating myself at the courtyard table while Charlie vanished, returning a few minutes later with two tall glasses containing a pale-yellow liquid.

'One of your cocktails?'

'Pineapple Downfall,' he said, 'but without the rum, as I'm working this evening.'

'You work every evening?'

'No, not every evening and remember, I have tomorrow afternoon off.'

'Ah yes, the wildlife park.' I smiled and took a sip of my drink, which was cold and sweet and delicious, and we chatted about England, spending an enjoyable half hour comparing notes on the places we had in common. I sensed he was deliberately avoiding the subject of the postcard, and was grateful, and soon, Dolly and Frank were back and introductions were made. Frank was a charming northerner with puppy-brown eyes, and a friendly smile, and clearly adored Dolly, and the next hour flew by. It was almost like being part of a family again as the conversation flowed, mostly driven by Dolly, spoiled only slightly by Mathilde giving me a smaller portion of *ratatouille* than everyone else, and banging my plate down with unnecessary force, but I was the only one who apparently noticed.

'Elle's our wedding photographer,' Dolly announced to Frank (I'd almost forgotten about that) and when he asked what my job involved, I realised I'd built up a wealth of material.

'Women in boudoir poses were popular for a while,' I said, after explaining the basics. 'They'd turn up with exotic lingerie and feather boas, and it was usually a bit of a laugh, but occasionally men would come in and ask for nude pictures of them for their wives, but I couldn't do it.'

'Who wants a picture of their hubby's twig and berries on the wall?' said Dolly, and when we'd stopped laughing, I told them about the portfolio of headshots for a woman who went on to be the face of a well-known yoghurt brand, and seeing how interested they were was struck by the fact that mine wasn't the worst job in the world. I just wasn't sure whether I wanted to do it any more. Not that I was about to say so, having committed to one last wedding.

One last wedding? Yes, I decided. After Jess's, I wasn't going to do any more. Petra could take over that side of things – all of it, in fact. It felt like my thoughts were moving too fast, and when Dolly invited me to stay longer, I declined.

'It's been lovely,' I said, standing up, 'but I said I'd pop round and see Marie.' At least, that was what I'd told Henri; my excuse for not seeing him that evening.

'Say hello from us.' Dolly smiled at me warmly. 'She didn't join the knitting group in the café this morning, but I know she's busy at the moment. It's more of a winter hobby, really.' She got up and checked my hand, peering under the plaster like a nurse, and whispered, 'Go and see Dee in the morning, before you come in.'

My heart jumped. 'I will.' I was aware of Charlie rising from the table.

'Mum's right,' he said, and I couldn't think what he meant until he added, 'You do look like that actress.'

'Oh?' I gave an awkward half-laugh, not making any assumptions after my faux pas with Marie.

'Marilyn Monroe, only prettier,' he said, with awkward gallantry.

Dolly looked as ecstatic as though he'd proposed marriage. 'You do,' she said, gripping my upper arms and giving me a little shake. 'But *much* better, because you're *real*.'

'It's true,' Frank agreed, but he was looking at Dolly.

I couldn't remember a time when my cheeks had felt hotter, but then Mathilde came out to glower at me and brought me back to reality. 'Thanks,' I mumbled, wondering whether Mathilde had a broomstick stashed somewhere.

'Shall I walk you back to the house?' offered Charlie.

Dolly nodded, her eyes like stars.

'Honestly, I'll be fine,' I said, smiling as she let me go. 'It's still light and you've got to work.' I could hear people passing outside, footsteps pausing as though checking to see if the café was open for business. 'I'll see you tomorrow.'

'It's a date,' he said, with a little salute, and Dolly gave a sharp intake of breath. 'It's a figure of speech, Mum.'

But as I turned to leave, she winked at me, and I could almost see her thinking, *It's only a matter of time*.

Maybe it was. Not for me, but for Tegan.

Lucky Tegan.

Chapter Twenty-Two

In the end, I didn't go to Marie's. When I got back, I heard her chatting with Ted and Miranda on the terrace, and didn't want to intrude (or get embroiled in a controversial debate), so I had a long shower and an early night. But the following morning, she caught up with me as I left the house, pushing her bike with the basket on the front.

'Are you not going to the café this morning, Elle?'

I held up my palm. I'd removed the plaster to let some air at the wound. 'Cut my hand on a piece of glass,' I said. 'I've got today off.'

'That looks very hurtful.' She averted her eyes. 'I am sorry, I get a little…' She pressed her lips together. 'I do not like blood,' she said apologetically.

'Me neither.'

We exchanged smiles. 'Would you like to see the market?' she said. 'It is a very nice one.'

'I'd love to, but I have to do something first.' I tightened my grip on my bag. 'Could I meet you there?'

'Of course.' She looked pleased, her eyes bright in the morning sunlight. 'You know where it is?'

'I'll find it,' I promised.

As she cycled away, skirt flapping around her calves, I checked my phone for the address I'd tapped in earlier: rue des Caillotières. I was going to go straight to the florist's to talk to Dee. My heart beat steadily in time with my footsteps as I followed the directions on my phone. I didn't just have the postcard in my bag, I'd brought the shawl and bracelet too. No pussyfooting around, I'd decided before leaving the house, or worrying about the consequences. I'd woken early with a fully-formed thought in my head: that giving up a baby, whatever the reason, meant you had to be prepared for a fully-fledged adult to rock up on your doorstep one day, demanding answers – whether you liked it or not.

Probably not.

If it turned out to be Dee and she wanted nothing to do with me, that was fine, providing I got the answers I was looking for. I'd tried to work out exactly what they were as I ate an apple for breakfast, and drank a cup of coffee at the kitchen table, but in the end, decided to simply produce the items and ask her outright whether she was the M who'd given a baby to Russell Matheson, thirty years ago. And if she wasn't, did she know anyone in Chamillon who might be; or anyone who *knew* anyone who might be.

Nerves threatened to overwhelm me as I reached the street more quickly than I'd expected, and saw the shop on the corner, with wicker baskets of flowers arranged outside, and a black and white cat snoozing in the sunshine.

Not stopping to think, I strode into the bright interior, pausing for a second to admire the vivid arrangements, before heading to the driftwood counter at the back, where a tall, very thin woman, with spiked-up red hair and round glasses on the end of her nose, was poking greenery into a bouquet of pastel pink flowers.

'Do you speak English?' I said, because if she didn't, this was going to be tricky.

'I think you will find that most shopkeepers on the island speak very good English,' she said smoothly, in very good English. 'It is necessary when so many visitors do not speak our language.'

It felt like a (well-deserved) reprimand, but she was smiling over her glasses in a friendly fashion, her small, very dark eyes (everything about her seemed 'very') appraising me with mild curiosity. I waited a beat for the smile to falter; for her to drop the bouquet and say in a hoarse whisper, 'You look like someone I knew a long time ago. Are you… are you his… *our*… daughter?' but although she *did* lay the bouquet down, it was only to free her hands to adjust a hairband nestled among the spikes. 'How may I help you?'

'Are you Dee?' I said, suddenly dry-mouthed. 'Madeleine…' I realised I didn't know her surname, but it didn't matter because she was nodding, hands resting neatly on the counter. Her nails were very short, and she wore a gold band on her wedding finger. I searched her face for something familiar, but felt nothing – other than a fleeting admiration for her perfectly aligned eyebrows.

'You would like some flowers?'

'What? Oh, no. Thank you,' I said, opening my bag. I hadn't realised my hands were shaking until I drew out the carrier bag, watching her closely for signs of recognition. *Nothing.* Hardly breathing, I drew out the shawl and bracelet and laid them on the counter beside the flowers, and placed the postcard on top. It would have made a lovely photo for Instagram. 'Do you recognise any of these?'

'I do,' she said, her eyebrows arching as she bent forward to look more closely and my heart shot into my throat. 'Isn't that Café Belle Vie?' As she picked up the postcard, I saw that her nails had a layer of soil underneath, and wanted to snatch it off her. She clearly had no idea; didn't even look at the back, just continued staring at the picture.

A polite smile tilted her lips, which were as thin as the rest of her. 'It has not changed much since then.'

'What about this?' I said dully, nudging the bracelet forward, knowing it was pointless. 'Have you seen it before?'

For a second, something like recognition flickered over her face. 'It is pretty,' she said. 'I think a friend had one like this, a long time ago.'

My heart stuttered. 'What was her name?'

She fingered it, gently. 'Lots of us had charm bracelets like this,' she said. 'I cannot remember exactly who it was.'

'Might her name have begun with M?'

'Maybe.' Her eyes flicked up to mine. 'Are you selling it?' she said.

'No, of course not.' My tone was sharp with disappointment, and she gave me a startled look. 'What about the shawl?'

'It is very beautiful.' As her fingers edged towards its delicate edges, I whipped it away, like a magician pulling a cloth from under a table setting. 'It doesn't look familiar?'

'Again, I…' Her eyebrows pinched together. 'It does look familiar. It is the kind of shawl for wrapping babies up, I think.'

My heart gave a kick. 'That's right,' I said, imagining myself swaddled in it, in my birth mother's arms.

'But I think… a lot of babies, they will have a shawl like this one.'

I felt a sag of resignation as I thrust everything back in the carrier and stuffed it in my bag. 'I'm sorry for wasting your time,' I said.

'What is this about?' I had her full attention now, her eyes sharp on mine. 'You are looking for someone.' It wasn't a question.

I nodded. 'It's a long story,' I said, as I had to Charlie when he'd asked why I lied to Jess about being in Greece. 'I thought you might be her, but…' I mustered a smile. 'It was a bit of a long shot.'

She shook her head, and pushed her glasses up to meet her eyes. 'I do not know what a long shot is, but I think you are seeking someone with an initial like mine – maybe from the postcard.' It was still on the counter and she picked it up and turned it over, eyes skating across the words.

'Eloise,' she said. 'Is that you?'

It was such a direct question, I could do no more than nod. 'So, M,' she pointed to the initial at the bottom, 'she is your…'

'My birth mother.' I felt as though I'd put down an armful of logs, and wished I'd said it sooner. 'I thought she might still live in Chamillon.'

'And you wish to find her?'

'I… yes.'

'You have shown other people?' She pointed to my bag, as if it was full of contraband. 'Other women, like me?'

'There aren't too many whose name begins with M.' I mustered a smile. 'She didn't leave us much to go on.'

'No.' Dee looked thoughtful suddenly, as if picking up the trail. 'You have talked to Marie Girard?'

'I have.' I mustered a smile. 'I'm staying in the house next door.'

Dee nodded, her eyes narrowing.

'She explained that…' I hesitated, not wanting to give away Marie's confidences. 'It's not her,' I said quickly.

'She could not have children.' Dee sounded sad and I realised they must go back a long way, and were probably still good friends. Maybe this was where Marie bought her flowers for the guest house.

'Let me think about this,' said Dee. Her gaze was shrewd and sympathetic and hard to look away from. 'Maybe I can help.'

'I'm only here for a few more days.' I took a deep breath. 'I think it's impossible, but thank you.'

I found the market easily, and spotted Marie right away, browsing an array of brightly coloured fruit and vegetables. There was a bunch of radishes peeping out of her basket, and she was weighing a small green melon in one hand. As if sensing my approach, she turned, her face lighting up the way Mum's used to do when Jess and I got home from school.

'You're here,' she said, as if she'd doubted I would make it.

'This is nice.' I did a slow spin, taking in the rows of brimming stalls, which seemed to sell everything from meat and cheese, bags and espadrilles to cooking pots and china. Perhaps I could buy some crockery to replace what I'd smashed at the café.

'Did you finish your *errand*?' Marie stressed the word errand with a smile, as if it was a word she'd recently learned and had been waiting to use.

'I did,' I said brightly, pushing aside the sense of failure I'd felt while hurrying away from the flower shop. Maybe Dee could help, but I doubted it, and there were no more Ms in Chamillon. The only other possibility was Dolly's social media route, or Charlie's idea of a piece in the local paper, but there didn't seem much point. Birth records didn't lie, and it was unlikely there was someone here who hadn't been registered; someone female, whose name happened to start with M. Once I'd ruled out Margot, that was that.

'This would be very nice on you,' said Marie, pulling me from my thoughts.

I looked round to see that she'd pushed the melon beside her radishes, and some mint-green balls of knitting wool, and had turned to a stall selling clothes, attractively hung beneath a wavy-edged canopy. 'See?'

She'd picked out a silky, sleeveless V-neck top the same shade as the sky. 'It is perfect with your eyes.' She held it against me with such clumsy shyness – as though she'd never done anything like it before – that my eyes unexpectedly filled with tears.

'I love it,' I said, hugging it to me, blinking to clear my vision as I stooped to peer in a little round mirror on a stand. I couldn't see it properly, but the colour seemed to sum up everything about Chamillon, and I knew that whenever I wore it, I'd remember my time here. 'I'll take it,' I said, trying to open my bag with my uninjured hand, but Marie had produced a wallet-style purse and was pulling out some notes.

'Please, I would very much like to purchase it for you.' Her cheeks were pink with pleasure, her eyes full of light, and I couldn't bring myself to argue.

'That's so kind of you, Marie.'

'Do not mention it.' She instructed the stallholder to wrap it carefully, then seemed unsure what to do with it. 'It will not go in your bag,' she said, glancing at it doubtfully. It was bulging with the carrier bag containing the shawl and bracelet.

'Perhaps you could take it home, and I'll pick it up later,' I said. 'I'm going out with Charlie this afternoon, so I won't be going back to the house right away.'

'Charlie from the café?' She tucked the parcel carefully into her basket, and gave me a curious look – as if there was another Charlie I didn't know about.

'Yes, Charlie from the café.'

She gave an approving nod. 'He is a very nice young man,' she said as we moved to the next stall, which was piled with china, and where an American was attempting to barter with the trader. 'He works very hard.'

'He loves his job.'

'That is a good thing.' Marie picked up a plate circled with tiny blue dots and I wondered whether she was going to add it to her collection at the guest house, but she put it down again and said, 'You did not bring your camera.'

'No,' I said, reaching for a leaf-patterned cup with a large handle. 'I haven't really had time to take any photographs.'

'But you are going out.' She seemed puzzled, sweeping a hand round to encompass the surroundings. 'It is a good opportunity.'

'I worry about taking my camera out of its bag, in case it gets stolen, or I drop it,' I confessed. 'My father bought it for me, a few birthdays ago.'

She seemed to consider for a second. 'It holds close to your heart,' she said, as though she'd just understood something important.

'Something like that.' *Exactly* like that, I realised. Away from the studio, I tended to use an older model if I wanted to take pictures (though away from work, I didn't often feel like it), or even took snaps on my phone, which made me feel guilty, as if I wasn't a proper photographer. 'He died eighteen months ago, so…'

'I'm very sorry,' Marie said, sounding it. 'You are too young for such loss.'

'I'd already lost my mum, so I'm kind of used to it,' I said in the usual flippant tone, and felt bad when Marie's eyes went wide with shock. 'It was a long time ago,' I added.

She looked at me for a long moment. 'You are a remarkable young woman, Elle. She would be proud of you.'

When I was sure I wasn't about to cry, I said, 'That's nice to hear, thank you.'

'You look like her?' She was studying the line of my jaw, as if she'd known my mother and was searching for similarities.

'Actually, I take after my father,' I said. 'Everyone says so.'

She nodded, slowly. 'I am like both of my parents.' She pointed to her small, straight nose. 'My father.' She patted her hair. 'My mother.'

'Actually, she wasn't my biological mother,' I said, unexpectedly. 'Because we were both blonde with blue eyes, nobody ever knew unless we told them.' The Chamillon Effect was happening again, making me say things I never normally would to virtual strangers – or even people I knew well. 'She *was* my mother though, if you see what I mean.'

'Yes,' Marie said slowly. 'Yes, I do see.'

For a second, I thought things were going to turn awkward, but then she pointed to a stand with a stripy awning and said, 'Would you like to get some ice cream?'

My spirits lifted. 'Only if you let me buy them.'

The veil of sadness that had settled across her face lifted with a smile. 'I will let you.'

'What about your bike?' I looked around and saw it chained to some railings.

'It will be safe,' she said, and we wandered companionably to the stand and joined the small queue, and once we'd chosen our flavours – we both preferred vanilla – strolled away from the market and settled on a bench, Marie's basket on the ground between us.

'This is nice,' I said, as much about the view of sand dunes, beach and sea as my ice cream, which tasted of every summer I'd spent at my grandparents' house in Cornwall.

'It is so familiar to me.' Marie dabbed ice cream from her chin with her paper serviette. 'Once, I could not wait to leave Chamillon, but when I returned, I knew this was where I would stay.'

'I can understand why.' I watched a couple pass with a little girl, her hair streaming behind her as she ran ahead, reminding me of Jess. 'I'm coming back at the end of the month to take photos of Dolly's wedding.'

'You are?' Marie's smile couldn't have been any wider. 'That is wonderful, Elle. I hope I will see you then. You must stay with me,' she said. 'I insist.'

'That would be nice.' I looked at her. 'Do you have any family left here, Marie?'

She took a second to reply. 'No more, but I have good memories of them.' As sadness filled her voice once more, I wished I hadn't brought it up, then her smile returned. 'I am godmother to my friend Jeanne's daughter,' she said. 'I see them often, and I have so many friends, and my guests, it is impossible to be lonely.'

'Maybe you'll meet someone special again. He could help you to run the guest house.'

Her laugh sounded youthful, and brought colour to her face. 'I think I have become used to living privately,' she said. 'My husband… he was an actor you could not follow.'

'You mean, a hard act to follow?'

She nodded and continued, 'We do not all have the happy ending we might have wanted, but I have found contentment.'

I discreetly studied her face as we finished our ice creams – watched by a row of hungry-looking seagulls – and hoped that one day, I'd feel the same sort of certainty about myself.

Chapter Twenty-Three

'It's so weird being in a car again,' I said to Charlie, as we hurtled towards the wildlife park outside La Rochelle. 'I don't think I could get used to driving on the opposite side of the road.'

'It's a bit scary to start with,' Charlie agreed. He was sitting in what would have been the passenger seat back home, which was disorientating. 'Not that I drive here as often as I used to in the UK.'

I suppressed a squeal of fright as a car shot past on the 'wrong side' and he flashed me a look of alarm. 'Do you want me to pull over?'

'No, no, I'll be OK.' I dug my nails in my palms, and squealed again when pain lanced through my hand.

He glanced over, to see me staring at the cut, which had opened up again. 'I told you, you should have put a fresh plaster on,' he said. 'There's some in the glove box.'

Leaning over, I opened it and took one out. 'You keep plasters in your car?'

'Never know when you'll need one,' he said. 'I've got cough sweets, scissors, string and a toolbox in the boot.'

Smiling as I covered my cut, I said, 'I'll let you know if I get a tickle in my throat.'

Arriving at the café at noon, after walking Marie back to her bike and thanking her again for the top she'd bought me, I'd found Charlie waiting outside, and my heart had lifted further at the sight of his smiling face.

'Good morning?' he'd said.

'Really nice.' I hadn't mentioned seeing Dee, and he didn't ask.

Instead, he'd requested to look at my hand, and told me off for not keeping the wound covered up. 'You don't want to get an infection,' he said, and I'd had to hide a smile because he sounded funny when he was cross.

Dolly, watching through the window, had turned to Madame Bisset, and I'd easily lip-read the words, 'Don't they make a lovely couple?' before she raised her eyebrows at me, asking silently whether I'd spoken to Dee, and I'd given her a thumbs down, turning away before Charlie could see.

Now, I put the plaster on gingerly and sat back to enjoy the view, but we were travelling along a busy motorway, so there wasn't much to see, and I shut my eyes when Charlie pulled out to overtake a lorry.

'Why haven't you brought your camera?' he said, after he'd pulled back in.

My eyes flipped open. 'I can take pictures on my phone.'

'But you've got a fancy camera.' He gave me a curious smile. 'I saw it, remember?'

'I know, but I… forgot it,' I said. 'I told you, I met up with Marie and we went to the market, and I didn't have time to go back to the house and get it.'

'Do you even like taking photos?'

'What?' My head whipped round.

'You've already told me you don't enjoy doing weddings.'

'That's because of the stress,' I said. 'I don't mind the other stuff.'

'Wildlife, landscapes?'

'I don't do landscapes, I do people.'

'Maybe it's time for a change.'

'There's no money in landscape photography,' I said. 'You can't do it from a studio.'

'How do you know?' He flashed me a look. 'That there's no money in it, I mean?'

I folded my arms, realised I looked defensive and uncrossed them. 'I don't, but I wouldn't need a studio if I was a landscape photographer and then Toni and Petra, my assistant, would be out of a job.'

'Not if you got someone else in, or promoted your assistant and left Toni in charge.'

He made it sound appealingly simple. *Maybe it was.* 'You've missed your calling,' I said. 'You should have been a career counsellor.'

'I do give good advice.' His teasing smile was impossible to resist. 'So, you're definitely doing Mum's wedding?'

'Definitely,' I said.

He looked relieved – no doubt glad I hadn't decided to pull out. 'You won't mind coming back to Chamillon?'

'Obviously, I mind, but I've said I'll do it now.' When his smile vanished, I said, 'I'm joking! Of course I don't mind coming back. Who wouldn't want to be here?' I gestured to the window and screamed as a motorbike roared past, too close to my door.

'Jesus,' said Charlie, slowing and clutching his chest. 'He was joining the motorway from the slip road, that's all.'

'I forgot it was on that side,' I said, heart banging. 'I thought he was going to hit us.'

Looking shaken, he said, 'I'd better take the scenic route back.'

*

The wildlife park, nestled at the heart of a pine forest, was crowded but clean with the usual assortment of animals, but seeing the Caribbean flamingos against a backdrop of brilliant blue sky, surrounded by trees and a waterfall, made it seem more exotic.

'It says here that the park plays an important role in the conservation of endangered species, and finances protection programmes, such as the one for the orangutans of Borneo,' said Charlie, reading from the pamphlet he'd purchased with our tickets. 'Your sister would approve.'

I grinned at him. 'She would,' I said, feeling instantly better about being there, pleased to see plenty of staff around, and that the enclosures all looked roomy. 'She loves an orangutan.'

'According to this, they've saved quite a few species from extinction.'

I looked at him scanning the leaflet for nuggets of information to reassure me, and some impulse made me reach up to kiss his cheek just as he turned his head. Our lips collided, yielding for the briefest moment before we jolted apart.

'What was that for?' He looked at me with startled eyes, something in their depths I couldn't read.

'Sorry,' I mumbled. 'It was meant to be a thank you, but went a bit wrong.' *Or right.* 'Sorry about that.' My heart was beating furiously. I could feel the imprint of his mouth on mine; taste mingled flavours of coffee, cinnamon and peppermint. 'I wasn't expecting you to move.'

'What were you thanking me for?' His voice had gone gruff, and I was annoyed with myself for embarrassing him.

'For this.' I swung my arm around, trying to make light of it. 'You could have done anything with your afternoon off and you've ended up here with a madwoman.' He was looking at me in an intense way that was almost… *sexy.* 'Look, I know you've got a girlfriend,' I said, in case he thought I'd been coming on to him. 'Can we forget that just happened?'

'Forget *what* happened?' He gave a lopsided smile and I managed to return it. 'Let's go and find some goats.'

On the way, we stopped to pet a rhinoceros, got sidetracked by some meerkats ('They really look like the ones in the adverts,' Charlie said, his bewildered amusement making me laugh) and I was glad there was no lingering awkwardness, even though our eyes kept clashing, forcing us to look away. He insisted on feeding the giraffes before we went any further. 'They make me feel tiny and insignificant,' he said, buying a bag of green stalks, and passing them to the giraffe under the watchful eye of the keeper.

Further on, I got out my phone to take a photo of Charlie being eyed up by a strutting ostrich, and a passing couple offered to snap us both.

'I couldn't really say no,' I said, joining Charlie in front of the wire fence.

'Just smile,' he said through a cheesy grin, obligingly wrapping his arm around my waist.

'It looks like the ostrich is trying to remove your wig,' I spluttered, when we looked back at the picture. 'What were you doing with your hand?'

'Er, trying to stop it from ripping my hair out?' He peered over my shoulder, cupping his hand around the phone screen. 'At least *you* look normal.'

I'd angled my head close to his so it looked as if I was leaning on his shoulder, and I was surprised to see that I looked what magazines would call 'radiant'. 'I think I've got a bit of a tan.'

'Makes your eyes look really blue,' said Charlie. He was so close I could smell warm skin and hair, and wondered whether it was the sun – high and hot – that was making me feel light-headed, or something else.

'Time for refreshments,' he said, flapping the hem of his shirt and blowing his hair off his forehead. 'I don't know about you, but I'm roasting.'

There weren't many places to buy food, just the sort of Portakabin affair usually associated with football grounds, and we ended up with a hot dog and a cold drink, both surprisingly tasty. When we'd finished eating, Charlie checked the map outside the seating area.

'To the goats!' he said, like a warrior entering battle, and we worked our way through the crowd, which seemed to have doubled since we arrived, but when we got there, I was disappointed to see the goats were part of a petting zoo, queues of children lining up to stroke them.

'I don't think this is going to work,' I said, after trying to line up a picture on my phone that didn't contain small children. 'The colours are wrong for a start, and they don't have the right kind of horns.' I looked round to see Charlie struggling not to laugh. 'That's not very helpful,' I said. 'What am I going to do?'

'Try zooming right in, so you can just see an eye.' He made a frame with his fingers. 'It'll look like a goat, without giving too much away.'

I gave him a long look.

'What?' he said. 'That was me being helpful.'

'There should be mountains in the background, like this.' I brought up an image on my phone of a kri-kri clinging to a rock face, its distinctive horn curving over its back. 'Not quite the same,' I said, turning to watch a toddler pushing a piece of popcorn at a billy goat. 'It hasn't even got a horn.'

Charlie shook with silent mirth, a fist pressed to his mouth.

'Charlie!' I whacked him with my phone, but couldn't help laughing too. 'This is the stupidest idea I've ever had.'

He pulled himself together with an effort. 'Why don't you pull a picture off the internet and send her that?' he suggested. 'She probably won't know the difference as you're a professional photographer.'

'She'll probably ask some in-depth question I won't know how to answer and I'll be rumbled.'

Charlie crossed to a patch of shade beneath a tree and I followed, glad to escape the sun's glare.

'You could tell her the truth,' he said.

'Which is?'

He leaned against the trunk and folded his arms. 'That you're here to find out who your birth mother is.'

The sensation of falling was so real, I put out a hand to steady myself. 'You read the postcard?'

'I took a lot of French classes when I came here, and most of it stuck.'

'I… I wasn't sure.'

'I honestly thought the postcard was Mum's, but when I read the message on the back, I got the gist,' he said. 'Eloise. That's how you introduced yourself, remember?' I did. 'And you don't know anything about her, other than her initial?'

I shook my head. 'Only that she had dark hair and eyes, according to my dad, and grew up here, according to the postcard.' I clasped my arms around my waist, meeting his gaze full on. 'I'm so sorry I didn't tell you the truth,' I said. 'I told your mum, and she offered to help in exchange for me working at the café, but I asked her to keep it to herself.'

'I get that,' he said, and I could tell that he did. 'But I'd like to help, if I can.'

'You know as much as we do, except she left me a shawl and a bracelet too, but they're not much use.'

'How come her name's not on your birth certificate?'

'She didn't hang around to register the birth,' I said. 'My parents did that, so my Mum's name is on the certificate. My dad didn't know her name. My birth mother's, I mean.'

'Do you think she was already married, or something?'

'Maybe.' I nodded. 'She obviously didn't want me to find her.'

He leaned his back against the tree. 'Maybe she wasn't thinking straight at the time.'

'She could have changed her mind, but she didn't.'

He was silent for a moment, his expression focused.

'I only found the postcard a few months ago,' I said. 'I think... I don't think it really sank in until I got here.'

He looked like he was imagining it, his forehead furrowed. 'It must have been a shock.'

'I always knew she was out there somewhere, but it didn't seem to matter. Now... I want to know more,' I said. 'I agreed to help at the café because I thought it would be a good way to find out more about the locals.'

'I guess it worked,' he said, passing his hand over his jaw. 'Getting to know the locals, I mean.'

'Yes, but I'm no closer to finding out who she is... was.'

'Is it really that important?'

I frowned. 'I wouldn't be here if it wasn't.'

'But, if you had good parents and a happy childhood, does it matter if you don't know the woman who made all that possible?'

'When you put it like that...' I slipped my foot out of my sandal. The grass felt wonderfully cool between my toes. 'I know biology isn't everything, of course I do, but it feels like unfinished business, and I must admit, I'm curious,' I said. 'It seems odd to know nothing about the woman who gave birth to me.'

Charlie pursed his lips. 'Would you be looking if your parents were still alive?'

'Probably not,' I admitted. 'But losing them both…'

'Go on.'

'It makes you question everything, I suppose. And finding the postcard… it gave me a purpose, I guess. Once I had it, all these questions flooded into my head and I knew I couldn't move on until I'd tried to find her.'

'What happens if you don't?'

'I'll go home and get on with my life.' The thought was oddly depressing. 'I'm kind of expecting it,' I said. 'I just have a feeling she's not here, despite what the birth records say.'

'Don't give up hope yet.' Charlie pushed a hand through his hair. 'If you speak to Dee—'

'I did that this morning,' I confessed. 'She's going to "have a think".'

'Well, that's something, I suppose.'

I looked at my watch, and glanced once more at the goats with a sigh of defeat. 'I suppose we'd better head back.'

He sprang to attention without question, as if relieved to draw the afternoon to a close, and I tried not to let my disappointment show. 'The scenic route?'

'Yes, please.'

We drove back with the windows down to let in the sea-freshened air, our hair blowing about, and I managed to relax this time. Charlie pointed out some landmarks, and I asked if it ever rained on the Île de Ré.

'Not often, but when it does, it looks like any old seaside resort,' was his rather damning response, and we debated whether even the most unremarkable places would look pretty in the sunshine ('Probably not warzones,' Charlie said) and then he tuned the radio to a music station, and by the time we arrived at the café, I was starting to doze off.

'Sure you don't want me to drop you at the house?' he said as I stretched and yawned. He'd parked up on the kerb to let me out before taking the car round the back of the café to park it.

'No, it's fine. The walk will wake me up.'

'I hope you have a nice evening,' he said, rather stiffly, and for a split second, I couldn't think what he meant.

'Oh right,' I said, 'the fishing boat.'

'Are you going to tell Henri you know he's not a humble fisherman?'

'No,' I said. 'I'm going to let him tell me.'

Charlie's face split into a grin. 'Good luck with that.'

As I opened the car door, I spotted a familiar face through the café window, and recognised the woman who'd been sitting with Henri the day I ran my suitcase over his foot.

'Is it true that his sister's a swimwear model?'

Charlie followed my gaze. 'It's true,' he said. 'Why do you ask?'

'I just saw her in the café, and it reminded me of what he'd said.'

He followed the line of my gaze. 'Where?'

'There.' I pointed, then tried to look like I hadn't been pointing when she looked over at us.

Charlie frowned. 'That's Thérèse, she works at the bank,' he said. 'She's not Henri's sister.'

Chapter Twenty-Four

After telling Charlie I'd made a mistake about the woman being Henri's sister – I could see he wasn't convinced – I went straight back to the house, feeling annoyed that seeing her had taken some of the shine off the day, and called Toni.

'So, shagging the sexy fisherman's off the agenda?' she said, when I'd let off steam.

'I never said it was *on* the agenda.' I stopped rifling through my clothes for something suitable to wear. I hadn't even decided yet whether I was going out. 'I just said he's got too many secrets.'

'For a very good reason.' Toni sounded amused. 'Two minutes ago, you said you can understand why he didn't mention he's a billionaire.'

I was starting to wish I hadn't called her. Apart from anything, Henri would be turning up any minute, and I still hadn't decided what to say to him.

'He's not a billionaire,' I said. 'I looked him up, he's a millionaire.' The Durands were a very big deal in France, his grandfather having built his kingdom from the ground (or sea) up, and his parents lived in a house that looked like the French equivalent of Downton Abbey.

'Oh, well, he's not worth bothering with then,' joked Toni. At least, I thought she was joking.

'I just wish he hadn't let me think the woman he was with in the café was his sister.'

'But he didn't actually *say* that?'

'No, but he implied it, which meant it was another one of his exes.'

'Or a friend.'

'Even so,' I said. 'He knows a *lot* of women.'

'Doesn't mean he's sleeping with them all.'

'I get the impression his libido is rather massive.'

'Hopefully, it's not the only thing.'

'Toni!'

'Well, I suppose with someone like him there's going to be a dark side, Elle. Isn't it more fun than knowing everything at once?'

'You mean someone like Declan,' I said, though in truth, Henri was much more of a gentleman than he'd ever been. Declan would never have left things at the door the night before, for a start.

'Yes, but you don't want to fall for another Andrew.'

'As it turned out, I didn't fall for Andrew,' I pointed out. 'And I'm not falling for anyone.'

'Not even in lust?'

I rolled my eyes. 'What are you up to this evening?'

'Stop rolling your eyes and changing the subject,' she said. 'You know we'll be tip-toeing around until Freddie's asleep before nodding off in front of the telly as usual.'

'Living the dream.'

'Not my dream,' she said, but I knew she didn't mean it. 'So, there's no news about your birth mother?'

'You'll be the first to hear if there is, but don't hold your breath.' I felt drained after taking her through everything that had happened since we'd last spoken. 'I'd better go,' I said. 'He'll be here any minute.'

She started singing, 'Thou shalt have a fishy on a little dishy, when the boat comes in,' and I ended the call with a smile – which vanished when I heard a knock at the front door.

Henri looked as handsome as ever, in navy jeans and rugged boots, and a white T-shirt that complemented his tan, but I couldn't help viewing him differently in light of Charlie's disclosure. Was the bed-tousled hair, ordinary clothes and lazy (sexy) smile all part of an act, or was he really a humble fisherman at heart, looking for a woman who wasn't interested in the trappings of a privileged lifestyle?

'You look… amazing,' he said, eyes travelling over my outfit. At the last second, I'd wriggled into the 'Riviera' dress because it was made from the sort of fabric that didn't need ironing. I'd dressed it down with a cable-knit cardigan I'd had for years, and a pair of trainers I'd brought in case… I wasn't sure why I'd brought them.

'I thought it might get chilly,' I said, fingering the cardigan buttons, though I still wasn't certain I wanted to get on his boat. Apart from anything, I'd forgotten to pick up some anti-seasickness pills.

Now that Henri was in front of me, his powerful scent having its usual effect on my pulse, my resolve to confront him weakened. I decided to go with the flow – something Toni was always telling me to do.

'The colour suits you,' said Henri, and I assumed he was talking about the dress and not my putty-coloured cardigan. His eyes loitered on my lips, and my mind flashed back to kissing Charlie at the wildlife park. I hadn't mentioned it to Toni out of embarrassment – though, ironically, I hadn't minded telling her why we were there in the first place. She'd laughed for quite a long time at the thought of me trying to photograph a goat that didn't exist in France.

'I'll just get my keys,' I said to Henri. I picked up my bag and took out the shawl and bracelet and laid them on the stairs before stepping outside. 'No bike?' I said, spotting a taxi parked across the road.

'Not tonight.' Henri twirled his hand. 'I thought we'd travel in style, mademoiselle.'

Not the sort of style you're probably used to. Still, it *was* a nice taxi. And he really did look gorgeous.

As I locked up, Marie came out, looking surprised to see Henri. 'Good evening,' she said, dipping her head, and I realised she was probably slightly in awe of his status – Henri Durand, son of the richest family on the island.

'Madame Girard.' His smile was warm and friendly. 'I hope your guests enjoyed their scallops the other day.'

'*Oui, merci.*' She turned to me. 'I was bringing this round for you.' She held out the parcel containing the top she'd bought me.

'Oh, Marie, thank you,' I said. 'Can I pick it up tomorrow?'

'Of course,' she said, her gaze moving between Henri and me, and I thought she looked concerned. 'I hope you have a lovely evening.'

'We shall.' Henri bestowed her with another smile (a 'Lord of the Manor' smile, or 'we're all equals' smile? I suddenly couldn't tell). Taking my elbow, he guided me into the waiting taxi, and seemed not to notice that I was quiet on the journey to Saint-Martin. He chatted animatedly about a scallop war that had broken out in the English Channel, following a long-simmering row over the rights of fishermen from both countries.

'The British claimed they were insulted and pelted with rocks, and they requested protection from the Royal Navy.' He shook his head, as if he couldn't believe it.

'What does a fisherman *do* every day?'

It wasn't the sexiest question, but seeming pleased that I'd asked, he detailed an itinerary that sometimes lasted three days, starting at 4 a.m. involving tides, nets, trawling, winching and planning for all possible outcomes. 'On the water every decision is one of survival. Mistakes can be deadly.' His face was alive with passion. 'Fishermen have to know the fish they are after, how best to catch them, how best to bring them in and how to keep them fresh until they deliver to the buyers. They have to know the sea, the way it changes and how these changes affect their boat, their gear and the fish.'

'I had no idea there was so much to do.'

He smiled. 'It's important to me that if I marry again, my wife understands my job.'

'Was Bernice not a fan?'

'She liked some elements of what I do for a living.' His mouth tightened, and although he didn't elaborate, I knew he was talking about money and not a surplus of mackerel.

'So, fishing is pretty much your full-time job?' *I'm fishing*, I thought, and almost tittered at my joke.

He turned to face me and said with great expression, 'I want so much for the next woman I love to share the experience with me.' Taking my hand, he squeezed it, and although I breathed through the pain, he must have seen me wince.

'Too much, too soon?' He hoisted his brows, a humorous gleam in his eyes. 'It's OK, I'm prepared to wait for someone I think is worth it.'

I waited until he'd released my hand before saying, 'I don't think I'm that person, Henri.'

'You don't know everything about me yet.'

You'd be surprised.

The car drew up at the harbour and I climbed out, assuming Henri was going to pay the driver, but all they exchanged were a few words before he joined me, and I realised the driver must be on the payroll.

A gust of wind caught my hair, whipping it over my face, and Henri pushed it back and gently cupped my cheek. As our eyes locked, he cradled my other cheek, eyes deep with intent, and he looked so serious all of a sudden, I couldn't stop a giggle escaping.

He pulled his head back.

'Sorry,' I said.

Puzzlement flashed over his face, then his mouth advanced towards mine. An image sprang up, of Charlie's lips, and this time, I pulled back. Kissing two men in one day was excessive by anyone's standards.

'So, where's this boat?' I said in a bracing voice, and a woman walking past with a tiny dog on a lead stopped and glanced at us, her raven-black hair swinging around her shoulders.

'Henri?' Her almond-shaped eyes widened, and she said something to him in French that sounded insanely sensual – but then, most things did, especially when the speaker was so attractive. Her waist was smaller than one of my thighs, and her features perfectly arranged. She reminded me of a doll I'd had as a child, whose hair grew to her waist when you wound her arm around.

Henri said something back to her, but didn't introduce us, and she shot me a superior look before jogging away, dragging the dog behind her as if she wished it was me.

As though we hadn't been interrupted, Henri – apparently forgetting he'd been on the point of kissing me – said, 'The boat's down here.'

Ignoring his palm, outstretched to help, I hoisted up the hem of my dress – *why the hell had I worn a dress?* – and stomped after him like a stegosaurus. Down a short flight of stone steps, I found myself up close to the boats in the water and knew that now would be a good time to tell him I didn't fancy getting in one. *On one?* Then I thought of the way he'd spoken so passionately about fishing, and felt a squeeze of curiosity. Perhaps on the boat, where he was most comfortable, he'd talk more openly – perhaps even ask me something about myself that wasn't money-related. I could draw him out while he fiddled with his lobster pots, and if the water remained as calm as it looked in the harbour, I'd probably be fine. It was so long since I'd been on a boat, it was possible I'd outgrown my chronic seasickness.

'Just a bit further,' he said, leading the way with steady strides to what could only be described as the mucky side of the harbour, away from the shiny yachts, to where the fishing boats were moored. Although painted in jaunty colours, most looked battered compared to their shiny neighbours, and I felt a flash of panic when Henri pointed to the smallest and most… *industrial*-looking one.

'Isn't that a trawler?' I drew the edges of my cardigan around my chest. The breeze was stronger here, and the boats were bouncing about on the rippling water. 'I thought we'd be going in one of those.' I pointed to a big red and blue one that looked like a cartoon tugboat.

'Those are for tourists,' called Henri, leaping on board the vessel, its deck layered with fishing nets, rope, hooks and other equipment I didn't recognise. The word 'rigging' sprang to mind. 'I wanted to show you the real thing.'

I felt a pop of annoyance that he hadn't explained how basic the boat would be. It was obviously a test to see how I reacted, just as he'd probably 'tested' a string of women before me. 'I'm not dressed properly.'

'It's OK, you don't need special clothing.'

My stomach clenched a warning. 'It's too close to the water.'

He laughed as though I'd said something delightful, and when he reached for me, I allowed him to help me onboard, half-annoyed with myself now, for wanting to show I was 'game'.

'Good job you're wearing trainers,' he said as I slipped and clutched at his arm, wishing I was the type of woman capable of leaping on a trawler and taking charge.

'Aye, aye, skipper,' I said, in a Long John Silver voice, determined to prove a point – though what it was, I was no longer sure.

He laughed again and gave me a tight hug. Feeling the contours of his arms and the breadth of his chest, I told myself there were rewards for stepping way beyond my comfort zone.

He let me go and reached for a life jacket, while I looked around, noticing a lot of seagull poo, and what looked like a fish eye peering up at me from a wicker basket. A strong smell of exhaust fumes hit my nostrils and my stomach began to churn. *Great.* I'd only just stepped on board and already felt sick. 'Does it always move around this much?'

Henri laughed as though I'd made a joke, and handed me the life jacket. 'You'd better put this on,' he said. 'There's only a small storm forecast, but it's best to be on the safe side.'

'Storm?' My voice was a squeak of alarm and Henri, pulling on a yellow oilskin, looked at me as he zipped it up.

'It'll pass quickly,' he said. 'I've been out in force ten gales and never had any problems.'

Force ten gales? As he helped me into the life jacket, I decided I'd better confess, though my face was probably a giveaway. On the ferry trip to Belgium, a teacher had said she'd never seen anyone's face actually turn green before. 'Henri, I'm not very good on boats.'

'Don't worry,' he said, circling round to start the engine, clearly in his element. 'You'll soon find your sea legs.'

My legs were fine, it was my stomach I needed to find. 'I don't think so.'

Bending, he flipped open a cool box and pulled out a bottle of beer. 'Once we're out there, we can have a drink,' he said, with a devilish grin. 'That should settle your stomach.'

Settle it? The thought of alcohol made my stomach rise. 'I need to sit down.'

Henri was revving the engine and didn't hear me. The smell of fuel intensified and I clamped a hand to my mouth as he expertly swung the boat around and directed it towards the mouth of the harbour.

Oh God, there was so much choppy sea.

Ducking down to avoid looking at it, I spotting a slatted bench at the back of the boat, and crawled across the deck, past caring that I might be touching fish guts.

The seat was splattered with droppings, but I dragged myself up and lay down on it, drawing my knees to my chest. Spotting another oilskin lying on the deck, I pulled it over me like a blanket as the boat continued forward, rising and falling like a fairground ride. I began to whimper, remembering that this was exactly how I'd felt on the ferry to Belgium, and why I'd stayed away from boats ever since. I'd read some people never get used to the motion of the sea, and I was clearly one of them.

'Elle?' called Henri, as if suddenly realising I wasn't where he'd last seen me. 'Are you OK?'

'Do I look OK, you tosser?' Nausea was making me cranky, but he didn't hear, my words disappearing on the wind, which seemed to be gathering pace.

The boat carried on lurching, belching out fumes, until I couldn't have cared less if Henri came over and chucked me overboard like a substandard flounder. If anything, it would be a blessing.

After several more interminable minutes, my face was damp with sea spray, I was covered in goosebumps, and my whole body was wracked with shudders.

'Hey, what's wrong?' Henri loomed over me, his face hard to see with the light behind it. The sun had gone in and there was an ominous tinge to the sky, as if it was full of rain, waiting to burst out.

'Feel a bit off-colour,' I mumbled, the waxy sleeve of the oilskin pressed to my mouth. 'Might have to go back.'

'Go back?'

I nodded, a tear seeping out and running into my ear. I wanted so badly to be back at the house, my head sinking into the pillows on Natalie's bed, fresh air flowing through the window. What I *didn't* want was to be lying on a poo-splattered trawler in the middle of the Atlantic Ocean, heading into a gale.

'What are you laughing at?' I said bad-temperedly, hearing the sound of his chuckling above the howling wind.

He squatted down, bringing his face close to mine, and brushed a lock of damp hair away from my cheek. 'Why didn't you tell me you were seasick?' His eyes were creased with sympathy – or maybe it was amusement, I couldn't tell any more. 'It would help if you sat up and kept your eyes on the horizon.'

'Bit late for that.' Nevertheless, I hoisted myself into a sitting position and pointed my eyes at the harbour wall. It was a shock to see it was so close, and to realise the wind was nothing more than a strong breeze. With all the pitching and rocking, I'd been certain the boat was already in the eye of the storm. 'Why didn't you tell me the truth about who you are?'

Henri sank back, and when I risked a glance, I saw he was looking sheepish. 'Charlie told you?'

Switching my eyes back to the boat masts in the harbour, I said, 'I suppose all that stuff in the restaurant was you psychologically profiling me.'

'Stuff?'

'Trying to find out how much I earned, and whether I wanted to marry for money.' Overheard, a seagull screeched, as though expressing its disapproval. 'You should have been honest.'

'You understand why I wasn't?' He sounded as if he wished he had been. 'I don't want to waste my time with someone who's only interested in how many houses, or pairs of Louboutin shoes I can provide.'

'I think, these days, many women are happy to make their own living and not rely on a man.' I was impressed I'd managed to get the words out, when all I wanted was to jump over the side of the boat and swim to dry land. 'Not everyone's like your ex-wife.'

'You'd be surprised.'

'Well, you're obviously meeting the wrong women.'

'Exactly.' He sprang forward and grabbed my sore hand, which was practically numb with cold so at least I didn't feel any pain. 'But now I've met you, and you're different,' he said.

'Because I don't like oysters, have my own business and I got on your stupid boat, even though it's making me want to die?'

When he laughed, I noticed how even his teeth were. They must have cost a fortune. 'Yes,' he said, nodding to prove it. 'You make me laugh and I think…' He paused. 'I think you like me too.'

'Henri, I do, but we only met a few days ago.'

The stiff breeze was blasting his hair around, revealing more of his perfect bone structure and his perfectly shaped ears. 'As soon as you ran over my foot with your suitcase, I felt something,' he said.

'Probably your toes breaking.'

He lowered his head and when he raised it, his eyes were alight with laughter. 'See?' he said. 'You're funny.'

I slid my hands from his and tucked them under my armpits. My stomach was heaving in time with the boat, and I wasn't sure how much longer I could last. 'I'm a novelty,' I said. 'When it wears off, you'll realise we have nothing in common.' Somehow, I couldn't imagine telling him about my birth mother yet, in the end, it had come easily with Charlie – even though I'd only known him for the same amount of time. His vision of me seemed so much more real than Henri's.

The look that Henri was giving me was long and probing, and I wanted to tell him to get a move on and say what he had to say. 'You look like a mermaid in that dress.'

'Brilliant.' My teeth started chattering. 'Just what I wanted to hear.'

He began to shake with amusement again. 'Will you at least give me a chance?' He spread his hands. 'Now everything's out in the open?'

I looked at him, outlined by the lowering sky, hair tossed by the wind, dark and piratical – such a contrast to Charlie at the wildlife park, haloed by light and sun. It felt like a metaphor and as my stomach started to tip, I said, 'I can't see you again, Henri, I'm sorry.'

'You're saying that because you feel horrible right now.' My words seemed to have slid right off him, like rain off his oilskin. 'I'll ask again when you're feeling better.'

'Fine,' I snapped. 'Now take me back.'

'You don't want me to show you how to—'

'NO!' I practically roared, and as he shot to his feet, I threw up on his boots.

Chapter Twenty-Five

'What's happened to you?' said Dolly, coming into the kitchen as I was tying my apron the following morning. 'Have you got an infection?' Before I could speak, she took my hand and closely checked my palm. 'It doesn't look too bad, but make sure you wear rubber gloves so it doesn't get wet.'

Wet. Just the word made me shudder, bringing back memories of last night. I was sure I could still feel the motion of the sea, and was certain I was swaying slightly.

'She went fishing,' said Charlie, coming through with a tray of milk jugs, giving me a curious look. He'd been talking to Gérard when I came in, and I'd managed to slip past without being spotted.

'Fishing?' Dolly looked baffled, as though she couldn't understand why anyone would do such a thing. 'There are better things to do in the evenings than go fishing.'

'I know that now,' I said, recalling Henri's latest proposal as he'd deposited me, pale and unsteady, at the house. The storm had passed and the sky had cleared, and in a burst of optimism he'd said, 'We'll go dancing next time.' I'd had to admire his persistence in the face of adversity. He was no closer to finding a woman to share his love of deep-sea fishing than he had been a week ago, but was set on doing something we *would* enjoy.

I hadn't answered as I'd wanly waved him off before crashing into bed, certain that when he thought about it, he'd realise he was wasting his time.

'I thought boats made you seasick.' Charlie looked at me closely, and I hoped my hot shower and vigorous tooth brushing had chased away any lingering smells.

'They do,' I said grimly.

'Then why did you go?'

'I thought I might have grown out of it, OK?'

His expression softened. 'Have you eaten?'

I shook my head, aware of Dolly watching our exchange as if hoping it would end in marriage. 'I couldn't face anything.'

'I'll make you one of my ginger and peppermint cocktails,' he said, wiping his hands on his apron. 'It's good for settling stomachs.'

As he left the kitchen, Dolly looked almost tearful. 'He's going to make such a lovely husband for some lucky lady.'

'Not cool, Mum,' he said, popping his head back, and I almost smiled when Dolly blushed and hurried to the oven to take out some brioche rolls studded with chocolate chunks.

'What happened with Dee?' she said when we were alone.

I briefly explained, glossing over the details – more because I felt sick than because I didn't want to talk about it. 'It wasn't her,' I said flatly, relieved when Charlie returned and left the drink on the side.

Dolly patted my arm with a worried expression before taking the rolls into the café, and I sipped my drink slowly as I loaded the dishwasher.

When Charlie came back with an almond croissant, I ate it quickly and felt almost restored when I'd finished. 'Thanks,' I said, the next time he came through, with a mountain of dirty crockery. A coachload of visitors had descended on the café. 'I feel much better.'

'You're welcome,' he said, with a smile. I noticed a strip of redness across his nose from where he'd caught the sun the day before, and heard myself say, 'I know I shouldn't have got on that boat, but I was hoping he'd tell me the truth.'

Charlie transferred some plates into the sink. 'Did he?'

'No,' I said. 'I forced his hand in the end. He guessed you'd told me.'

Charlie turned. 'Was he mad?'

'Not really,' I said. 'I got the impression he was sorry he'd lied, though.'

'Good.' He turned on the tap and water jetted out all over his shirt. 'Shit,' he said, leaping back. He brushed at his chest. 'I'd better go and get changed.'

As he ran upstairs, I stood for a moment, feeling as if I'd been cheated of something, but didn't know what it was.

For the next hour or so, there was a steady stream of washing-up and I was startled when Dolly came through and said in an oddly charged voice, 'Dee wants to speak to you.'

I tightened my fingers around the cup I was holding. 'To me?'

'That's what she said.' Dolly's eyes were big. 'What exactly did you say to her yesterday?'

I paused. 'I told her the truth,' I admitted. 'It sort of popped out.'

'And?' Dolly's face was avid.

'She said she'd have a think.'

'Well, it looks like she did.' Dolly grew brisk. 'You'd better get out there and speak to her,' she said. 'The woman looks fit to burst.'

Dee wasn't hard to spot with her Lisa Simpson hairstyle. She was by the window chatting to Margot, who was nodding a lot, the sun sparkling off a diamanté clip in her hair. When she saw me, Margot said, 'Ah, here is my muse,' and blew me a kiss, which seemed to confuse

Dee. She moved too quickly, knocking the edge of the table, causing Margot's coffee to spill.

'What's going on?' she said anxiously, and I resolved to talk to her as soon as I'd dealt with Dee. If only she wasn't so fragile, hands fluttering to her throat, eyes flicking about, clearly desperate to escape into her fictional world.

'Nothing,' I said, feeling an urge to reassure her.

She looked relieved, and blew me a kiss before opening her laptop.

'You wanted to talk to me?' I said to Dee.

Her lips were drawn into a tight line and turned down at the edges. She nodded, indicating we move somewhere quieter, though the café was busy, the noise levels too high for anyone to overhear, and once we were out of earshot of Margot, she said, 'I have been to talk to Marie and she told me that you were here.'

My stomach flexed. 'Why did you talk to Marie?'

'I needed to say something to her.'

My heart began thudding, even though what she was saying didn't make sense. 'And… now you want to talk to me.'

'To tell you that you must go and speak with her.' Behind her glasses, Dee's dark eyes were grave. 'She is upset.'

'Upset?' Panic rose in my throat. 'What did you say to her?'

'Go now.' Dee flipped her fingers urgently. 'It cannot wait.'

My limbs felt watery. 'Dee, what's going on?'

'Go,' she repeated, her glasses slipping down her nose. 'You will see.'

I nodded, fingers fumbling with my apron. 'OK.'

I flew out to get my bag with Dolly hot on my heels. 'What did she say?'

'I have to talk to Marie.'

'Marie?'

'I'm sorry, Dolly, but I have to go.'

'Go where?' Charlie appeared in a fresh white shirt, arms dusted with fine gold hairs, and I had a powerful urge to throw myself into them.

'She has to go and talk to Marie,' supplied Dolly as I checked my bag for my keys.

'Do you think it's to do with...?' Charlie widened his eyes.

'That's what I was thinking,' said Dolly, swapping a glance with him. I guessed he must have told her that he knew, and felt bad all over again that I'd asked Dolly not to tell anyone in the first place.

'I really don't know,' I said. 'I'm sorry, but it sounded urgent.'

Charlie reached out and his fingers brushed mine. 'Come back when you know.'

'I will,' I said.

Dolly's hands pressed my shoulders. 'Let us know if there's anything we can do.'

'I will.'

I half-ran to rue des Forages, arriving sweaty and out of breath and desperate for a wee. I hovered outside Marie's, but couldn't wait to use the bathroom, so let myself into Natalie's house and dashed upstairs. I was washing my trembling hands when I heard a noise downstairs that made me freeze. It was a wail, like that of an animal in distress, and my lungs seemed to shrink with fright. *Marie?*

I crept onto the landing and peered down, to see her sitting on the stairs. 'I was on my way round, but needed to use the loo,' I said stupidly as I began to descend the stairs.

'I saw you,' she said, but her voice sounded weird – as though she had laryngitis. 'I could not wait. The door was open, so I came and I... I saw this.' She was clasping the shawl that I'd left on the stair the night before, one hand pressed to her mouth, as if to stop another noise coming out.

'Marie, what is it?' I approached slowly, as if she was a wounded animal that might lash out.

'This is yours?' Her voice had dropped to a whisper.

I sank beside her and nodded.

'And this?' The bracelet was nestled in the folds of her skirt and she picked it up, twisting it in her fingers, her face a mask of hope and disbelief.

'It's... they're... they're not mine.' My voice shook. I knew that whatever happened next would define everything going forward. 'I mean, they don't belong to me, as such, they were a... a sort of gift.'

'Gift?'

'I... I found them,' I said.

'Where?' Bewilderment radiated from her in hot waves. She blinked a few times, looking from me to the shawl and back to my face. 'Where would you find such things?'

'They were... they... I found them, in a bag, in my father's wardrobe when I was clearing out his things.'

'Your *father*?' She buried her face in the shawl, a sob shuddering out of her, the sound of it sending a shock wave through me.

'Marie?' I touched her shoulder, my breathing uneven. 'You're scaring me.'

'This...' She drew the shawl away from her face, and turned to me with tear-soaked eyes. 'I made this.' Her voice was ragged with emotion. 'And the bracelet... I bought this.'

'I... don't understand.' I was struggling to hold onto a sliver of calm. 'What are you talking about?'

'My friend Dee, she came to see me this morning.' Marie's voice grew faint, as though her strength had been drained. 'She told me that you went to her shop and showed her these things, and that there was a postcard too. She said that you were trying to find the woman who gave birth to you.' She didn't wait for a response, which was just as well, because I felt incapable of speech. 'She thought she recognised the shawl and the bracelet, and said you should speak to me, but you told her you already had, and that it couldn't be me.'

'That's right.' I crushed my hand to my mouth as what she was saying began to sink in, speaking through my fingers. 'I *did* tell her that I'd spoken to you.'

'But you did not show me these when we spoke.' Marie lifted the shawl and jangled the bracelet in her hand. 'Dee thought you had, and that I lied to you; denied that I recognised these things. She wanted to know why.'

Dizziness made my head swoop. 'I know I didn't make it clear to her,' I said. 'I didn't think it mattered. You told me you couldn't have children, so…' My words dwindled to nothing. *Had Marie lied?* Everything was spinning. I could barely form the words I needed to ask; couldn't believe that the time had come, that all along, she'd been right there, next door… 'Marie, are you my birth mother?'

Her face seemed to collapse. 'Oh, my lovely girl.' Her voice trembled with emotion. Pushing the shawl into her lap, she reached for my hand. 'I wish so much that I was, but no. No, I am not.' Tears spilled down her cheeks. 'I am not your birth mother, she…' Her breathing faltered. 'I'm so sorry to tell you that she died, many years ago.'

Died.

Such a final word. And yet… I think I'd known all along that she was no longer in the world, and hadn't been for a long time. I was gripped by sadness that I would never be able to meet her; thank her for giving me to Dad and Paula, and for letting me have Jess as my sister. Or, to ask her *why*?

'But you knew her?' My hand rested in Marie's, a current of feeling flowing between us. 'If you knitted the shawl, was it for… did you know she was pregnant?' I shook my head, and realised my cheeks were wet. 'I don't get it,' I said. 'How could you recognise the bracelet?'

'Oh, Elle, it is so much more than I could have hoped for.' She was smiling now through her tears, laughing almost, with a look of such joy in her eyes that I found I was smiling and crying too, and I didn't have the first clue what was going on.

'Marie, what are you trying to say?'

'She was my sister, Elle.' Her fingers tightened around mine. 'Emmeline was my sister.'

Chapter Twenty-Six

Emmeline. Em. M. All this time, I'd been chasing down the wrong path.

'It is how she signed her name,' said Marie, when I'd showed her the postcard, and she'd cried over the message, stroking the words with her fingers as if to absorb them. 'It is what she instructed your father to call her, so he did not know who she really was.'

'My name could be a letter too,' I said in a daze. 'Elle... L.'

'Oh yes, that is true.'

I knew I'd come back to the name later, but... 'You're my *aunt*!' It hit me forcefully that I'd come to Chamillon and gained an actual relative. 'You're my Aunt Marie.'

'You are my *niece*!' she said. 'It is the same word in English, I believe.'

We looked at each other and laughed, our fingers entwined, and when she leaned over and hugged me tightly, I hugged her back and realised now why I'd felt a connection the first time we'd met. It was because – unbelievably – we were related. 'Aunt Marie,' I said, trying it out as she hugged me tighter.

'I knew there was something,' she said at last, drawing back and cupping my chin with her hand. 'There is something about the way you hold your head that is like her.'

My heart felt in danger of exploding. 'That's why you thought I was familiar.'

'I could not think why. It was… what do you English say? It was *bugging* me.'

We laughed again, searching each other's faces, trying to absorb the magnitude of it all. 'I didn't expect this,' I said.

'I did not expect this, *ever*.' Her eyes were soft as she rested her palm against my hot cheek. 'I think this is the best day of my life.'

We sat for a moment longer, making room for our discovery, which felt like a miracle. Seeing the effect on Marie was somehow even better than finding my birth mother – partly because she hadn't given me away, but mostly because I'd started to know and like her. She was someone I would love having in my life, and it had been clear since we'd met that she'd like me in hers.

'I thought it might be Miranda,' I said. 'Because Henri said something about her lost daughter. That's why I came round for breakfast – to meet her.'

'Miranda?' The look on Marie's face made me giggle a little hysterically. 'I do not think you would like her to be your birth mother,' she said.

I was glad she'd followed my lead and not simply said *mother*. 'I've so many questions.'

She nodded. 'There is a lot to talk about.'

'Do you… could I see a picture of her?'

'Of course.' Her eyes spilled tears again, and she tugged a handkerchief from the pocket of her flowered apron and pressed it to her nose. 'We shall go to my house and I will tell you everything I know.'

My birth mother was beautiful. Tall, with long dark hair, just as Dad had described, with smiling eyes to match, but looking through the album Marie had taken down from her bookshelf, I didn't feel any connection to the woman in the photographs. It was a relief somehow that I wasn't immediately flooded with longing and regret; just a powerful curiosity about what had led to me being here, in the house where she'd grown up with her sister and parents.

'She was a ballet dancer,' said Marie, which made sense of all the pictures. 'We both were for a time, but when I met Victor, I knew I wanted to marry and have a family with him, but Emmeline, she wanted very much to please our parents, who had very big plans for her.'

'She didn't want to let them down.'

'She was their firstborn. They had such high hopes and they pushed and pushed for her to do well. Me, the second child, I was more...' She hesitated, seeking the right word. 'I liked to daydream and read my books. Our parents, they were more forgiving of me.'

So, Dad had been right about the parental disapproval, and I wondered afresh whether they'd talked more that night than he'd ever let on.

'She had so much talent, but she'd worked hard too,' Marie continued. 'Harder than I ever did.'

'I don't suppose a baby fitted in with their plans.'

'Probably they would not forgive her.' Marie seemed lost in memory for a moment. We were sitting at the table on the terrace where I'd sat with Ted and Miranda the day before. They were in Saint-Martin, Marie had explained, and wouldn't be back until late, and her American couple were out too.

'You said she didn't want my father to know her true name, so does that mean she told you about their... about him?'

'No, I did not know then.' Marie went back inside and came out with a yellowing envelope. She pulled out a letter and handed it to me.

I looked at it for a moment, at the untidy scrawl that matched the writing on the postcard. 'It's in French,' I said. 'I'm afraid I can't read it.'

'Of course.' With a little shake of her head, Marie took it back and settled down to read it out, her face tight with emotion.

'Marie, I am sorry to have not been in touch for so long. Something happened. It is not true what I said, that my leg was badly broken and that I needed time out to recover. The truth is that I met someone – a man – on tour in London. It is a poor excuse, but I was lonely…'
Marie paused, as though this admission still pained her, before continuing in a halting voice as she struggled with the translation.
'I did not expect to fall pregnant from this encounter. I was always so careful, but I had too many drinks that night. Marie, you can imagine how angry and devastated Maman and Papa would be. They wanted so much, they will never forgive me if I do not have the career they have sacrificed everything to pay for, the lessons, the outfits, the competitions, the travelling – you know what they were like, it would break them for me to become a statistic; a single parent.
'It is true,' Marie said sadly. 'Emmeline was their prodigy. They told everyone she would be famous one day, like your Margot Fonteyn, or Anna Pavlova.'

I nodded for her to go on, not trusting myself to speak.

'I was so scared,' Marie continued. *'I knew what you would say if I told you. You would beg me to come home, but I knew I could not do that, that I would not be welcome by them, so I stayed. You will hate me now for not confiding in you, but you had just met Victor, you had your life to live. I could not put this on you. I cannot even*

explain why I decided I would go ahead with the pregnancy, only that I wanted to bring this baby into the world, even if I could not keep her. Yes, I had a baby girl! She was born in June, as the sun was rising. An easy birth in a local hospital, and I took care of her for one week. She is with her father now, in England. He is a good man, Marie. I could tell from the second we met.' My eyes blurred with tears to hear Dad described so accurately, and to hear how Emmeline had wanted me, when it would have been so much easier for her if she hadn't. *'He is to be married soon and they will give her a good life. I know she will be happy here. Please, do not be too angry. I hope we can still be friends. I took the shawl you made, remember, to wear when the nights were cool. I have left this with her father, along with the bracelet you bought me for my birthday. He will give them to her, if he thinks it is the right thing to do, so maybe they will be returned, in time. He has the postcard of the village that I took the last time I was home. I wrote a message, so she will know where I was born and one day may come to find us. Maybe I will be there with you when Maman and Papa are gone and I am no longer dancing. Please, do not ever tell them about her. It would not be fair, and I could not bear it. Sometimes, I cry because I miss her. I wish I could have made different choices, waited to know her, but I had to be strong and let her go. I called her Eloise and she is beautiful.*

M.

I was crying by the time Marie had finished, and so was she.

'Eloise was our grandmother's name.' Marie's voice was hoarse with feeling. 'It moved me that she chose it, but I *was* angry with her at first.' She folded the letter away and dabbed her face with her handkerchief.

'I told myself I could have raised her baby, but in truth, my relationship with Victor was new, I was in love for the very first time and...' she shook her head '... I do not know how I would have acted, and my parents, they would have made everything so difficult,' she said. 'I do not think we could have given you what your parents did, but if I had known then that I would never have my own children...' She took a slow but shaky inhalation and I covered her hand with mine.

'What... what happened to her?'

Sorrow shadowed her face. 'Soon after the letter arrived, Emmeline won a place with the Boston Ballet Company. Our parents were overjoyed. She flew out to join the company, but the car taking her from the airport was in an accident.' Her voice caught with emotion. 'Emmeline... she did not survive.' Marie's face was knotted with grief and I understood that the air of sadness she carried was for her sister, as much as for the children she'd never had. 'Emmeline was so young,' she said. 'Only twenty-three.'

Younger than my sister – than both of us.

'I'm so sorry, Marie.' I remembered how it had felt to lose Mum before her time, and knew how devastating it must have been for Marie – and her parents. 'You never told them about... about the baby?'

She shook her head. 'I do not know how it would have helped,' she said simply.

'Did you... had you made up with her?'

She nodded and dabbed her eyes. 'She was so happy the last time we spoke,' she said. 'That was some comfort. I had forgiven her, of course, and we did not speak about the past, only her future. I think she felt she had to be even better now, to make her sacrifice worthwhile.'

We were silent for a moment, our hands joined, lost in thought.

'So, you've known all this time that I existed?' I said at last.

She nodded. 'Often over the years, I wondered about you.' A faint smile rose to her lips. 'It's so silly, but I went to London after Victor and I divorced, before I came back to Chamillon.' She gave an embarrassed shake of her head. 'I wanted to see where Emmeline had been living while she was there, but the house had gone. I walked around for a long time. I think I expected to see you, but, of course, I had no idea where to look.'

'Oh, Marie,' I said, overcome. 'I wish I'd known.'

'I am so sorry if this is not the outcome you were hoping for, Elle, when you have suffered so much loss already.'

'I'd already lost her,' I said gently, wiping my eyes with my hand. 'And I've so much to be grateful for.' I wondered how things might have turned out if Dad had known that Emmeline had died. Would he have shown me the things she'd left for me; perhaps offered them as mementoes? But the past had happened and couldn't be changed, and there was no point imagining different outcomes. Maybe it was better I'd found them when I had – that they'd finally brought me here and delivered me to Marie's door.

'I want to celebrate having an aunt,' I said, a feeling of rightness washing over me. 'You have to meet my sister, Jess.'

'I would love that.' Marie reached out and our fingers laced together. 'What is it?' she said, as my eyes filled with tears once more.

'My sister,' I cried. 'She thinks I'm on holiday in Greece.'

Chapter Twenty-Seven

'I literally cannot take this in,' Toni said, half an hour later.

'How do you think *I* feel?' I'd come back to the house, promising Marie I'd return when I'd made a few calls, sensing she too needed a while to adjust to this new reality; perhaps make some calls of her own. I knew Dee would be eager to hear from her.

'All week I've been asking questions and it turns out her name didn't even begin with M.' I was lying on the grass in the garden, looking up at the sky, because I needed a space big enough for my thoughts. 'It's unbelievable, really.'

'It's like the plot of a film,' Toni agreed. Her familiar voice had brought fresh tears to my eyes when she'd answered her phone with the words, 'Please tell me you shagged the fisherman.'

'And you're really OK with it not being what you were expecting?' she said now. 'Honestly, Elle, I should be with you for this.'

'I didn't know *what* I was expecting.' I brushed my knuckles over my eyes. They felt swollen after all the crying. 'It's awful what happened to Emmeline, but it's so much worse for Marie, and, to be honest, it's a bit of a relief to not have to deal with a birth mother.' I wasn't wording it very well, but Toni seemed to get it.

'It would have been complicated,' she said. 'Mum keeps telling me it's easier being a grandparent because she worries less, and gets to do all the fun bits and hand Freddie back at the end of the day, so it must be bit like that.'

I laughed, but I knew what she meant. 'Marie's so nice,' I said, stretching a hand up to the sky. 'Right from the start, it was as if I knew her from somewhere.'

'Well, you do share DNA.'

'That's so weird.'

'No other relatives knocking about?'

'She has an uncle and a couple of cousins just outside Paris,' I said. 'She's going to introduce us, and she wants to show me where Emmeline is buried.'

'Oh God, Elle.'

'It's fine. I know it sounds a bit grim, but I want to see it. I want to say thank you for… you know, for her giving me to Dad.'

When Toni spoke again, her voice was thick with tears. 'You know you're going to have to tell Jess.'

I closed my eyes as the sun shifted over the roof of the shed. The inside of my eyelids turned orange, and I thought of the sofa upstairs at the café, and wondered what Charlie would make of this. I badly wanted to tell him and Dolly.

But Toni was right. First, I had to talk to Jess.

I delayed the moment by checking the time in Borneo. It was evening. She'd likely be eating dinner, and although part of me wished it was the middle of the night so I could put it off a bit longer, I knew it would only eat away at me.

I rehearsed a few lines, pacing the garden, then returned to the house to say them in front of the mirror.

'Jess, I haven't been honest with you.' My eyes were bright and shiny rather than swollen, and more freckles had appeared on my cheeks. I'd never looked so healthy. 'I'm not in Crete,' I continued in my business voice. 'That's why I haven't seen any goats, apart from the ones at the wildlife park.' Too long-winded. 'Jess, I'm sorry to call with news like this out of the blue…' No, she'd think I was ill. 'Jess, there's something I haven't told you, and it's to do with a bag I found in Dad's wardrobe a few months ago.' She might think it was money – that I'd found a fortune stashed away, and be disappointed by the truth. It might be better than the actual truth. But Jess wasn't interested in money. 'Oh, for God's sake.'

I called her number and as soon as she answered, blurted out, 'Jess, I'm not in Crete, I'm in Chamillon in France, and I didn't tell you because I came to find out about my birth mother, because I found a postcard in Dad's wardrobe and she'd written a message, and her name doesn't begin with M, like we thought. It's a really long story, but basically, I have an aunt called Marie, she's French… obviously… but my birth mother, Emmeline – her name was Emmeline, which is where the M came from… EE, EM – well, she died a year after I was born, but I didn't come here because I thought I needed a new mum, I would never do that—'

'Hang on, Elle,' Owen's voice interrupted me. 'I'll hand you over to Jess.'

'Why didn't you answer your phone?' I said when she came on, my voice wobbling on the edge of tears. 'I can't say all that again.'

'It's OK, I heard it.' It sounded as though she was smiling, which couldn't be right. 'Owen put it on speakerphone because I was feeding Bobo.'

'When will he be on solids?'

'The females nurse their babies for eight years,' she said. 'But as long as there's plenty of fruit around, it probably won't be that long.'

'Right.' My voice grew smaller. 'I didn't mean to say it like that, Jess. I'm so sorry.'

'I knew you weren't in Crete,' she said, in her matter-of-fact way.

'*What*? How?'

'The selfie you sent. Your location setting must be on, because it came up on the picture.'

'Oh, God.' I moved to the sofa and dropped down. 'Why didn't you say something?'

'I was waiting for you to tell me,' she said. 'Here, take the bottle.'

'Sorry?'

'I was giving Bobo to Owen.'

'I'm sorry I lied.'

'It's OK.' She let out a soft sigh. 'I guessed why you'd gone there.'

'You did?'

'We knew your birth mother was French,' she said. 'You've never been to France before, and one minute you're talking about selling the house and packing up Dad's things, and the next you're taking a holiday.'

'It's not unreasonable to take a holiday.'

'You never take holidays, and definitely not somewhere like Crete, on your own. I knew there was more to it, and your photo confirmed it.'

'You're not mad with me?'

'Why would I be?' She sounded surprised. 'I mean, I didn't know about the postcard, but if you'd told me, I would have told you to go.'

'Really?' I wasn't sure why I was so surprised. The only time I could ever recall Jess being mad at me was when she discovered my favourite peanut butter contained palm oil, which led to 'rainforests being destroyed' and I wouldn't give it up until the jar was empty.

'It's normal to look for answers if there's a clue,' she said. 'Instinctive.'

It was a typical Jess response, but I was so grateful, I wanted to reach through the phone and take her in my arms – orangutan and all. 'I wasn't trying to replace Mum.'

'I know,' she said, and I could tell it hadn't even crossed her mind to think otherwise. 'It must be good to get some answers.'

'That's all I wanted, really.' I swiped at my eyes, which were leaking tears again. 'I don't feel any more French than I did before, but I do understand now why she gave me up. She really was doing what she thought was best for me.'

'Are you anything like her?'

'She was a ballerina, so no, but apparently, I have her jawline.' I gave a choked-sounding laugh. 'She died so young, Jess.'

'It's a shame Dad never knew,' she said, taking me by surprise. 'I think he worried a bit that she'd come for you, one day.'

'It wouldn't have made any difference.'

'I know,' said Jess. 'I'm glad you're my sister, Elle.'

I smothered a sob – she never said things like that. 'I'm glad too.'

'I'd like to meet your aunt one day.'

'She wants to meet you too,' I said, sniffing. 'I'd better make do with showing her a photo for now.'

'Send me a picture of her.'

'I will.'

With a burst of excitement, I imagined telling people back home – except… apart from Toni and Mark, and possibly Petra, no one would really care. And while it was acceptable to have acquired an aunt in Chamillon, revealing the circumstances to friends and neighbours in Wishbourne would only raise questions about Mum and Dad and our relationship. Gossip would spread like a virus, and Dad would have hated that.

More people here cared, than back in England.

'You need to take some time now, to figure out what you want,' Jess said, as if privy to my thoughts. 'I know you've had enough of being at the studio.'

I started. 'How could you know that?'

'Toni told me when I called to tell you that Owen had proposed,' she said. 'She seemed worried about you.'

I couldn't help smiling. My emotions were swinging wildly. 'She really didn't tell you where I was?'

'No,' said Jess. 'She does go on a bit, though. It sounded as if she was hoping you'd have lots of sex while you were away.'

I inhaled and started coughing. 'I haven't had *any* sex,' I said, when I'd caught my breath. An image of Charlie's lips slid into my head. 'That's not why I'm here.'

'But now you've solved the mystery of your origins, you can do anything.'

You can do anything. Her words gave me a soaring sense of hope. 'That doesn't mean I'm going to rush out and have sex.'

'Toni said there'd be plenty of man candy where you were.'

'Ugh. *Man* candy?'

'I think she was trying to be urban.'

Jess sounded so puzzled, I laughed. 'I need to have words with her.'

'Mating's a biological urge,' said Jess. 'If you pick the right person, I don't see why you shouldn't have lots of sex.'

'I don't think I like it when you say sex.'

'Toni calls it shagging, which is worse.'

'That's *so* true.'

'You can invite her to the wedding, if you like.'

'Oh, she's expecting an invite. She's probably choosing a dress as we speak, and a little suit for Freddie.'

'I was talking about Marie.'

'Oh.' I dropped back against the cushions. I felt wrung out, but in a good way – as if something I'd been putting off for years had finally been accomplished. 'She'd like that,' I said.

'And Petra can take the photos.'

'What?' I sat up. 'Jess, I—'

'I want you to be my maid of honour,' she interrupted. 'I know it's old-fashioned, but I think Mum and Dad would have liked it.'

'Oh, Jess. I wish they could be there.'

'Me too.'

'I'd like to tell them one more time how much I love them.'

'Yeah, me too.'

'Do you think they'd understand why I came here?'

'I know they would,' said Jess. 'Don't torture yourself, Elle.'

'Apparently, Eloise was my great-grandmother's name.'

'Do you want us to call you that now?'

I didn't need to think twice. 'No,' I said. 'I like my name as it is.'

A suckling sound punctured the silence that fell.

'Is Bobo still feeding?'

'That's Owen, eating a watermelon.'

We talked a bit more, about the wedding and the orangutans, and I relayed most of what Marie had told me about Emmeline, until I could barely keep my eyes open.

The signal started to fade as Jess was telling me why captivity was bad for animals, after I confessed to visiting the wildlife park to look for a goat I could photograph. We said goodbye and hung up, and I messaged her *Love you X*, hoping she'd see it before she went to bed.

Chapter Twenty-Eight

Before returning to the café, I knocked at Marie's and she invited me to join her for supper that evening. 'I have so many photographs I think you will like,' she said, practically glowing with pleasure. 'And when you come back to do the wedding for Dolly, I would like to make a party, so all my friends may meet you.' She looked at least ten years younger, despite some tell-tale pinkness around her eyes.

'That would be lovely,' I said, feeling a flare of happiness. 'I can't believe it's my last day here tomorrow.'

'I cannot bear for you to go.'

'It won't be for long,' I said. 'Apart from the wedding, I have a *tante* to visit now.' I'd been practising saying *tante*, but it still didn't sound very French.

Marie's cheeks rose in a smile. 'I'm so glad I already said that you will be staying here.' She looked around the little hallway that was fast becoming familiar.

'Will there be a spare guest room?'

'You are family,' she said. 'There will always be room for you.'

Family. I gave her a hug and she responded fiercely, pressing a kiss to both my cheeks. I thought of doing the same, but worried it might go wrong, so pulled away with a smile and said, 'I'll see you later,' and as I walked away, I felt her gaze on my back like an invisible cord, and liked knowing it was there.

Chamillon was busy with visitors in holiday mode, eating al fresco, or browsing the shops, and I spotted Mimi coming out of a craft store, wearing a purple kaftan, hair as shiny as a blackbird's wing under the blazing sun. 'Find your dad's girlfriend?' she greeted me, as if we were old buddies.

I smiled and said, 'In a manner of speaking,' which made her raise her sunglasses to give me a closer look.

'Talking to you in the caff made me think about my marriage.' Her voice was several decibels too loud, drawing some curious looks from passers-by. 'I had a look for Jason Bellamy on Facebook as soon as I got home.'

Oh dear. 'Really?'

'Hadn't thought about him in yonks till you asked me all those questions,' she said, her smile revealing a layer of plum-coloured lipstick on her two front teeth. 'I remember how we couldn't get enough of each other. In the bedroom,' she added, in case I was in any doubt. 'He's single now, as luck would have it – I reckon I spoilt him for anyone else – so I've invited him over next month.'

My mouth was open. 'What… what about your husband?'

Mimi's bosom bounced as she hoisted her raffia bag onto her shoulder. 'He's going to Yorkshire to visit his mother,' she said. 'With any luck, he won't be back.' She looked at me again, this time over the top of her sunglasses, and I wondered fleetingly whether she wore them all year round. 'You did me a massive favour,' she said, seeming to smile with her whole body. 'I already feel like a new woman.' She paused for effect. 'And so does my husband!'

Roaring with laughter, she moved off before I could comment, not that I had any idea how to respond. At least Stefan would be safe from her flirting – providing Jason was still a match for Mimi.

As I approached the harbour, I spotted Charlie in the throng, outside a restaurant called La Croisette, talking to a woman easily recognisable by her gleaming hair as Tegan. She was straddling her bike, her endless legs emerging from tiny pink shorts, listening closely to whatever he was saying. There was a flash of teeth as she laughed, so it was clearly something funny. Charlie *was* funny. Not in a trying-too-hard way, just naturally amusing.

I hadn't expected to be seen as I passed, but Tegan called out in a friendly fashion, 'Hey, how are ya?'

'Good, thanks!' I threw her a smile as I slowed. 'On my way to the café.'

'Poor you.' She pouted her generous mouth. 'I'm trying to talk Charlie into coming to La Couarde-sur-Mer.' Her French sounded even worse than mine. 'I fancy going jet-skiing.'

Recalling Charlie's confession that he wasn't fond of water sports, I said, 'Good luck with that.'

She dialled her beam down. 'Excuse me?'

'I said, have fun!' I gave a bland smile as I hurried away, managing to avoid Charlie's eyes, feeling deflated that he was busy when I'd wanted so much to tell him about Marie.

I thought I heard him call my name, but when I looked back, all I could see was a stream of cyclists heading towards me. I froze while they swerved around me, shouting over their shoulders, and when I looked again, Tegan was leaning over and kissing Charlie's cheek.

'What does brool-ohn-lawnfer mean?' I asked Dolly, who – despite several customers trying to claim her attention – was making a fuss of a pile of ginger fur on Madame Bisset's lap.

'*Brûle en l'enfer?*' She looked up, startled. 'Burn in hell, why?'

'No reason.' I backed away as Madame Bisset held up the fur for my attention.

'Oh my *God*, he's—'

'*She.*' Dolly widened her eyes at me. 'Delphine's a girl cat, aren't you puss-puss?'

'She's… lovely,' I lied, reaching to stroke her head. As if she knew I was fibbing, the cat shot out her claws and raked them across my wrist.

'Don't worry, I'm fine,' I said, as blood bubbled to the surface, but Madame Bisset was kissing Delphine's scary face, as if *I* was the one who'd attacked her.

Dolly ushered me to the kitchen, and Stefan put down the croque monsieur he'd been about to sink his teeth into, and hurried through to the café. 'So, what happened?' she said urgently, running cold water over my wrist at the sink. 'You were gone so long, we were starting to worry about you.'

'I'm sorry,' I said, 'I know you're busy, and poor Stefan—'

'Never mind that. Stefan's already had one lunch today.' Dolly grabbed some kitchen roll and dabbed my wrist, and when it was dry, I was relieved to see nothing but a faint pink line. I'd never sustained so many injuries as I had in the last six days, and had seen enough blood to last for the next ten years. 'Now, do you feel up to telling me what's going on?'

I nodded, and let myself be led out to the courtyard, compliant as a child.

Once seated at the picnic table, I started from the beginning and halfway through – back from seeing Tegan – Charlie came out with three coffees and slid onto the bench beside me. He listened intently as I told them about the letter from Emmeline, and how Marie had always known she had a niece somewhere.

Dolly was snuffling, her face shiny with tears. At one point, she blew her nose on her apron and muttered, 'Sorry, carry on.'

I kept talking until I'd run out of words, and when I'd finished, Charlie spoke for the first time.

'That's a lot to take in.' His face was puckered with feeling. 'Are you OK?'

'I am, now that's it's sinking in.'

'I'm glad,' he said, nodding slowly. 'Marie's a good person to have as an auntie.'

The way he said *auntie* made me smile, even though I'd been on the verge of crying while telling them about the letter. 'Actually, I feel lucky,' I said. 'Marie's so happy, it wouldn't feel right to be sad.'

'I knew Marie had a sister, but it's not something she ever talks about,' said Dolly, patting her face with her apron. 'Not to me, but now I understand why.' She reached over and took my hand. 'I'm so pleased for you, love, I really am, but what a shocker!'

'I can't thank you enough for all your help.'

'Not that it mattered in the end,' she said, with a watery smile.

'It felt good to have you on my side.' I turned to Charlie. 'I'm sorry I didn't tell you the truth right away.'

'It's not important,' he said. He'd moved closer while I was talking, his arm so close to mine, I could feel its heat. Or maybe it was the rich sunlight, slanting across the table, warming my skin.

'Well…' Dolly cleared her throat and smoothed her fringe. 'I knew you weren't here about a job from the get-go.'

Charlie and I swapped a look – the first since he'd sat down. He seemed unusually subdued, now I thought about it – as if he was wishing he had gone jet-skiing with Tegan after all. 'What do you mean?' he said.

Dolly stirred her coffee, which had developed a layer of skin on top. 'I was bringing out an order and I saw you fly through the door and knock

Elle over, then pick her up again.' Her gaze darted between us and back to her cup. 'I thought you made a lovely couple, and when I heard Charlie ask if you were here about the job, I had this idea of asking you to come in.'

'Mum, for God's sake.' Charlie drew his hands down his face. 'Not this again.'

'It's not like with Natalie,' Dolly protested. 'I just had a feeling—'

'So, you thought you'd offer her a job, even though you knew she wasn't looking for one?'

'I didn't know *why* she was really here, not at that precise moment.' Dolly rolled her eyes, as though Charlie was being deliberately obtuse. 'I just wanted to get her into the café so I could talk to her,' she said, as though I wasn't there. 'I'd just offered the job to someone else, if you must know. Mathilde's grandson.'

'What?' I said.

'Mum, that's hardly fair.'

'As it happens, he can't start until next Monday, so it worked out perfectly.' Dolly was on the defensive. 'Even if Mathilde doesn't believe you're only filling in.'

I stared. 'That's why she hates me.'

'Don't worry about her, she has a suspicious nature.' A smile settled on Dolly's face. 'When you told me why you were here, it seemed natural to offer to help, and I knew it would make you feel better to do something in return.'

'What if Elle had said no?' Charlie seemed set on pursuing the matter. 'What would you have done then, Mum? Kidnapped her?'

Dolly tutted. 'I'd have thought of something,' she said. 'Because I'd seen the way you looked at each other.'

'*What?*'

Charlie and I spoke as one, not quite meeting each other's eyes this time. 'She was in shock, because I sent her flying,' he said.

'I saw her before, standing outside, and thought what a beauty she was.' Dolly's voice had taken on a dreamy note. 'There was an air of mystery about her, something a bit lost, and I just knew.'

'Sounds like *you're* in love with her,' said Charlie, and the silence that ensued had a weird fizz of expectation. It was as if they'd both forgotten I was there.

'Look, it worked out perfectly in the end,' I said. 'And I've met some lovely people, which I might not have done if I'd tried to do this on my own.'

'See, my instincts were right.' Dolly pointed her spoon at Charlie. 'I knew I was doing the right thing from the minute you followed me inside,' she said, pointing the spoon at me. 'I'm not crazy.'

'I never said you were crazy, Mum.'

'You're not crazy, Dolly.'

'And now Elle knows the truth about her birth mum, and you two have got to know each other pretty well, so—'

'Mum, just leave it.' For a second, I wondered whether Charlie was going to tell her he'd already met someone, or reiterate that he wasn't in the market for a relationship, but instead he stood up and said, 'I'd better get back to work, it's pretty busy in there.'

He paused, a hand hovering near my shoulder before it dropped to his side. 'I'm glad you're OK,' he said, and went inside.

A bird flew down and landed on the table, then took off as though it had made a mistake.

Dolly sniffed, and wiped her apron beneath her eyes. 'I've messed up again.'

'I think he just wants to, you know, find someone naturally, without… without—'

'His mother interfering?'

'Well, yes,' I said, smiling. 'You know that song, "You Can't Hurry Love"? It'll happen when he's ready.'

'I just had this feeling, you see.' She pressed her knuckles to her heart, reminding me of Jess's words about humans having instincts just like animals, and how we often ignore them. 'I'm sorry, love.' Dolly gave a quick smile. 'The last thing you need is me going on, after the day you've had.' She looked at her watch. 'Do you know, I've not taken so much time off work in ages as I have this week with you.'

'Thanks,' I said. 'For letting me "work" here.' I made quotation marks.

'You don't have to any more,' she said. 'Now you've found your M. Or should I say EM?' Realising it sounded exactly the same, we laughed.

'I'd like to finish my shift, if that's OK.'

'Of course it is, but don't come in tomorrow.' She came round and squeezed my shoulders. She seemed to have a thing for shoulder squeezing and it was comforting. 'It's your last day, so spend it with Marie – do whatever you want.' She dropped a kiss on top of my hair, as if it was the obvious thing to do. 'Maybe get your camera out and take some pictures, love.'

Chapter Twenty-Nine

After a leisurely shower, I slathered myself in coconut-scented body lotion from a basket labelled 'guests' and slipped into the top that Marie had given me before I'd left her house. *A gift from my aunt, who lives in France.*

I found a pair of white jeans to wear with the top, which fitted perfectly and made my eyes look brighter, the V hinting at a cleavage – though I knew it was just an illusion.

I dabbed on some lipstick and smoothed my eyebrows, and, in a fit of vanity, combed on mascara and dusted bronzer across my cheekbones.

I held my hair off my face, studying the tilt of my jaw. It was nice to know there was something of my birth mother in me, after all. I wondered whether Dad had ever seen it, but they'd spent so little time together, it seemed unlikely.

Questions came in waves. Would Dad have loved me as much if I hadn't looked like him? What if I'd stood out, so that people were constantly asking why I didn't look like my parents, like Jess? Would my relationship with my sister have been different? If I'd looked like my birth mother when I was born, would she have given me up so easily?

Letting my hair fall, I gave myself a hard stare. I would never have a *Sliding Doors* moment and know for sure, but believed in my heart that none of those things would have made a difference. I'd been loved, and that was all that mattered. I was *still* loved. And I had an aunt, who was cooking me dinner next door.

As I ran downstairs, a familiar knock resounded through the house, and I smiled as I slid my feet into my sandals, realising I would miss it when I got home. 'Hello, Henri,' I said, pulling the door wide, enjoying the sight of him spot-lit by the sun – in the same way I would enjoy a beautiful building or a sunrise. 'How can I help you this evening?'

'Elle, you look…' He took a step back, as if to get a panoramic view, eyes sweeping over me like lasers. 'You look amazing,' he said, almost awestruck – as if he'd got used to seeing me at my absolute worst and hadn't expected anything different. Which, in its way, was flattering.

'Thank you,' I said, surprised to find that my pulse rate hadn't risen. 'You look pretty good yourself.'

He looked down, as if to say, *oh, these old jeans and sneakers?* but probably knew he looked like he'd stepped from the pages of a men's magazine – a sporty one, where the men looked rough and sexy, and not like they were trying too hard, even though they were. 'You're ready to dance?' He waggled a set of car keys. 'I'm driving tonight,' he said. 'I know a nice place not too far from here, and we can have something to eat first.' When he gave his heart-stopping grin, my heart didn't miss a beat. 'No oysters,' he said. 'And definitely no boats.'

I smiled. 'I appreciate the effort, Henri, and again, I'm so sorry for being sick on your boots last night, I do feel bad about that, but I've made plans for this evening.'

'Plans?' For a moment, it was clear he thought I was joking. His chin pulled in and he narrowed his eyes, a smile playing over his lips. 'What plans?'

'I'm having dinner with Marie.'

His gaze flicked to her house and back. 'I don't think she'll mind if you tell her I'm taking you out.'

'No, but I would.'

Still sure of his powers of persuasion, he lifted his eyebrows and executed a sexy hip wiggle, while thrusting a hand through his hair. 'I promise you I can dance.'

'I don't doubt it,' I said, still smiling. 'But I told you last night that I didn't want to go out with you again.'

'You were serious?' His brows drew together. 'I thought it was because you were feeling sick,' he said. 'Honestly, Elle, whatever you want to do tonight, we'll do it. Walk among the sand dunes?' He did a few pantomime steps. 'There's a jazz festival in Saint-Clément.' He played a pretend trumpet, puffing out his cheeks. 'I like a bit of jazz.'

'I'm not a fan,' I said, adding, 'Like I told you, Henri, I'm seeing Marie tonight and on Sunday, I'm leaving the island.'

All the humour left his face as he realised I was being serious. 'I was hoping to tempt you to stay longer,' he said. 'I'm sure I could wear you down eventually.'

I laughed. 'You would want me on those terms?'

'If that's the only way I can get you.'

'Oh, Henri.' I rested against the doorframe, and wished for a second that I *could* fall in love with him – wondered whether I would, given time.

'I haven't kissed you yet,' he said. 'A bit of lip-action will put me in a better light.'

About to make a laughing response, I saw his attention snag on a pretty cyclist, and knew it would always be like this, being with someone like him. Wondering whether he was going to lose interest and move on to the next bright, shiny female. I'd had a relationship like that once, and didn't want another.

'Hey, Elle, how're you doin'?' the cyclist called with a high-voltage smile, and I realised it was Tegan.

'Hi!' I gave her a wave and she glided by, her hair catching the light. She was wearing a little denim skirt that revealed a flash of white gusset as she pedalled past, and I saw that Henri had noticed. I wondered whether she was on her way to meet Charlie, and briefly wished she'd fall off and suffer a very mild concussion.

'You know her?' said Henri, tracking her to the end of the street before dragging his gaze back to mine. *Was he already moving on?*

'She's called Tegan,' I said. 'She's Australian, and very sporty.'

'She does have a sporty vibe.'

'She would have been great on your boat last night. She loves the water.'

'Really?'

I almost laughed, seeing how interested he was, even though he quickly refocused his attention back on me. 'Is there nothing I can do to tempt you to come out?' he said, pushing his hands in his pockets.

I shook my head. 'I'm sorry.'

'I could come and visit you in England.'

'Don't,' I said gently. 'You'd be wasting your time.'

His chest rose in a sigh. 'So, this is goodbye?'

'I'm coming back at the end of the month,' I said, and his face brightened in a way that made me believe he really thought we might have a chance. 'But as far as a relationship goes, it's definitely goodbye.' No point beating about the bush.

'Break it to me gently, why don't you?' He knew his British accent would get a smile, and I didn't disappoint.

'I have to go now, Henri.'

He looked at me a moment longer, as if debating whether or not to continue pleading his case, then pressed his fingers to his lips and gently placed them on mine. 'Goodbye, beautiful Elle.'

I watched him cross to a nondescript car, tossing and catching his keys, turning to wave before getting in and driving off, and although I felt a pinch of regret, I knew that with so many fish in the sea – *another marine-related pun* – he would soon find one happy to swim alongside him. *That's enough now, Elle.* Someone like Henri wouldn't stay single for long. In fact, it wouldn't have surprised me to know he'd caught up with Tegan, and asked her out on his boat.

'So, what are your plans when you return to England?' asked Marie, after we'd eaten a delicious dinner of mussels in white wine, and tarte au citron that she confessed was shop-bought. 'Baking is not my talent,' she'd said, moving lightly around the kitchen, refusing to let me help as she brought everything through to the dining room, clearly happy to be cooking for 'family' instead of guests.

'I told them I had the headache,' she'd said, touching her temple and feigning a pained look that made me giggle. 'I have never said such a thing before, but I am…' she'd swung her head from side to side '… I am so giddy, like a young girl.'

We'd barely stopped smiling at each other while we ate, exchanging information about our lives in little bursts. She'd wanted to know everything, and murmured often how wonderful my parents sounded, how sorry she was not to know them, and told me about hers, who'd sounded – if I was honest – quite scary. More so where Emmeline was concerned – like those helicopter parents I'd read about, taking an excessive interest in the life of their child.

'Ballet was our life for a long time,' Marie explained. 'It was all we talked about, but Emmeline was better than I was, more dedicated. I did not get the shows as often as she did. Often, I was a waitress, to make money.' I remembered her saying she'd worked in hospitality. 'It all happened the way it had to,' she said.

Now, in her living room, surrounded by photographs, the shawl – which I'd said she must keep as it had belonged to her, draped over the chair, Emmeline's charm bracelet on her wrist – she wanted to know my plans for the future.

'I'm going to give up working at the studio,' I said, surprised in the end it was such an easy decision to make. 'I want to sell the house, because being there feels like living in the past, and I don't want to do that any more.'

'I don't feel that.' Marie looked around her. 'My memories here are of the good times, and I have lived here long enough, with so many people coming in and out, that it has…' She made a movement with her hands, 'it has a different shape now.'

'It's different for me.' I tried to find the right words. 'Mum was ill for a while, so there's that, and after she died, Dad really struggled for a few months. He couldn't work, and Jess and I… we coped by working too much, so for me, that's what I think of when I'm at home – there's too much sadness.'

'Then you should go, and make happy memories somewhere new,' she said, passing me a picture of her parents. It was clear where Marie had got her looks. Her mother had Bambi-wide eyes and a sweep of glossy hair and her father was tall and film-star handsome, but neither was smiling, as if life was a serious business. 'You will always carry your parents in your heart, wherever you go,' she said, patting my arm, and I felt a twinge of sadness that I'd never known my grandparents – even though they'd driven Emmeline away.

I left around eleven, just as Ted and Miranda were returning, pink-cheeked, from a club in Saint-Martin, where Miranda had tried to limbo and almost broken her back (according to Ted).

'I hope they will go quickly to sleep,' Marie whispered, as they weaved upstairs singing, 'How Low Can You Go'. 'Usually, they are very noisy lovers.'

I clung to her, giggling, as we said goodnight, and she held me for a long time as though trying to absorb every molecule of me. 'Come again tomorrow,' she said. 'We still have so much to catch up on.'

I didn't need to be asked twice.

Before I went to bed, I called Toni, hoping she'd be awake as it was an hour earlier in the UK.

'Was in a deep sleep,' she mumbled, just as I was about to hang up.

'Oh no, I'm sorry.' I kicked off my sandals and sat in the kitchen, the only light from Marie's house spilling across the garden; probably Ted and Miranda's bedroom. 'I thought you'd be up with Freddie.'

'Mark's parents have got him for the night.'

'And you're not out clubbing?'

'Very funny,' she said. 'All we could think about was getting nine hours of uninterrupted sleep.'

'Which I've ruined.'

'Which you've ruined,' she agreed. 'You'd better have shagged someone, or I'm hanging up.'

But she didn't hang up, even when I explained about Henri (though she said I should still have shagged him anyway, for the experience) and I told her I didn't want to work at the studio any more.

'About time,' she said, when I explained that I wanted to try my hand at other types of photography, maybe do some courses. I wasn't sure what, but I was definitely done with weddings. 'You've been on autopilot for ages.'

'Your job's safe,' I said, moved that she hadn't mentioned it. 'Petra's too, she can do my job and you'll be her boss.'

'Hang on,' she said, 'I'll be officially in charge?'

'You can have a pay rise to prove it.'

'Woah,' she said. 'How's that going to work?'

'I'm selling the house,' I said, 'So that'll give me some capital.'

'But you'll need to buy somewhere else to live.'

I hesitated. 'I know, but… I don't know yet where that's going to be.'

I heard the sound of the kettle boiling in the background. 'Elle, are you thinking of moving over there?'

'Would that be totally mad?'

'You'd be mad not to, now you've got an auntie and access to hot men,' she said. 'And stunning scenery for your photos, obviously.' I could tell she was being humorous to hide being upset.

'It's not far, so you'd be able to come over and visit, and I'd be over there a lot,' I said. 'It's just…'

'Apart from me, there's nothing tying you here.' She'd adopted her brave voice, the one she'd used when her first boyfriend broke up with her and she tried to pretend she wasn't bothered – that she'd been ready to dump him anyway – and again when she was rejected at her first job interview. *It's their loss.*

'I'll always be tied to you,' I said. 'You can't get rid of me that easily. I'll be over there all the time, I don't want Freddie to forget who I am.'

'I know we don't have nights out like we used to, I've turned into a boring mum.' She was sounding weepy now. 'Sometimes I envy you, Elle, not having any responsibilities.'

'Ah yes, but remember your parents are still alive, and your grand-parents, and Mark's parents treat you like their own daughter and—'

'OK, OK, you win.' She gave a snotty laugh. 'There's no way I can compete with dead parents.'

'Anyway, I don't even know if it's going to happen yet. I just know that being here this week, it's… I feel different,' I said. 'I'm not stuck any more.'

'I'm glad, Elle.' Toni sounded as if she had a tissue pressed to her nose. 'I've been waiting a long time to hear you say that.'

The light next door went off, and above the silhouette of the shed roof, I saw stars as bright as pins in the sky. 'Look out of the window.'

'Do I have to?' she said. 'I've just sat down with a cup of tea.'

'Go and look.'

Tutting, I heard movement – the sound of a curtain being pulled back. 'It's still a bit light,' she said, surprised. 'It felt like I'd been in bed for hours.'

'Look at the sky.'

'What for?'

'Can you see any stars?'

There was some huffing, the sound of a light being clicked off, followed by a clunk as if something had been knocked over, then Toni saying, 'I can't see anything apart from the bloody great street light outside our window.'

'That's a shame,' I said. 'I was going to say something profound about how, wherever we are in the world, we share the same stars, or something.'

'I'm so glad you didn't.'

We laughed, and I heard her take a slurp of tea. 'I'm glad you woke me up, Elle.'

'Me too,' I said, washed with emotion. 'Thanks for listening, Toni, and for being there, and for always being a brilliant friend.'

'I was going to say, I'm feeling horny as hell for the first time in months, so I think I'll wake Mark up, but you're welcome.'

I was still laughing as I took off my make-up, and when I got into bed, I felt as though she was with me, like the sleepovers we'd had at each other's houses growing up, and fell asleep still smiling.

Chapter Thirty

After a quick breakfast of toast and marmalade – Natalie's food tastes were quite English – I popped next door to wish Marie a good morning.

'You look like an English rose,' she said, approving of my stripy cotton shorts and the one and only strappy vest top I'd brought. 'Beautiful skin.' I sensed the words 'like Emmeline's' hovering, but she didn't say them. It must have been hard for her not to keep seeking comparisons, but I didn't mind – I knew how much it meant to her to have a little bit of her sister back in her life.

'You look nice too,' I said, eyeing her simple, lilac shift dress.

'You are going to take pictures?' She pointed to my camera and I raised it and snapped one of her. 'I look… young,' she said, when I showed her the image on the LCD screen. 'How did you do that?'

'It's not magic,' I said, tickled that she thought I'd deployed some secret skill. 'It's just the light coming through the front door has caught your eyes, and you're smiling, because I caught you off-guard.' It was a lovely picture, and closing my hand round the camera body, I felt a small thrill. It would be wonderful to take some photos that weren't posed, or in a studio. Just natural shots that didn't require a fixed smile and perfect make-up. 'I'm going to send it to Jess,' I said, and Marie looked thrilled.

'And now?'

'I'm going to wander about being a tourist,' I said. 'After I've been to the café to say goodbye to Dolly.'

'I would like to come with you, to show you things,' said Marie. 'But Ted and Miranda, they are not up out of bed yet and they will want breakfast.' She made a face, and said in a confidential voice, 'I wish they would bugger off.'

'Marie!'

Her eyes sparkled. 'Marty taught me that,' she said. 'It sounds so funny.'

It did, coming from her. 'I'll see you this evening for dinner,' I promised, and thought for a moment she was going to clap her hands.

'I will make Emmeline's favourite, *coq au vin*.'

'Oh, you're taking pictures,' said Dolly as I entered the kitchen to find her rolling out pastry and took a photo of her.

'I've got to have something to remember you by until I come back.'

She looked pleased. 'Hope I haven't broken it,' she joked.

'I thought I'd better ask you for some details.'

'Details?'

'For the wedding.'

'Ooh, the wedding,' she said, returning to her pastry. 'I can't wait!'

'Well, I need to know a few things, like how many guests; do you have any particular poses? Are there any venue restrictions? You can message me, if that would be easier. I'll give you my email address.'

Her mouth was hanging open. 'I want you to turn up and take pictures,' she said. 'We're not Meghan and Harry!'

'No, but…'

'Honestly, love, if you could take some nice, natural photos that would be perfect. I want you to enjoy it too.'

'That would be a first.' I felt drenched with relief. 'I think I can manage that.'

'Just be here on the thirtieth. Sooner, if you like.'

She made it sound so simple, but really… *it was*.

'We're so glad you're coming back, Elle,' she said, and I could tell she meant it. 'We were saying how much we'd miss you.'

'We?'

I looked over at the young man efficiently loading Basil, who looked a lot like Stefan but with less hair. 'Oh, that's Stefan's brother, I wasn't talking about him.' She gave a hooting laugh. 'I meant Charlie.'

I gave her a sceptical look, certain he wouldn't have said any such thing. 'Is he… is he here this morning?'

'He's popped out,' she said. 'He said he had to talk to someone.'

Tegan. Maybe things were hotting up and he was on the verge of introducing her to Dolly.

'I'll leave you to it,' I said. 'I probably won't see you before I leave, so I'll say goodbye now.'

'You mean *au revoir*,' she said sternly, flapping her floury arms for me to give her a hug. 'Definitely not goodbye, my love. You'll be back in no time.'

I couldn't remember being hugged as much as I had in the past week, and it felt good; almost like having Mum back, though no one's hugs would ever be quite that special.

'Let's have a look at your hand,' Dolly said, and I obediently held it out. 'Much better, but make sure you look after it. Put some antiseptic cream on.'

'I'll be fine,' I said. 'Shall I pay you for all the stuff I've broken?'

'Don't be silly.' She tut-tutted. 'Shall I pay you for helping out?'

'Of course not.'

'There you are, then,' she said. 'Let's call it quits.'

'I'm glad I didn't have to talk to Margot,' I said, hearing her call out to someone in the café. 'I could have really upset her.'

Dolly bit her lip, then said, 'I've decided to have a chat with her, thanks to you.'

'Me?'

'If the rumours are true, I think it would do her good to take some action,' she said. 'That child might be waiting for her to turn up and tell him she loves him.'

Moved, I said, 'He might not.'

'No, but it's better to do something. Look at you,' she said, 'you're like a different person to the one who arrived.'

'Not everything works out.'

'No, but I'm still going to talk to her.' She gave her pastry a final, determined thump and said, 'Charlie would want to see you before you go.'

'It's OK,' I said, close to tears. 'Tell him good… tell him *au revoir* from me.'

I turned back to the café, pausing to let Stefan pass.

'You are taking pictures?' He struck a pose with the tray, and blinking hard, I obliged, realising I'd miss him. That I'd miss them all – smiley Celeste, Gérard and Hamish, Margot and her laptop and even Madame Bisset; minus the cat. But as I surreptitiously photographed them all, I knew I'd be back, and not just when I returned for Dolly's wedding.

I wanted to be able to drop into the Café Belle Vie whenever I wanted.

*

It felt deliciously lazy to wander around the harbour and down to the beach like a sightseer. I even had a paddle in the sea, though I wished I'd brought a towel when I ended up with sand embedded between my toes.

There were photo opportunities everywhere, and once I'd exhausted the sights of Chamillon – and the seagulls were getting annoyed with me pushing my camera into their business – I took a taxi ride to La Couarde. I found a bustling ice-cream shop, where I opted for a scoop of salted caramel, made with *fleur de sel* which the owner – a silver-haired man with a big, round tummy – explained was the salt from the sun-bathed marshes around the island. It packed quite a punch and I needed a drink soon after, and sat with an iced coffee outside a café overlooking the sea, feeling vaguely disloyal to Dolly.

Browsing the gift shops, I bought some chocolates for Toni – hoping they wouldn't melt before I got them home – and a little donkey in a pair of trousers for Freddie, which reminded me of Charlie, telling me about the donkeys in pantaloons in Saint-Martin.

I wondered whether he was still with Tegan or back at the café.

Finally, footsore, sunburnt, tired of jostling through the crowds and desperate to put my camera down, I summoned a taxi to take me back to Chamillon.

It was a relief to flop on a chair in the garden in a shady spot with a glass of water and flick through a few more copies of *An Expat's Guide* – and I wondered whether I'd be subscribing myself soon, if I became an 'expat'.

The thought of possibly having two homes, and not being tied to the studio any more, was indescribably exciting. I could hardly believe I'd let so many years drift by, doing the same old thing. If I hadn't decided to clear out Dad's wardrobe, who knew how many more years I'd have carried on?

It was quiet next door, and although I wondered whether Marie was having a siesta, I suspected she was busy preparing for our supper that evening.

I decided to double-check my flight times, and smiled when I saw that Jess had replied *love you too X* and attached a selfie of her and Owen, with Bobo squashed between them like a furry baby.

The thought of going back to the UK was nowhere near as depressing as it might have been if I hadn't known I was returning in a few weeks – and if I hadn't found Marie – but I realised I was looking forward to seeing Toni. I was also looking forward to having the house valued, and making new arrangements at the studio.

I wasn't due at Marie's for a couple of hours and, suddenly restless, decided to pack for tomorrow, and book a taxi for 9 a.m. to take me to the airport.

It didn't take long to stuff everything in my suitcase as I hadn't unpacked properly in the first place – *why, oh why, had I brought all those socks?* – and I would have to leave my toiletries until the morning.

The bed looked inviting, even though I'd forgotten to straighten the duvet that morning, and I lay down, thinking I might compose a note in my head for Natalie when she returned. Or maybe I should have a tidy-up – I'd trailed sand into the house – and wash my vomit-and-seagull-poo stained 'Riviera' dress, which was lying where I'd stepped out of it the night before. Or wash my hair, and rub some after-sun cream into my shoulders. I hadn't got any, but there might be some in the cabinet in the bathroom…

I woke with a start and a desert-dry mouth, and realised the Chamillon air had worked its magic again – or maybe it was Natalie's bed. I only had a few minutes before I was due at Marie's, and had nothing decent to wear apart from my new blue top and white jeans. I pulled them on again, wincing as I tugged the jeans over my sunburnt legs. I brushed my teeth and hair and ran downstairs, and had just tipped the remaining sand from my sandals and put them on when someone knocked on the door.

'Henri,' I said, annoyed, as I yanked the door open that he wasn't getting the message. 'I thought…' I stopped.

It was Charlie.

'Hi, Elle.'

'What are you doing here?' I noted my rising heart rate. 'I was… I'm just on my way to Marie's.'

'She's only next door,' he said, pointing. 'Sorry, but you made it sound like it was miles away.'

I couldn't stop staring at him. It really was Charlie, his hair awry, as if he'd run here, a tinge of pink to his cheeks. He was wearing his café uniform of trousers and shirt, but had never looked more handsome. 'Do you want to come in?' I said when he peered behind me with a hopeful expression. 'Just for a minute.'

'Thanks,' he said, and as he came in, I realised this wasn't the first time he'd been inside the house.

'I'm sorry it's not very tidy.' I kicked aside one of the trainers I'd worn on Henri's boat, feeling nervous, and as if I was blinking too quickly.

'It looks fine,' he said. 'You've seen where I live, right?'

It sounded so intimate, I flushed, remembering I'd peered in his bedroom. 'Good point.'

He was looking around as though he didn't know where to put his eyes. 'I just wanted to…'

'What did you want?' I said at the same time and laughed. 'Sorry, I didn't mean what do you want, like *what do you want*?' I did a furious voice. 'I mean, it's nice to see you. You weren't at the café when I dropped by to say goodbye to your mum.'

'I know,' he said. 'I'd gone to see Tegan to—'

'You don't have to explain,' I cut in. 'I was just... you don't owe me an explanation. Or anything. You don't owe me anything.'

'I know,' he said, thrusting his hair off his forehead. 'I'm not here because I owe you something.'

'So, why *are* you here?'

'I told Tegan I didn't want a relationship,' he said in a rush. 'With her, I mean.' He scratched his head. 'It wasn't going anywhere, and... well, I told her.'

I was aware of something unfurling inside me – something I hadn't dared put a name to. I still wasn't sure what it was. 'Did she... was she OK about it?'

'Oh, she'll be fine.' Charlie gave a wry little smile that made my stomach leap. 'She's probably already looking for someone to go jet-skiing with.'

'Henri, maybe,' I said. 'I think they'd be quite well-suited.'

'Too alike. I reckon they'd argue a lot.'

Our eyes met.

'So that's what you came to tell me?'

'Well, yes.' He rubbed the back of his head. He was obviously out of his comfort zone, but so was I. My heart felt like it was going to fly out of my mouth. 'Also, I was wondering whether I could come and visit you in England.'

'Sorry?'

'My friend Ryan's invited me to his stag do next weekend,' he said. 'I wasn't going to go – stag nights aren't really my thing, to be honest. They're not his thing either, but he sort of got bulldozed into it. *Any*way… Mum's good for staff and, well… I thought I'd go, and I wondered whether you'd like to meet up, maybe on Sunday, I'm staying for a few days. You don't have to, there's other people I can visit, but—'

He stopped abruptly and looked at me, his expression both hopeful and vulnerable – so different from the man who just days ago had said casually, *Marriage is one institution I hope never to enter. I'm not in the market for a relationship.*

'You came to tell me you want to go to your mate's stag do and maybe meet up with me if you've nothing else to do?'

'What?' He looked startled, as if I'd quoted a passage from the Bible. 'No, I'm saying, I'd like us to meet up because I really like you, and I want us to get to know each other better.'

I was looking at his mouth. The mouth that had been saying all the right things since he'd picked me up off the cobbles outside the café and somehow I'd crossed the room and was pressing my lips to his and kissing him properly and thoroughly – a film kiss, shoving my hands through his glorious hair, and he was kissing me back, tightening his arms round my waist, and I wanted to stay there forever, but needed some air.

'I thought you didn't date staff?' I said, looking right into his eyes.

He looked right back in a way that sent my senses spinning more than they already were. 'You're not staff any more,' he said, and kissed me again.

'I thought you'd changed your mind,' said Marie, coming out of her house as Charlie and I stepped outside. We'd straightened our hair, but there wasn't much I could do about my mouth, which felt bruised with all the activity.

Charlie looked slightly punch-drunk. 'Hi, Marie,' he said, still looking at me.

'Hello, Charlie.'

'I'm going to go now,' he said, looking as if all he wanted to do was kiss me again, and keep on kissing me for hours while I kissed him back. 'I'll see you tomorrow.'

'Tomorrow?'

'I want to give you a lift to the airport, if you'll let me.'

'I'll let you,' I said with a smile, my heart so full it felt too big for my chest. 'Nine o'clock?'

'I'll be here,' he said.

'Me too.'

As he walked away, Marie reached for my hand and drew me to her side, as though she knew something momentous had happened. 'I think he will make you happy,' she said.

'I think so too.' I rested my head on her shoulder and we watched as Charlie reached the end of the street and turned, as if checking I was still there. There was a moment where it seemed he might come running back, and knowing he wanted to was everything.

'It seems a bit greedy,' I said to Marie. 'Finding a boyfriend *and* an aunt.'

She smiled, eyes overflowing with love. 'It is a happy ending.'

'Beginning,' I corrected, smiling back. 'It's a happy beginning.'

A Letter from Karen

I want to say a huge thank you for choosing to read *Summer at the Little French Café*. If you did enjoy it, and want to keep up-to-date with all my latest releases, just sign up at the following link. Your email address will never be shared and you can unsubscribe at any time.

www.bookouture.com/karen-clarke

It was a lovely treat to return to Chamillon to write Elle's story. I'd had an image in my mind for a while of a young woman finding a mysterious postcard that would take her to the Île de Ré, and that was my starting point for Elle's search for her birth mother. I was keen for Charlie to have more involvement, as I loved writing his character in *Escape to the Little French Café*, and I wanted Dolly to have a bigger role too. I like to think she becomes the mother figure that Elle has been lacking! Family is so important, but can take many forms, and I hope that comes through in my story.

If you loved *Summer at the Little French Café*, I would be very grateful if you could write a review. I'd love to hear what you think, and it makes such a difference helping new readers to discover one of my books for the first time.

I love hearing from my readers – you can get in touch on my Facebook page, through Twitter, Goodreads or my website.

Thanks,
Karen

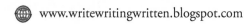 www.writewritingwritten.blogspot.com

 karen.clarke.5682

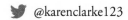 @karenclarke123

Acknowledgements

A lot of people are involved in making a book, and my heartfelt thanks go to Oliver Rhodes and the brilliant team at Bookouture for making it happen. Thanks to Abi (for the last time) for being a brilliant editor, and a total pleasure to work with. Thanks also to copy editor Jane, proofreader Jane, cover designers Nikki and Emma, and to Noelle, Kim and the marketing wizards, who work so hard to spread the word.

As ever, I'm enormously grateful to my lovely readers, as well as the blogging community, whose reviews are a labour of love, and to Amanda Brittany for her tireless feedback and friendship.

And last, but never least, thank you to my family and friends for not getting fed up with me talking about my books; my children, Amy, Martin and Liam, for their unwavering support, and my husband Tim, for your support (especially when things get frenzied!) and all the cups of tea – I couldn't do any of it without you.